RISE OF THE RAYS

A DCI MICHAEL YORKE THRILLER

WES MARKIN

ABOUT THE AUTHOR

Wes Markin is the bestselling author of the DCI Yorke crime novels set in Salisbury. His latest series, The Yorkshire Murders, stars the compassionate and relentless DCI Emma Gardner. He is also the author of the Jake Pettman thrillers set in New England. Wes lives in Harrogate with his wife and two children, close to the crime scenes in The Yorkshire Murders.

You can find out more at:

www.wesmarkinauthor.com

facebook.com/wesmarkinauthor

BY WES MARKIN

DCI Yorke Thrillers

A Lesson in Crime

One Last Prayer

The Repenting Serpent

The Silence of Severance

Rise of the Rays

Dance with the Reaper

Christmas with the Conduit

Jake Pettman Thrillers

The Killing Pit

Fire in Bone

Blue Falls

The Rotten Core

Rock and a Hard Place

Better the Devil

The Yorkshire Murders

The Viaduct Killings

The Lake Killings

The Cave Killings

———

*Details of how to claim your **FREE***
*DCI Michael Yorke quick read, **A Lesson in Crime**,*
can be found at the end of the book.

PRAISE FOR WES MARKIN

"An explosive and visceral debut with the most terrifying of killers. Wes Markin is a new name to watch out for in crime fiction, and I can't wait to see more of DCI Yorke." – **Stephen Booth, Bestselling Crime Author**

"A pool of blood, an abduction, swirling blizzards, a haunting mystery, yes, Wes Markin's One Last Prayer has all the makings of an absorbing thriller. I recommend that you give it a go." – **Alan Gibbons, Bestselling Author**

"Cracking start to an exciting new series. Twist and turns, thrills and kills. I loved it." – **Ross Greenwood, Bestselling Author**

"Markin stuns with his latest offering... Mind-bendingly dark and deep, you know it's not for the faint hearted from page one. Intricate plotting, devious twists and excellent characterisation take this tale to a whole new level. Any

serious crime fan will love it!" – **Owen Mullen, Bestselling Author**

Text copyright © 2020 Wes Markin

First published 2020

ISBN: 9798429055992

Imprint: Independently published

Edited by Jenny Cook and Jo Fletcher

Cover design by Cherie Foxley

For Janet and Peter

1918

T HE PIGS WERE quiet this evening.
Unusually so.

The circling raven welcomed it. Not because this farm was its destination. Pigs weren't its thing. Instead, this breed of killer was targeting a neighbouring yard where it could feed on the eyes and tongues of new-born lambs. However, quiet pigs meant undisturbed, sleeping lambs, and the raven enjoyed its advantage.

Below, on the pig farm, another breed of killer welcomed the silence.

This species came in a pack. Six in total. Each of them driven by the same reason to kill. Not for food, like the bird above, but for vengeance.

It was past midnight and the pack weaved through the pig pens towards the rear of the farmhouse.

The pigs remained still.

These animals had been the most critical part of the plan. The noise these beasts made, especially when disturbed in this manner, could raise the dead and would almost certainly bring out the mad farmer. He was rumoured to possess a Pattern 1913 Enfield rifle. Although they could probably have taken him with their Webley Pistols, souvenirs from the Royal Navy, they did not want to risk any loss of life.

So, despite the men's great loss, which was torturous, and nagged at them constantly for a rash response, they'd been patient. Over several clandestine meetings, they'd formulated a plan. The pigs had been drugged by a man who had been working on the farm for the past few months. It hadn't taken a king's ransom to convince him. The man had seen 'depraved acts', referred to his employer as a 'vile individual', and had considered it his 'solemn duty as a god-fearing man' to assist in the plot against him.

One soldier pointed overhead at the raven. It circled and drew dark veins on the full moon.

'It means bad luck,' the soldier whispered.

'When they come in twos or threes, maybe. There's only one,' another hissed.

'Even so, I think the luck of the bastard farmer has just run out.'

The pack of wronged soldiers came in their uniforms. They were proud of their achievements. They'd fought for King and Country. *Won* for King and Country.

The least they could expect was a welcome return. One full of happiness and love.

Into the arms of their families. Except ...

There was a problem. The pig farmer had taken their children.

2015

PAUL SAW THAT there was no reception on his mobile phone, and he shivered.

But really? What had he expected? The middle-of-nowhere had always been very good at cutting off contact from the outside world.

Acknowledging his foolish actions, he glanced back at his mother's vehicle; illegally driven here because he was only sixteen and had no driving licence. He'd parked it alongside several gnarled trees.

A branch curled out of the largest tree like a finger beckoning to him. He struggled to tear his eyes away from it. It was a significant branch on a significant tree. Dripping with history.

This was why he'd come here. For history. *His* history.

He turned back to the farmyard. It was a cold night, but not a wet one, and the skies were clear. A large black bird rose and fell above him, etching inky black lines into the full moon.

While questioning the wisdom of this impulsive trip, he began his journey into the eighty-eight-acre farm. The grass came up to his knees and shrubbery clawed at him, but despite the explosion of life that nature brought, the place itself felt long dead.

Fences that used to house the pigs lay broken and smashed. Barns looked decrepit and the farmhouse that he drew near to looked skeletal. Parts of the roof had fallen away, and ivy had torn through the walls.

Maybe that was all he needed. Knowledge that the place had fallen. That it was all over. That the Rays were no more.

So, why was he still going? Why had he not turned back for the car?

Because the fact that the Rays were no more wasn't strictly true.

He was a Ray.

Not his mother. No. She'd had a lot of misfortune in her life but that wasn't part of it; she'd only married into the diseased line and adopted the name. So, he was potentially the last of the Rays – depending on whether his aunt, Lacey Ray, was still alive. *And,* he thought, *it would probably be better if she wasn't.*

As he neared the farmhouse, he started to sweat despite the cold. The weight in his left hand was becoming a real burden.

He stopped metres from the farmhouse, he closed his eyes and pictured that young nurse broken and bloody on the pathway, riddled with pellets. He turned and looked at the old barn to his left. The nurse's murderer, Thomas Ray, had been found dead and mutilated in there years later.

He wasn't at all surprised that this place had been a thorn in the council's side for so long now. This place would never be bought. These may be less religious and superstitious times, but after what happened here, could anyone really deny the existence of evil?

He took a deep breath and looked up at the circling black bird.

Now the last of the Rays was back. Back in *this* blood-drenched hell hole.

He marched down the pathway lugging the plastic fuel can.

1918

T HE PACK OF wronged soldiers had found it easier than expected.

Despite the monster's heinous actions against their own children, these were men bound together in morality. They had fought the Germans in the name of decency and justice for many arduous years and weren't about to sacrifice their righteousness now, no matter how acidic their desire for vengeance was. So, they had spared the children. Seven-year-old Andrew Ray had put up a fight and had kicked one of them ferociously in the shins, but it hadn't been hard to overpower him and his younger sister, Dorothy.

The children had been locked beneath the stairs and spared the fate that was facing their father. He would not live to feel the pain of losing his own kin. The same pain that plagued every second of the soldiers' now sleepless lives.

No. For the wronged soldiers to kill children would serve no purpose, except to destroy what little soul they had left. It wasn't an option.

The fate of the mother, Gladys, was still undecided.

Her involvement in this affair was still unclear. 'Surely, she must have known?' had been commonly uttered in their clandestine meetings. 'But suspicion is not evidence,' Douglas, the wisest of the soldiers, had often asserted.

Gladys would watch as justice came to her husband. Then, she would be tried, and judged too.

William, the eldest of the soldiers, and the natural leader among them, grabbed the farmer while he slept and lugged him down the stairs.

At the bottom of the stairs, he threw the farmer through the open front door. He crashed into his hand-carved rocking chair on the front porch. Made of heavy wood, the chair didn't move; instead, the little farmer bounced off it and hit the floor face-down, with a crunch.

William marched over and put his hand on one of the arrow-shaped spindles on the back of the chair. He rocked it, waiting for the farmer to turn onto his back. 'Skilled with your hands, aren't you?'

The farmer quivered, and a strange noise came from him. *Was he sobbing?*

'Is this where you sat while you planned to destroy all of our lives?' William spat at him.

It was becoming clearer that the farmer wasn't sobbing.

Anything but.

He was laughing to himself.

From the door emerged Gav, the largest and strongest of the soldiers. He had enveloped Gladys in his massive frame and his hand was pinned over her mouth. Her white nightgown billowed around her as she fought in his grip. She also tried to slam her heels into his shins, but Gav did not allow enough distance between them for her to build up any force.

The farmer continued to quiver with laughter. It was a

hollow sound. One that was very different from anything they'd all heard before.

William felt a rush of blood and approached the downed farmer. He held one of his ammunition boots above the bastard's head. He closed his eyes and imagined driving the iron heel-plate and the studded leather sole into his skull. He imagined doing it again and again. Grinding, if necessary.

Wiping him off the face of the earth.

'You must have known this day was coming, Reginald,' William said.

Reginald Ray turned slowly onto his back. The moon was full and bright enough to offer them, for the first time this evening, a clear view of his face. Or what was left of it. It was covered in scaly patches. Most were dry, but some were open, and wept.

'What is wrong with you?' William said and backed away with his hand to his mouth.

'The plague!' David, the youngest of them, cried, putting his hand to his mouth also.

Gav hissed in Gladys' ear. 'Tell us now. What is *wrong* with him?'

He uncovered her mouth so she could respond. 'Nothing, you filthy pig!'

'Nothing? Look at his face! It's falling apart!'

'It's always been this way. *Reginald has always been this way.* It's not infectious. It just flares sometimes.'

Not infectious?

'*Are you sure?*' David said.

She spat her words. '*It's always been this way.*'

The soldiers took their hands down and looked at each other, sharing their relief that this wasn't infectious. They now knew why this man had been a virtual recluse in Little Horton. A skin condition such as this one would certainly have driven him to avoid the public eye.

'Whatever you think he's done, he hasn't. We are good folk. He has nothing to do with your missing children. I swear it on the lives of our own,' Gladys said.

But Reginald continued to laugh.

William looked down at him, wincing over the sight of the old farmer's sores opening and closing with each grotesque chuckle, and said, 'He doesn't seem to agree?'

Gladys shook her head. 'I don't know. Maybe the fall stunned him? Reginald ... why are you laughing?'

Reginald continued. He rocked his sore covered head from side to side.

'Reginald, please, now, stop this ...' Gladys' voice was starting to crack under the weight of her tears.

'I've had enough,' David said, stepping forward and slamming his boot into Reginald's side.

Reginald curled up into the foetal position, but it did not halt his laughter.

'Let's just get on with this,' David said. 'We know he did it.'

Reginald pulled back his lips, and exposed his sore, infected gums. He had no teeth. The words he then muttered were muffled and quiet, but understandable. 'It's true. I know where your children are.'

Apart from the one holding tightly to Gladys, the soldiers moved in closer.

'Where are they?' William said.

The words that came out of his decaying face were worse than any bullet from a German's gun.

Gladys wailed, while most of the soldiers pinned their

hands again to their mouths – this time in disgust, rather than through fear.

'Say that again and I'll kill you right now,' William said.

At that point, the raven returned, gorged on lamb tongues. It swooped low and caught the words.

'*We ate them.*'

2015

THE BACK DOOR was hanging off, so Paul Ray entered that way.

The kitchen was dark, and he used the torch on his phone to look around.

It was like a large Victorian kitchen; a school trip had taken him to one just like it, in a hall owned by the National Trust. There was a cast-iron stove; alongside it, copper pans hung from the wall. As he moved deeper into the kitchen, it became more chaotic. Some of the more modern cupboards were falling to pieces, and drawers lay smashed on the floor.

Despite the place being deserted, there was a meaty aroma that seemed remarkably fresh. This peculiarity forced Paul to consider the atrocities that must have occurred in this kitchen a century ago.

As a child, it had been terrifying to hear the story from another boy. He had introduced it with a question which had only one aim – to bully him. 'Do you know what your great-great-grandad did?'

His parents, and the parents of others, would often dismiss this story as Wiltshire folklore. Their children's minds were vulnerable, after all, and needed protecting. When Paul *did* eventually find out that it was true and that the records of this event existed, he'd lain awake all night, scribbling other words the bully had used that first time. Over and over again.

He ate children ... he ate children ... he ate children ...

The bullying had worsened before it had improved. Paul had earned the nickname *Hanzel* due to the references to cannibalism in that classic tale. He'd had his schoolbag filled with dogfood and the children had laughed at him for bringing a 'minced baby' to school with him. Kids could be cruel. These had been for a long time.

Of course, it had all come to an end, when he was twelve and he'd almost died. He'd been kidnapped, and his father, murdered. After returning to school, the bullies had rounded on him and Paul kicked the living shit out of two of them.

That had been the end of that.

Paul often considered this moment of triumph with a smile across his face. But not this time. Not while he was in a farmhouse passed down from murderer to murderer, breathing in rank odours, and lugging litres of petrol around with him.

At the kitchen door, Paul put the plastic fuel can down for a moment, to catch his breath, and wipe the sweat from his brow with his T-shirt. It was a cold night but lugging this weight over that farmyard had taken its toll.

It was only now that he realised that he was shaking and his stomach was turning over. He was terrified, but who wouldn't be?

He needed to get this done quickly.

He left the petrol can at the kitchen door and moved into the hallway. The most important thing to do now was check that there was no one here. The last thing he wanted to do was burn the place down with a potential squatter sleeping upstairs.

The check didn't take long. The house was smaller than it'd looked on the outside. He was also careful to call out warnings before going into any room to avoid being ambushed by someone.

The first part of his warning was very honest. 'I'm about to burn this house down.'

The second part, less so. 'I'm not going to come in to check and I'm just about to strike a match.'

When no one emerged, he went in. Paul may have been a Ray, but he wasn't like any of the other Rays. Life may have been cheap to them. It wasn't, and never would be, to him.

This was where the legacy of the Rays truly ended.

Here. Tonight.

Then, he would change his name. He was sixteen now. The law would allow him that mercy.

He knew exactly where he wanted to start the fire. He returned to the living room. Here a stuffed Dachshund whiled away its time on a white rug.

He unscrewed the can and emptied petrol all over the Dachshund. He held his breath and moved back quickly as he poured; he knew the fumes would attack his eyes otherwise. The petrol gushed out over the floor and the walls as he weaved backwards through the hallway. Some splashed on his shoes and trousers, but he wasn't worried. He'd be some distance away before the flames went up. He manoeuvred carefully around the kitchen so he could hit the cupboards, the drawers and all the work surfaces without doubling back on himself. Finally, he was outside with petrol to spare.

He pulled a Zippo lighter out of his pocket and read the engraving: *Happy Birthday Joe!*

'For you Dad,' Paul said and lit the Zippo. He threw it into the kitchen and listened to it clatter against the ground. The sound of the ignition was soft but, considering the silence, significant. The flames rose quickly. Surprised by the speed, Paul turned to run.

There was a man standing there in overalls. There was a loose white sack over his face. It wasn't tied on, but eyeholes had been cut out so he could see. He held a mallet in his hand.

Paul was already mid-sprint, so suddenly turning back again caused him to lose his footing. He fell to his knees. He noticed a black bird sitting on the ground in front of him. Then, he heard and felt the thud in the back of his head, and everything disappeared.

1918

THE RAVEN FOUND another tree from which to watch. Close enough to see but not to be seen. The bird was still heavy from its late-night feast and it didn't want to add a frantic escape to its agenda. It so desperately wanted to watch. This was its favourite kind of show. One which involved death.

The soldiers had been quick in their ambush of Reginald Ray. Now the beating they gave the old farmer as they marched him across his farmyard was swift and brutal. Their hatred for this man burned. Other men may have moved slowly to savour the experience; let the farmer *feel* each blow and then suffer for a short time before landing the next one.

But no. These men were soldiers and they behaved as such. They were trained to move quickly and efficiently to get the job done. Enjoyment would be a distraction. So, they pounded him as they moved at pace.

The screams from both Reginald and Gladys were thick and desperate. Screams were punctuated occasionally by a soldier's war-cry. 'You are going to burn in hell tonight for what you've done.'

Sometimes, one soldier would warn another. 'Not the face. Don't hit him in the face. It'll come off all over you.'

Eventually, the screams subsided, and to the raven, it looked as if they were now simply dragging a corpse.

Only when they reached the tree did Reginald indicate that he was still alive. 'I've spent a long time in Hell already.'

'Well then, you won't mind staying there permanently,' said the leader, William, as he seized Reginald under his armpits and hoisted him up. 'Turn and face me.'

Reginald complied. William looked him up and down. His buttoned cotton pyjamas were grass-stained and muddy. 'What the hell is wrong with you? Your face—'

'—looks like a piece of rotten fruit?' Reginald smiled, causing the largest sores on his cheeks to crack open, exposing the glistening soft tissue beneath.

'Yes,' William said and spat on the floor.

Reginald's hair was thinning peculiarly. It was as if someone had seized handfuls of it and torn it out, exposing patches of his scalp, which was also blistered and weeping. 'As I said, I've spent a long time in hell already,' he paused to lift his hand and point at the soldiers. 'I never experienced the youthful wonders that you did. Do you remember when you had the pick of the girls? When you could touch and feel all those bodies?' He touched his puffy top lip with the tip of his tongue. '*Inside and out?*'

'You're an animal,' William said.

At this point, Gladys, who was down on her knees several metres behind William and her husband, burst into tears again.

Reginald continued, '*Do you remember?* Remember all

that fuckity-fuck, fuckity-fuck? Well, I remember what I was doing in my youth.' He turned his finger back to point into his mouth. 'I was watching my teeth tumble out into the trough as I loaded the swill.' He then held up his hand. 'I watched my nails turn to the colour of shit.' He pulled at the sores on his cheeks. 'And I watched my face turn to rotten fruit. So, you want to talk about me going to Hell this night, soldier? Don't make me laugh. I was already there when all of you were fuckity-fuck, fuckity-fuck, fuckity-fuck!'

'It's a special day for me Reginald,' William said, gripping the farmer's shoulder. 'Today, my *only* son would have been fifteen.' He slammed his fist into his stomach. The old man crumpled to his knees, gasping for air.

Moments later, the breathlessness became an insidious laugh. He looked up with a toothless grin. 'No fuckity-fuck for him then!'

William kicked him hard in the face. It lifted him partially off the ground before sending him onto his back. William descended with his fists flying. It took three of his companions to restrain him. 'Let's do this properly, William,' Gav hissed in his ear, 'he's just trying to win whatever he thinks is left to win. Now's the time to end it.'

William pulled away and turned his back on Reginald. He looked down at Gladys. She was no longer being restrained. There was no need. Listening to her husband talking this way had broken her.

As the other soldiers prepared Reginald for his execution, William knelt and said, 'How could you allow this? You must have known?'

Gladys looked up at him with a red face. '*He took me.*'

'What?' William creased his face. 'I don't—'

'*He took me when I was five.*'

William widened his eyes. 'From where?'

'From the orphanage.'

'My God, *when you were five?* What the hell did he do to you?'

'Nothing ... at first. He treated me like a daughter, and I helped him with his illness.' She was crying hard, so she had to pause to get control of her voice. 'He treated me well. Until I was twelve. Until we had Andrew.'

William flinched.

She continued. 'And then he changed. All he cared about was Andrew, and later, Dorothy. I was his nurse then. Nothing more. To spit and shout at as his illness grew worse.'

Gladys was already speaking about him as if he was gone. Did she want the same thing that the soldiers did? An end to the madness?

William lifted her head by her chin and looked into her eyes. 'Did you know? Did you know what he was doing?'

'Unlike that man, I believe in God, sir, and I will swear to you on the lives of my children, I *knew nothing.*'

Reginald called out from behind William. 'She's telling the truth, soldier. She ate them ... enjoyed every mouthful, but she knew nothing.'

William turned. The noose was around Reginald's neck. Gav held him up by his legs. The old farmer didn't struggle. The rope had been thrown over the gnarled branch and then tied around the base of the tree.

'Why Reginald?' William said, taking steps towards the condemned man. 'Why did you do this to us? To our children?'

'The answer is simple really,' Reginald said. 'Their youth, their freshness, *their health.* I wanted it inside me.'

David vomited. Douglas cried, 'Jesus.'

'Why?' William said.

Reginald smiled. 'To make me better.'

'It doesn't look like it worked.'

'Eventually. I could feel the newness inside … building, growing.'

'Before you die, Reginald, can you tell us if our children suffered?'

Reginald paused before answering. 'No. Some questions are best left unanswered.'

'So you would deny us even that?'

'I would—'

'Monstrous fucking beast,' Gav said and released Reginald's legs.

There was no drop. They didn't want his death to be instant. Stop the flow of life had been the plan. Let him feel it leave him.

The raven chanced another two trees to get a better view.

It watched six soldiers in a semi-circle around the old tree. No more vomiting, or crying, just stony-faced appreciation of a demon being sent back to Hell. Even the wife, Gladys, had risen to her feet to bid farewell to the man who'd stolen her innocence.

Reginald Ray gripped at the noose around his neck, following an instinctive reaction to tear away the object cutting off the flow of blood and oxygen. The raven had flown near this man on many occasions. There seemed to be more peace in those eyes than ever before. Even when the capillaries in them began to burst.

After several minutes, Reginald Ray hung limply with his tongue protruding.

The soldiers took it in turns to spit on the body and then turned from it. They hoisted Gladys to her feet and told her that she would be spared on two conditions. The first was that she left Reginald Ray to the animals for a few days before he was cut down. The second that she was a good parent to those children.

Once they were some distance away, the raven flew over to the hanged man. It landed on his shoulder. It could feel the murderer's heart still beating. This didn't deter the raven. It really couldn't help itself.

It fed on the tongue of Reginald Ray.

2015

THE BACK OF his head throbbed.

The last thing Paul remembered looking at had been a black bird and, behind that, a burning farmhouse. Now, he was looking into a flame again, but this time, it was smaller, and less aggressive.

A candle.

He became aware of a deep, unwavering groan. Then his surroundings began to take shape. Candles were suspended in bulky silver candelabras which lined a long table. There was someone perched across from him and someone sitting to his right, at the head of the table.

His vision was swirling too much for him to focus on these figures and they were little more than ink blots on pale surroundings.

Memory flew to the man with the white sack on his head … the slits for his eyes … the mallet in his hand. His heart suddenly beating faster, he tried to stand up. Then, realising his legs were chained, he swayed on his feet, and felt his blood freeze.

'Stay seated, please.' The words were hissed, rather than spoken.

Paul disobeyed the order, despite knowing his options were limited. He couldn't run. The chains would bring him to his knees.

Shit ... shit ... not again ... Jesus, not again!

The moaning continued. His surroundings became clearer. There were bowls dotted around the table. Some contained bread, others fruit. There were sliced meats, and bowls of stew. It was a spacious room with a Victorian feel. There was a grandfather clock swimming out of the shadows, and some Victorian paintings. It was, in fact, a watercolour of a family gathered around a small stream on a beautiful summer's day, which brought his vision to full clarity.

And how, God, he wished it hadn't.

The moaning young man opposite him was disfigured. Identifying how exactly in the limited light offered by the candles were hard, but he didn't appear to have any lips, eyelids or ears.

Paul took a deep breath through his nose as the world swayed around him again. 'What's happening? Where—'

He stopped when he saw the elderly man at the head of the table. He also looked disfigured, but in a different way. His face looked sore. Patches of it looked scabby. He was thin and haggard, and there were many bald spots on his head. He was spooning stew into his mouth.

Paul tried again to step away, forgetting his legs were chained. The chains rattled and he stopped.

'You won't get far,' the elderly man said.

The young man opposite him, who appeared to have been doctored in some way, raised a hand to point at him ...

Except, there was no hand, just a bandaged stump.

The young man didn't speak and continued to groan.

'What's wrong with him?' Paul said.

The elderly man swallowed his food. 'Ah nothing, ignore him. I had him over for dinner, and I don't think this is what he expected. He hasn't even touched his food.'

The young man had a plate of sliced meat in front of him.

'Let me out of here,' Paul said. 'You don't understand. This can't be happening. Not again ... don't you understand? Do you know who I am?'

'No, who are you, young man?'

'I'm Paul Ray.'

The man put down his spoon. It clattered in his bowl. 'Well ... fuckity-fuck, Paul Ray! What were the chances of that? So, pleased to finally meet you.' He jumped to his feet and came around the table with his arms open to embrace him. 'I'm Reginald Ray.'

1

I N HIS BATHROOM mirror, Michael Yorke examined the lines around his eyes. He ran his hand over his beard. Would shaving it off give him a sudden burst of youth?

Probably not. He was forty-four. Besides, when had he ever really cared that much about his appearance anyway?

No, the beard stayed, despite the white patches; there was something about it that was comforting.

Yorke sighed. Not only was he aging at the speed of light, but in the space of less than two years, he had become a married father-of-two and *that* came with significant pressure.

When he'd been a Detective Chief Inspector with the Wiltshire police, the pressure had been immense. At times, intolerable. But fatherhood was a completely different planet. A different dimension even.

Beatrice Yorke, now nine months old, had not made a settled start to her life. She'd overcome her premature arrival easily enough, only to return home with colic, which had made her existence, as well as the existence of her parents, quite traumatic. Bouncing through every available concoction, both traditional and scientific, and all equally ineffective, had been costly, and exhausting. Eventually, the Yorke family had conceded defeat; they were never going to sleep again.

And then it suddenly stopped! Two months ago. But no sooner had they dared to accept the relief on offer than a problem with the other child began.

Yorke looked down at his adopted son Ewan's mobile phone screen and read the anonymous message again.

The thirteen-year-old boy was carrying one hell of a burden.

The message said: *Hey orphan.*

———

DS JAKE PETTMAN tried his best to get into bed with his wife, Sheila, without waking her, but failed miserably. As he so often did.

'*You seen the time?*' Sheila said, keeping her back to him.

'I'm sorry. It's this new case. The missing farmer's boy.'

He reached out to stroke her shoulder. She was wearing his favourite light blue nightie. The one that always excited him. But he was well and truly satisfied this evening. As he'd been most evenings this month.

'If I didn't know how shit your job was, I'd probably start suspecting you were having an affair,' Sheila said.

Jake flushed. He was immediately grateful that it was dark, and her back was to him. He faked laughter. 'Not sure I've got the time for any of that.'

Sheila turned over and put her arms round him. She nuzzled his wide neck and kissed his large face. 'Maybe tomorrow you could get back early? Frank was asking for you.'

Jake felt sick. He kissed her forehead. 'I'll try. I promise.'

'You smell like you've had a shower.'

'I had one at work,' Jake lied.

Sheila started to kiss his chin. She worked her way up and started to nibble on his bottom lip. Her hand slipped from his back and worked its way under the sheets. 'I like it when you smell fresh.'

He felt her hand on the front of his boxer shorts.

He reached under the sheets and took her hand in both of his. 'Sorry, Sheila. I'm *so* tired. This case too, it's tearing us all up.'

Sheila backed away and sighed. 'I understand ... goodnight then.'

After Sheila had fallen asleep, Jake lay awake for hours. He crossed his large arms behind his head and listened to the rain on his window.

Why had she started to be so nice to him now? After all these years of treating him with contempt when he'd only tried to do his best by her and Frank? Now, after driving him into someone else's arms, then she starts to behave like the loving wife ... was she sensing that she was losing him?

Jake sighed. *What the hell am I doing?*

Instead of counting sheep, he asked himself this question over and over until he passed out.

On his way to bed, Yorke decided to stop by Beatrice's room.

26

This is madness, he thought as he scooped her up.

Waking her would almost certainly condemn the Yorke household to a sleepless night. Right now, however, the risk felt worth it for the warmth she exuded and the contentedness she imparted to him.

There was an old armchair in the corner where Patricia often sat to breastfeed Beatrice during the more unsociable hours. With his tiny bundle, he settled back in the chair.

He looked down at her tiny face.

Baby Bea.

He stroked her cheek and she sucked in her lips. Yorke smiled. She was probably preparing to feed.

What he adored most about Beatrice, and what made him feel so content, was the absolute innocence, and the fact that she knew of nothing bad in this world around her.

Tears came to his eyes. With that button nose, and narrow cheekbones, Beatrice so resembled Danielle. The sister who'd practically raised Yorke when his mother hadn't wanted to know. Supporting him, influencing him, shaping him into the man he became. Danielle had been his everything. Until her drug addiction, and eventual murder by a drug dealer called William Proud.

Nine months ago, on the night that Beatrice was born, Yorke had confronted Proud. This had been the moment that Yorke had craved for so long. A chance for closure.

But instead of closure, the confrontation had cracked open a chasm of further questions, suspicions, and tragedy.

Proud had told Yorke that he wasn't the only one responsible for the death of his sister. *'I'm just the blunt instrument ... there's a bent bastard shitting in the same toilet as you...'*

Proud had died that night. Accidently. He'd been

backing away from an angry Yorke and had fallen down a ladder shaft. He'd broken his neck and died instantly.

Yorke didn't regret his death. The bastard had still executed his sister regardless of whether it was ordered by someone else or not.

But the death had repercussions. A suspension for Yorke while the fatality was investigated. It was found to be accidental, but Yorke had been acting alone when he should have called for back-up. His suspension was lifted but he was dropped a rank to DI.

He wasn't ready yet to work and, fortunately, the doctor had agreed. It hadn't taken much to convince him. He just told him the truth. That the thought of returning to work made him physically sick.

He was currently considering a career change. He'd probably have embarked on it already if it wasn't for one nagging question. *Who were these people who had ordered the death of his sister? And why?*

He had a painful feeling that he would have to remain in this job for an answer to that question.

———

DI Mark Topham rolled off Bobby.

With his back to the young man, catching his breath, he reached up to smother his sweat and tears.

'That was quicker than I expected,' Bobby said, stroking Topham's back.

Topham didn't respond. He wasn't interested in small talk. Bobby wouldn't be this man's real name anyway.

This whole situation wasn't real.

Hadn't been for months.

'I mean, I knew there was something there. Electricity, sparks, but wow, we flew there. *You really flew—*'

'You can go now.'

Bobby snorted. 'Shit! You are blunt! Most people at least chat for a few minutes afterwards.'

'You're a prostitute.'

A snort didn't suffice this time; he went all out with a gasp of surprise. 'So, it's okay to fuck me but not to talk to me?'

Topham wondered if it was even worth gracing this with a reply. He decided not. He felt the bed move as Bobby sat up.

'You know, you didn't seem to mind talking to me in the bar all night. But I guess it was all about the endgame.'

'The money is on the side.' Topham continued to face away. 'Please don't make a fuss on the way out of the hotel. I've paid you enough for your discretion.'

'*My discretion?*' He raised his voice. 'What do you want me to be discreet about? About the fact that you wouldn't fuck me with a condom?'

'Good night.' Topham closed his eyes. He listened to Bobby get dressed beside the bed and the door closed.

With his eyes still shut, he reached over to the floor beside him for the bottle of vodka. He sat up in bed and started to gulp.

As the spirit burned his throat he saw, in his mind, the words written on a card by a mute man who had seen Neil's corpse: *There were bits of him everywhere, Mark. He'd been stabbed thousands of times.*

His partner. His lover. His everything.

He gulped back more vodka.

Dead. Gone. Never to return.

YORKE STILL HADN'T MADE it to bed.

He wished he had because then he wouldn't have been sitting here watching the news. With wide eyes, he watched the burning farmhouse on the Ray pig farm.

As if the memory of William Proud's death nine months ago hadn't been enough this evening, now Yorke was faced with the memory of finding Thomas Ray's mangled body strung up in one of the old barns.

On the news broadcast, the firefighters were trying, and failing, to save the old farmhouse. Not that they had much of a chance; the place was old, wooden and very combustible. The fact that it was still standing at this point was a miracle.

'Police neither confirm nor deny foul play,' rolled across the info bar.

Yorke guffawed. It couldn't be anything but foul play! The property was abandoned, and in the middle of nowhere. It was unlikely to be a piece of faulty electrical equipment!

Add to that the fact that this property was owned by the most notorious family ever seen in Wiltshire. One that had terrorised the local community for several generations until Yorke and his team put a stop to it five years ago.

Police neither confirm nor deny foul play.

He laughed out loud.

He turned off the television.

Not his problem anyway.

UNDER THE GAZE of the burning farmhouse, an abandoned white Volvo V40 shimmered.

DCI Emma Gardner took a step away from it, leaned against the old tree and rustled in her pocket. A new officer noticed her searching and came over holding out a packet of cigarettes. 'Do you want one, ma'am?'

Gardner smiled. 'No thanks, Peter. Never smoked in my life.' She withdrew the packet of tic-tacs and turned to survey the scene.

It was busy, and not just with firefighters. Familiar faces, including that of Superintendent Joan Madden, were in abundance.

Gardner and several other colleagues had been pulled away from a missing person's case because this incident warranted immediate and serious investigation. This wasn't any old fire. This was the Ray farmhouse. Once a beating heart of evil.

'You'd expect fire in hell,' Gardner said, 'but it's been quiet for so long.'

'Too long,' DC Collette Willows said, approaching. 'It was only a matter of time.'

Gardner took a deep breath. She felt a twinge in her chest and coughed. A sharp reminder of the near-fatal injury she sustained almost a year ago.

'You okay, ma'am?' Willows said.

'Yes, Collette. You've got news on the car, haven't you?'

'I'm afraid so. It belongs to Sarah Ray.'

This wasn't any old fire.

She emptied the tic-tacs into her mouth and leaned back against the infamous tree on which Reginald Ray was executed.

From one of the twisted branches, the eyes of a black bird glowed.

———

In bed, Patricia turned to him.

'I'm sorry, I didn't mean to wake you,' Yorke said.

'Don't believe you! You're over the moon I'm awake ... there's something on your mind.'

He lifted his arm, and she edged in closer, so she was lying against his shoulder. 'You can read me like a book.'

She reached up and ran her fingers over his beard. 'Good ... still there.'

'Almost wasn't. I spent some time in the bathroom eyeing up the razor.'

'I guessed that's what you were doing.'

'Then I spent some time with Bea...'

She grabbed his ear.

'Ouch. That hurts!'

'Good. Hopefully, that will make you think twice next time. The milk machine next to you needs some rest.'

'There was no waking her.'

'Probably because she drained me an hour ago.'

Yorke considered telling her about the burning Ray farmhouse but decided against it. Despite his suspension being lifted, he was seriously considering his options. Heading back to law enforcement held little appeal right now. 'Sick to the stomach with it,' was his usual response to Patricia's attempts to broach the subject. If it wasn't for the ridiculous pay cut, he'd already be investigating a teaching qualification. Discussing the fire at this late hour might show he was interested in going back.

And he wasn't. He *just* wasn't.

Without really thinking about it, Yorke said, 'I noticed Ewan looked miserable, so I grabbed his phone for a look.

He's been getting some horrible messages. On one, they called him an orphan—'

Patricia sat up. '*You did what?*'

'*Shit.* I took his phone and read his messages.' He felt the colour drain from his face. 'You're about to tell me that was the wrong thing to do?'

'Yes! What were you thinking?'

'I was worried ...'

'He's a thirteen-year-old boy, you can't read his messages!'

'But surely it's okay if you think there is a problem?'

'Are you serious, Mike?'

'Sorry.'

'It's not me you need to apologise to. You can't police someone's life, Mike. That's not how it works.'

He ran his hand over his own beard. 'Even if the intention comes from a good place?'

'*Even if.*' She lay back down next to him. 'Talk to him tomorrow. Explain what you've done. I'm sure he'll understand.' She sighed and turned away from him.

'Aren't you forgetting something?' Yorke said. 'What about the fact that he's been called an orphan? Does that not shock you?'

'Of course, but I already knew.'

'How?'

'He showed me the messages.'

It was Yorke's turn to sit up. 'And you didn't think to tell me?'

'He didn't want me to.'

He felt as if he'd been punched and winded. 'Why?'

'For exactly this reason. Because he knew you'd go overboard!'

'Overboard? They're calling him an orphan! There's bullying and then there's full-on verbal assault!'

Patricia sat up and faced him. 'Behave.'

'So, that's it?' Yorke said. 'He tells you that and you write it off as nothing important?'

'Anything but. I contacted the school. It is being dealt with.'

'With what? *A detention?*'

'I don't know yet. But these are kids. Yes, they are bullying. Yes, it has to be stopped. But it won't be stopped with you marching in all gung-ho. That is the reason Ewan didn't tell you.'

There was a knock at the front door.

They both looked at each other and then looked at the clock by the bedside table.

'Wait here,' Yorke said and threw on his dressing gown.

He headed downstairs, quietly and quickly, not wanting to allow enough time for another disruptive knock at the door which could wake the children.

He looked through the peephole and felt a rush of adrenaline.

Sarah Ray.

GARDNER NOTICED Topham's car pulling up behind the other police vehicles. She left the infamous tree and jogged over to meet him. Along the way, she felt sharp reminders in her chest of the knife wound from nine months ago.

She wasn't going over to greet Topham. He'd spent the previous few months bashing the self-destruct button, so she wanted to see what state he was in before he ended up in the logbook.

It had been a wise decision.

Topham steadied himself against the roof of his car. His white buttoned shirt was untucked, his trousers were scuffed, and his hair was dishevelled.

Rewind one year and you would have a man who valued his appearance above everything else in the world. Except, maybe, Neil Solomon. His now dead partner.

'Tell me you didn't just drive here in this state.'

'I could tell you that if you want but would you believe me? You just saw me getting out of the car.' He smiled at her.

'Get back in the car, I'll take you back when I'm done. If Madden sees you, you'll be suspended ... probably wouldn't be a bad thing ... but I need to think. Get in the car. Sleep it off if you must. We will just have to make up some excuse about you and your car in the morning. Say you started throwing up or something.'

'I keep seeing him, Emma ... everywhere I look.'

'Neil?'

There were tears streaming down his face. 'God, no. I wish! I keep seeing the bastard who killed him.'

Gardner clutched his arm. 'Get in the car, and bloody well stay there.'

SARAH RAY LOOKED CONSIDERABLY BETTER than she had done five years ago.

Gone was the shoulder-length jet black hair, badly parted in the middle. Instead was a short bob, carefully styled, and tinged with red. She was a tall, broad woman and had replaced her loose-fitting, worn-out clothing with a close-fitting, fashionable outfit.

Unsurprisingly, the only way was up after a life freed from a serial cheater.

Yorke recognised the distress in her, and it brought all the memories crashing back. In fact, even before she told him, Yorke knew that her son was missing again.

It had taken several minutes for Yorke to untangle himself from Sarah's embrace. She'd cried uncontrollably on his shoulder. Little of what she'd said through mouthfuls of tears had made sense.

With a tray of steaming hot tea, Patricia had also come to his aid, and together, they had managed to get her onto the sofa.

When Patricia had placed the cups down on the wooden coffee table, Sarah sprang to her feet again. 'Coasters?'

'Of course,' Patricia said.

As Patricia went back to the kitchen, Yorke recalled Sarah's OCDs; her obsession with tidiness and cleanliness. In her current state of anxiety, they were bound to manifest.

'I *knew* it was him. Immediately.' Sarah sat back down. 'As soon as I saw the fire on the news, I just knew.'

'And you've tried phoning him?'

'Hundreds of times.'

'So, he's taken the car? No chance of it being stolen?'

'The keys are gone from the kitchen drawer. No one has been in my house – I'm certain.'

'Drink some tea, Mrs Ray.'

They all took a mouthful of tea, including Patricia, who had just returned with the coasters.

'But, ultimately, we've got a sixteen-year-old boy and a missing car. How long has it been?'

'Less than two hours.'

'So, if you went to the station now, they are unlikely to jump straight on this as a missing person...'

'Which is why I'm coming straight to you.'

Yorke put his cup down and stared at Sarah, uncertain of how to respond.

Patricia responded instead. 'Mrs Ray, I genuinely share your concerns. I really do. But my husband is not currently working. Michael has not been well—'

'And why did you think that I would respond any differently to my colleagues at the station?' Yorke said.

Sarah put her cup down and fixed Yorke with a stare. 'Because you were there, Detective Yorke. You saw what we saw. You saw evil that night. My god, have you seen anything like that since? If you have, I pray for your soul. You think a boy forgets what we saw that night? You think I forget? You think anyone can?'

Yorke did not respond.

'Did you forget, detective?'

'Of course not.'

Patricia jumped in again. 'Mrs Ray, I really think we should just contact—'

'Patricia, please,' Yorke said. 'Okay, Mrs Ray, you have my attention. But tell me, why now? Why did Paul get up today and burn the farmhouse down?'

'Because they came to him again ... and again.'

Yorke's heart beat faster. 'Who did?'

'The bastards he's descended from.'

'They're dead, Mrs Ray—'

'In his dreams, detective. Again and again. Every night. They come for him, and they want him.'

'That doesn't make any sense,' Yorke said.

'They're driving him mad. This last month he's barely slept and when he's awake at night, I sometimes hear him

37

crying. They won't leave him alone ... and now ... now ... he's gone and done this.'

Yorke felt Patricia's hand on his leg. 'Mike. This is not up to you.'

Yorke put his hand on Patricia's hand. 'I'm still listening, Mrs Ray, but could this not just be a coincidence?'

'I went to his room after I saw the fire on the news because I suspected he was involved somehow. I searched around, aimlessly. I was looking for anything to tell me where he could be. Then, I went into his bedside drawer, and ... and then I knew ...'

'What did you find in there?'

'It's what I didn't find, detective. His father's zippo lighter. He never took it out of his bedside drawer. It's his most treasured possession. And yet, tonight, when the Ray's farmhouse burns down, he what? *Coincidentally* takes it out with him?'

THE FIRE WAS ALMOST OUT, but the air was heavy with smoke. When Gardner first saw Yorke approaching her, she wondered if her eyesight was playing tricks on her in the poor visibility.

He stopped in front of her and PC Sean Tyler.

'Please to see you, sir ... I like the beard,' Tyler said, opening his logbook.

'Thanks,' Yorke said. 'But don't log me in just yet. I don't know if I'm staying.'

He looked at Gardner. She was lost for words and could only manage a 'sir?'

'Wrong way round now, ma'am.'

At roughly the same time that Yorke had been demoted, Gardner had earned a promotion to DCI.

'Yes ... sorry ... but Mike, why are you here?'

'Sounds ridiculous, I know, ma'am, but I kind of need my job back.'

'For God's sake, quit it with the ma'am, and walk this way with me.'

Gardner walked Yorke away from Tyler and towards her vehicle in which Topham was sleeping off yet another session.

'So, two days after you told me you were thinking about becoming a teacher, you decide to come back to work at ...' She paused to look at her watch. 'Quarter past twelve? And to a potential crime scene?'

'That's about the size of it, ma'am, sorry, Emma ... I got a visitor an hour ago which kind of threw the whole career-change plans on the backburner. The pipe, slippers and Shakespearian quotations will have to remain an elusive dream.'

'I think the teaching profession has moved on since your time in school, Mike, but get to the point - who is this visitor?'

'You wouldn't believe me if I told you.'

'Try me.'

'Sarah Ray.'

Gardner looked away. She was surprised but not in the way that Yorke expected her to be. She knew the Rays were involved already – the abandoned Volvo had indicated that. What surprised her was the fact that Sarah would immediately go to Yorke. 'Why?'

'She thinks her son drove here tonight.'

'*She told you that?*'

'Yes. She's got no evidence of it but she suspects it. Suspect being an understatement. She's *convinced*.'

Gardner held back. It wasn't the time to reveal the fact that they did have the evidence that he'd driven here. 'But still, why you?'

'A default reaction, I guess. I helped last time. I guess she thinks I'll help again.'

'Now, it's your turn to use an understatement. You more than just *helped*. You wrestled them away from some man-eating pigs in a barn.'

'Finding them was a team effort. We have only ever been as good as the sum of our parts.'

'Which is why I am so bloody glad to see you, sir ... Mike ... I hope I don't have to get used to that! I'm only standing in for—'

'Detective Inspector Michael Yorke,' Superintendent Joan Madden said. 'I thought you were sick?'

Yorke wanted to reply like he imagined a movie character might reply. A quick flick of the hair and the statement – *I said I'd be back.*

But Madden was not the kind of person to appreciate sarcasm and any display of bravado. Unless, of course, it was coming from her.

'I'm ready to come back, ma'am.'

She looked at her watch. 'At quarter-past-twelve?'

Yorke wanted to quip that he had déjà vu following Gardner's same observation but kept his dry comment to himself.

'Yes, ma'am.' He explained what had happened with Sarah Ray. The exact conversation, including the missing lighter.

Madden turned her back to him to look out over the farmyard and the smouldering farmhouse.

'Hard to believe that this place was once covered in pigs,' she said. 'Seems so quiet. So dead. Especially now the property has burned to the ground. You know that pigs can learn their names at just two or three weeks old? Do you think these animals ever knew? Ever understood the evil they were living with? I believe that they probably did. They say dogs can sense these things and pigs are more intelligent ... poor buggers. So ...' She turned back around. 'The Rays, eh? The worst thing that has ever happened to this bloody place. And you know that and that is why you are here. I commend you on that Michael. Emerging from that prairie of depression when you are needed. There is no keener sense on the force but to just come here and expect to muck in? Really? Do I look like an idiot?'

'Of course not, ma'am.'

'There are procedures. You are still signed off. You need a psyche evaluation. This isn't 1975.'

'I appreciate that, ma'am, but you know how crucial time is here. I'm not saying your team won't deliver on this but the more the merrier and do you really want to see me going through weeks of red tape when I'm willing to put in a shift?'

'Go home, Michael. You are not just walking into this crime scene. Go home and sleep off this sudden burst of enthusiasm which has dragged you from your stupor.'

Yorke lowered his head. 'Yes, ma'am.'

Madden turned away again and watched the final embers of the blaze fizzle away under a stream of water. 'So many times the Rays have put a crack through this community. So many times. And every time, just when it seems as if the community had healed, they come back to smash it open again.' She turned back. 'Be at HQ tomorrow morning at eight. I'll meet with you first and then DCI Emma Gardener can reinstate you.'

'Thanks, ma'am.'

'Don't thank me, yet. All I care about is Samuel.'

'Samuel?' Yorke said.

'Samuel Mitchell. The missing farm boy from last week.'

'You think this is connected, ma'am?' Gardner said.

'I *know* it is connected. When the Rays are involved, everything is connected.'

Yorke took a deep breath and nodded.

She was right.

2

F OR YORKE, IT felt strange to be back in a suit after
such a long period of time. It felt stranger still
wandering the halls of Wiltshire HQ and greeting
colleagues that he'd been quite close to but had opted not to
reach out to him during his suspension.

He conceded that it would have been awkward for
them, so he held no hard feelings; however, he did make a
mental note not to behave like that if the shoe was ever on
the other foot.

Being suspended had been a lonely experience.

DS Jake Pettman had been the exception of course.
He'd made an effort to keep in in touch. *Arguably,* too much
effort! He could be a right handful at times.

When Yorke sighted his close friend on the corridor as
he approached Madden's office, he opened his arms to him,
and they embraced.

Pettman was a giant of a man. His shaved head
wouldn't have looked out of place in the circle up at
Stonehenge.

Yorke backed away, catching his breath and rubbing his

ribs. 'I've missed working with you, big man, but I'll probably pass on the hug next time.'

'Well, there needn't be a next time because you're not going anywhere.'

Yorke smiled. 'Well, I'll be honest, up until last night, I'd probably have disagreed with you.'

'Yes, Emma mentioned you had your head turned by Sarah Ray.'

'Still talking about me behind my back then?' Yorke raised his eyebrows.

'Always, sir.'

'Well, you're right. Sarah turned my head. But those memories ... well let's just say they're raw. I don't feel a sense of responsibility ... or duty, really ... but ...'

'You feel sympathy?'

'Yes, I guess I do. Nobody deserves to experience what they experienced, and they certainly don't deserve to experience anything like it again.'

'And do you think they're going to?'

'I don't know, Jake. I hope to God, no.'

'I'm due in the incident room with Emma now,' Jake said. 'You coming?'

'No, I'm meeting Madden, and then I'll be catching up with Emma right after the briefing.'

As Yorke walked past, Jake clapped him on the back.

Yorke wanted to reply, but his best friend had again knocked the wind right out of him.

ALL THE WAY through the meeting with Madden, William Proud's words kept running through Yorke's head.

I'm just the blunt instrument ... there's a bent bastard shitting in the same toilet ...

Could it be Madden? His by-the-book lieutenant?

He'd already dedicated many hours of thought to this, but it just didn't ring true.

He wondered if this was what he was condemned to now he was back in HQ. Would he fall foul to continuous paranoia? Would every colleague be a suspect in the murder of his sister?

After promising to accept his demotion to DI graciously, and assuring her that he would attend all his reintegration meetings, especially the psych ones, he met Gardner in her office. His *old* office.

'It's only temporary,' Gardner said.

'No, it isn't. It suits you. You keep it tidier than I ever did.'

She smiled. 'We'll see.'

Yorke drank from a bottle of juice while Gardner opted for coffee.

'So, how was the briefing?' Yorke said.

Gardner sighed. 'Slow. They're a tough crowd. They think Samuel Mitchell, the missing young lad, is a goner, but I'm trying to keep them positive. I also introduced the suggestion that last night's disappearance of Paul Ray could very well be linked, and I was given many dubious looks. However, someone did suggest that Paul could have burned the farmhouse down and done a runner.'

'So why not take the car with him?' Yorke said. 'It was working I assume?'

Gardner nodded. 'Parkinson said that he might have been concerned about the car being reported stolen by his mother, so he abandoned it.'

Parkinson. The name made him wince. 'Still ... if I was

doing a runner from the arsehole of nowhere, I'd take the car. I wouldn't leave it there as proof that I was the arsonist.' Yorke took a mouthful of the artificially sweetened cordial. 'No. Paul's been taken again.'

Gardner eyed up Yorke's bottle. 'Why are you drinking that crap, sir?'

'It's a good question – I used to hate the stuff. Ewan started to get on at me about not drinking water. Juice is a compromise. I can't drink from a bottle of water all day. It's just too ...'

'Dull?'

'Yep, anyway. I want you to run me through Operation Bookmark from start to finish while I drink these chemicals.'

'Yes, sir.'

'And I have another request, not unlike the one you gave me last night.'

'Go on, sir?'

'For the last bloody time, could you please stop calling me sir?'

THREE DAYS AGO, seventeen-year-old farmhand Samuel Mitchell, had disappeared from his parents' farm. Samuel was renowned for being a polite young man, as well as an intellectually challenged one. His GCSE results the previous year had been poor, and he was supposed to be attending college to retake his English and Maths. Supposed to be. His parents were content to turn a blind eye to his absence while he was helping out on the farm. When really pushed on this, they'd admitted that they didn't think he had any hope of passing anyway and so had convinced him to snub the college and develop his trade on their farm.

Mitchell Farm was in The Downs, a stone's throw from the *Ray Pig Farm* in Little Horton. Gardner admitted that she'd thought about the association between this young man's disappearance and the Ray's vicious history before Paul Ray disappeared the previous evening, but it hadn't made it through to a briefing yet.

'It's a great farm for kids,' Gardner said. 'We took Anabelle up there a few months ago.'

Yorke smiled over the thought of his goddaughter. 'Is it a working farm?'

'Yes, for dairy. But they've got all sorts of things going on up there to attract visitors. Tractor rides, a petting zoo with gerbils, a park for children, a café selling homemade ice-cream. They've turned the place from a struggling farm into a goldmine. Twelve quid admission. When I first interviewed the parents, they said as much. They were about broke. With only a few loans, they established a day out for families, and their fortunes have reversed.'

'Interesting.'

'Getting quite common now. A lot of farms turning to welcoming in visitors. The only way they can keep going in the current economic climate.'

'So how did Samuel Mitchell disappear?'

Gardner opened a paper folder and showed Yorke an aerial photograph of a bush maze. 'Reynolds got very excited about sending his new drone up to snap this. He said the one on the internet wasn't fit for purpose. I was dubious, but I let him have his fun.'

Lance Reynolds was the Scientific Support Officer. His talents with a camera were legendary. Although the often-gruesome subject matter ensured that none of these photographs would ever be making it into an exhibition for the public.

Yorke ran his finger over the photograph of the maze. The centre was made up of four circular bushes, framed by four rectangular ones. 'It's massive. Must have cost them a fortune.'

'The maze is relatively new. They'd already made a reasonable amount of money before setting this up. So, anyway, the disappearance. At 2.46 p.m. an elderly man came to the front office of the farm to report his grandson missing. He claimed that the seven-year-old boy was lost in this maze. He gave his grandson's name as Jordan but did not provide his own name. Samuel's mother, Holly Mitchell, who was on the desk at the time, didn't think to ask; later, she reported to feeling uneasy over the man's appearance.' She paused for a mouthful of coffee.

'The man's appearance?'

'Yes, quite bad eczema, apparently. His face was covered in dry, red patches, some of which were scabbed over. By radio, she contacted her son, Samuel, to go into the maze and recover Jordan, the lost seven-year-old boy.'

Yorke pointed at the maze. 'And what did Samuel find in there?'

'We don't know. He never came back out.'

GARDNER LED Yorke into the incident room.

The automatic light burst into life. It was bright and hard and made Yorke feel like the spotlight had just been turned on him for the first time in a long while.

Welcome back, Michael ... let's see if you still have what it takes.

'Are you okay, Mike?' Gardner said.

Yorke smiled. 'Yes ... just got nostalgic for a moment.'

'Isn't nostalgia a positive thing? Some of the things we experienced in this room evoke anything but positivity in me!'

Yorke wanted to reply that these memories could be, in their own way, positive. The passion he'd felt in this room leading his team to success was unforgettable.

Gardner took his arm. 'Is it too soon?'

'No. I'm fine. Nice display ...' Yorke pointed over at the collage of images that filled the front whiteboard. 'Why don't we start there?'

Gardener's finger pointed at a tall boy with thinning hair. 'That's Samuel Mitchell.' He wore a goofy grin, and a T-shirt with 'KORN' written across it. The 'R' was written backwards.

'*Korn* are a heavy-metal band,' Yorke said.

'I always said you were down with the kids, Mike.'

'Well, you clearly aren't! They started out in the early nineties. They're bloody retro.'

'Everyone we've spoken to about this boy has only had positive things to say about him. Well-mannered, good-humoured with a passion for music and animals. No one has mentioned his low intellect in a critical way. Most people have been content to say that it is his simple manner that makes him so approachable. His parents, Holly and Ryan,' Gardner moved her finger to the photographs alongside Samuel, 'are obviously beside themselves. They kept telling me how much they adored his special nature.'

Gardner sighed and then continued to weave her finger around the crime tapestry until it fell on a forensic artist's sketch of the grandfather who'd reported his grandchild, Jordan, missing. Alongside it was a grainy CCTV image of the same man walking away towards the carpark at 2.48 p.m. – two minutes after making the report.

The wiry man's face was almost skeletal. His cheekbones were high and sharp. His eyes were burrowed so deep into his sockets that Yorke doubted that he had clear peripheral vision. Scaly red sores glowed from all over his face and he had bald patches all over his scalp.

Jake stepped up behind them at this point. 'Yep. God wasn't just content to make him ugly, he also decided to kick him around for good measure.'

'Hi Jake,' Yorke said. 'So, this peculiar man just walked away at 2.48 p.m., and no one noticed?'

'Why would they?' Gardner said, 'They were all worried about a seven-year-old boy lost in the maze. A fictional child by the way.'

'Can we be 100% sure that the grandson doesn't exist?' Yorke said.

'Yes. The same CCTV camera that caught the grandfather leaving, caught him arriving at 1.30 p.m. *Alone.*'

'Were there any more CCTV cameras in the carpark so we can identify the vehicle this man was in?'

'No.'

'And what time did Samuel actually go into the maze?'

'As soon as his mother, Holly, contacted him by radio. So, around 2.47 p.m.'

'What about other people in the maze? What did they see?'

Gardner shook her head. 'We've exhausted that avenue. People saw Samuel working his way into the maze, asking if anyone had seen a young boy called Jordan but no one had. Closing time for the farm is 3 p.m. so the maze was quiet at this point – as was most of the farm.'

'So, Samuel could have come back out of the maze?'

'Well, his father, Ryan, denies this happened. He was standing at the entrance to the maze.'

Jake jumped in. 'And there was definitely no other way in and out.'

'Thanks, Jake. I get how a maze works,' Yorke said.

'And all the times tally up?' Yorke said. 'The father was witnessed standing outside the entrance around 2.48 p.m. after his son had gone into the maze?'

'Yes,' Gardner said. 'By other workers on site. Plus, a small crowd of visitors, who gathered to see if they could help. We have had the Search Advisors and their dogs in the maze, as well as on the fields and in the wooded area immediately behind it. No sign. Helicopters have also scoured the same area. Again, nothing. Samuel Mitchell went in, and never came out.'

'It's not possible,' Yorke said. 'Unless he's still in there and I'm sure the Alsatians would have recovered the body if that had been the case.'

Yorke was still holding the photograph of the maze. He ran his finger around the outside rectangular bush. 'How well has this perimeter been checked?'

'What do you mean?' Gardner said.

'I mean that Samuel Mitchell must have gone over, through or under this outer bush.'

'Well, PolSA checked it over, but there was no damage to the bushes, and certainly no holes dug underneath it!'

'Which means he went over it ...'

'But why would he go over it, sir?' Jake said.

Yorke paused to think. 'Well, he was in there to rescue a missing boy. What if the missing boy was on the other side of that bush?'

'We don't think there was a missing boy, Mike,' Gardner said.

'Neither do I, but Samuel did. I want to go out to the farm now and I'd love it if you two came with me. By the way, where is Mark?'

Gardner and Jake exchanged glances.

'Bloody hell,' Yorke said, 'I've only been back five minutes and the secrets have already started.'

'It's not that, Mike,' Gardner said. 'I just think it's best if we explain on the way to the farm.'

It was the middle of April, so it was reasonably warm out in the open. The problem was when you strayed into the shade or the occasional blast of wind punctured your comfort with a shiver. The three detectives buttoned up their jackets and headed to the farm entrance.

Relatives were currently running the farmyard while the owners, Holly and Ryan Mitchell, desperately suffered at home. Family Liaison Officer Bryan Kelly was offering them a shoulder to cry on. He was good at playing the sympathetic ear. Less effective at being vigilant. However, Gardner had assured Yorke that he had learned from previous mistakes.

These relatives welcomed Gardner and her team, and they offered to clear the site of customers.

Yorke held his palm out. 'That won't be necessary, ma'am. We just want to look at the maze.'

Inside the farmyard, Yorke gazed around at the manufactured rural playground. The children's park sported large, tunnel slides and a range of climbing frames modelled on dinosaurs. The café they bypassed wasn't just a café; it was a two-story arena of activity. There was a colourful soft-play area on the ground-floor and a restaurant on the top floor. There was also a menagerie of insects and reptiles housed in a series of aquariums.

The thought of sharing his lunch with bird-eating tarantulas sent a shudder down Yorke's spine. His adopted son, Ewan, would enjoy it though. He had a thing for snakes and had lost his own pet corn snake at roughly the same time he'd tragically lost his parents.

As they approached the entrance to the maze, Gardner pointed out the petting zoo, where children could hold gerbils and rabbits. There was also a small enclosure for meerkats.

'Over there, they do sheep racing,' Gardner said.

'You can actually bet on a winner.' Jake grinned.

Yorke rolled his eyes. 'Get out of here!'

Gardner laughed. 'Not money, Mike. You can choose a sheep, grab a raffle ticket for free, and if yours comes in, you are entered for a prize draw to win some more tickets to come back again.'

Yorke shook his head. 'Farms were never like this when I was younger.'

Mind you, Yorke thought, *no one ever took me to one, so they might have been for all I know.*

His mind conducted a familiar rotation around a mother who couldn't care less about anything but men and drugs, and a sister who desperately tried to bring him up – and had no time for recreational visits to a farm.

They stood at the entrance to the maze. An elderly couple emerged. The man winked and said, 'I'd draw yourself a map if I were you! Getting in is the easy part.'

'I might just do that sir,' Yorke said, nodding his greeting.

'What are you looking for anyway?' Jake said.

'I'll let you know when I find it.'

Yorke pointed out that the sides of maze appeared to be connected to the sheep-racing course, and the children's park, and then said, 'So, if Samuel climbed over either of these sides, he would still be within the farm?'

'Yes,' Gardner said. 'At the time he disappeared, there were still some families left in the children's park. In the sheep-racing course, several farmers were tidying the site, and feeding the sheep. We spoke to everyone. No one saw Samuel coming over the bush walls. And they would have noticed, I'm sure.'

'So, it's as I said. He's gone over the outer wall into no-man's land,' Yorke said. 'Come on.'

They ventured into the maze. Out of his pocket, Yorke retrieved a copy of the aerial photo he'd looked at earlier. He'd already taken the liberty of drawing the route on the copy, so he didn't waste any time with dead-ends or doubling back on himself.

'Good thinking, sir,' Jake said.

Eventually, they hit the outer wall.

Yorke pushed his hand through the bush and rapped on the wooden fence behind it. 'That's what made it easy to climb over. Notice how thin the bush is here?'

He noticed Jake and Gardner looking at each other.

The fence was just over six-feet high. Yorke knelt, jumped and reached over the bush. He missed on his first attempt. He tried again and managed to grab the top of the fence. He levered himself up and used his feet to scramble up the bush wall.

He swung a leg over the top, looked down at Gardner and Jake, and said, 'Not bad for an old man.' He dropped down.

Being tall and muscular, Jake was able to give Gardner a leg up. She landed by Yorke with a thud and a grunt. Fortunately, she stayed upright.

Jake joined them, noiselessly.

'What did you do, step over it?' Gardner said.

Yorke ignored them and moved forward.

He looked out over the small patch of woodland and the acres upon acres of barren farmland stretching into the distance. 'So, after you climbed this wall, Samuel Mitchell, where did you go?' He took a deep breath. 'And who were you with?'

PAUL RAY WELCOMED HIS FREEDOM.

He knew it was a dream, but that did not deter him from enjoying it.

All around him was emptiness, ending only in blackness. It wasn't unlike the Ray pig farm; the insidious domain he'd vandalised earlier. Overgrown fields ringed by knotted trees, decrepit barns, and a farmhouse being consumed by the nature around it.

Yet, for all the loneliness, he was free, and it felt like a relief. Why that would be the case, he couldn't say. Strange how he knew that this wasn't real, and yet he had no idea what was happening back in reality.

As he walked towards the decrepit farmhouse, feeling the wind but, peculiarly, not feeling any cold, his father, Joe, joined him.

He looked across at his father who, surprisingly, looked full of life, despite being dead. He was also astonished by the fact that they were now both the same size. Last time, he'd seen him, he'd only come up to his shoulders.

'But the wild boars? He threw you in with them ...' Paul said, taking his father's hand.

'Yes, so I believe.'

'I've missed you, Dad.'

'I've missed you more than you could ever know, Paul. And your mother too. Has she moved on?'

'She's happier now.'

'Good. And you?'

'Not really, Dad. I keep dreaming.'

'About what?'

'About—'

'Paul, look!'

Paul looked ahead and saw a bulky man with long, straggly hair standing at the front door of the farmhouse. It was Lewis Ray. The man who had kidnapped him all those years ago and had murdered his father.

Paul and Joe approached and stood before him, looking up at his face. The cold-hearted killer stared off into the emptiness.

'You're dead too,' Paul said, 'my auntie, Lacey, killed you.'

Lewis continued his stare but offered a brief nod.

'And I'm glad,' Paul said, 'you are evil.'

'I am. *We are.*'

He noticed that his father was no longer standing next to him.

'You can't hurt me anymore,' Paul said.

'I can't, but others can.'

'Who?'

'Others like us, Paul.'

'I am not like you. I will never be like you.'

'Look behind you Paul.'

Paul turned.

The man in the white overalls with the loose white sack over his face was standing there. Paul could see the eyes moving behind the holes cut into the material. Paul looked down for the mallet which this man had hit him with earlier.

It wasn't there. Instead, he held another loose white sack.

The man offered. Paul shook his head, and then felt his arms being seized from behind.

He felt the white sack being forced over his head ...

... he coughed and snatched the sack off his head. He was awake and his mouth felt like it was full of chalk. His eyes darted around for the candle that allowed him to see earlier. It had gone. He'd been left to the darkness, and his dreams.

His eyes started to adjust, and he could see: the outline of the candelabra; the shape of the grandfather clock; and the shape of the mutilated boy opposite him.

It was silent. Wasn't the young man moaning before? Was he now sleeping?

As his vision began to claim more clarity, memories started to swirl in. He remembered the old man earlier, introducing himself as Reginald Ray, and then sliding over to where he was chained to a chair. He remembered Reginald holding a piece of sliced meat to his mouth, asking him to eat. He'd turned away from it, keeping his mouth tightly closed. Reginald had threatened to force it in, but Paul's tears and desperation to avoid the meat, which may or may not have been cut from the young man opposite, eventually deterred him.

'You will accept who you are without being forced,' Reginald had said.

A chemical-drenched rag had been forced over his mouth, and the dreams had begun.

Realising that everything was clearer now, Paul scanned the table, and saw the assortment of food was still present. When he lifted his eyes, he was relieved to see that Reginald was not here right now. But, when his eyes fell to the other captive, his breath caught in his throat.

The young man's head was no longer circular. It looked as if it had been flattened at the top. Smashed in perhaps.

He tasted bile in his mouth.

He stood up and felt the chains rattle against the chair legs. He vowed to get out of here even if he took the chair with him.

The door opened, throwing spears of light into the room. He pinched his eyes against the sudden sharp pain.

This time, when he opened his eyes, they adjusted quickly. The old man with the diseased face was standing in the doorway. Paul looked again at the young man with the misshapen head and put his hand on his mouth to keep the sick in.

Just above the young man's wide-open eyes, the top of his head was missing. A bloody saw lay on the table beside his dinner plate.

Reginald came into the room. 'Ready to eat, young man?'

3

I N AWE, GARDNER watched her former boss work. Not only because the officer she respected above all others was back, but because he was already making discoveries they had missed.

She had no right to be above him in the chain of command, but the fact that he'd accepted it so graciously, was further testament to the type of man he was.

Jake and Gardner stood back and watched Yorke move back and forth along the fence, stopping occasionally to prod it and, if something interested him, examine it further.

Eventually, he wandered back over to Gardner and Jake.

Jake raised an eyebrow. 'No, secret exit then, sir?'

'What was the weather like the day Samuel disappeared? Preferably, at the exact time?'

'Easy,' Gardner said, 'it was pissing it down all day.'

Yorke turned to face the fence again and instructed Jake and Gardner to do the same. 'Okay, imagine you were waiting at this fence for someone in the rain, where would you stand?'

'Also, easy,' Gardner said, pointing at a cluster of trees near the end of the fence. 'Shelter.'

'Yes,' Yorke said, 'follow me.'

Underneath the trees, Yorke pointed up. 'Lots of coverage here.'

The trees were old, and thick, and the overhanging foliage offered an umbrella over the position they stood in and stretched partway over the interior of the maze.

'Okay, humour me,' Yorke said.

'We are well-practised at that, sir,' Jake said.

Yorke flashed him a sardonic grin. 'Imagine if you are Samuel Mitchell on the other side of that fence calling out for this mythical seven-year-old boy, Jordan.'

Gardner's eyes widened. She'd received Yorke's hypothesis loud and clear. 'And then the abductor shouts 'I'm here' from this side of the fence.'

'Precisely,' Yorke said. 'And what's the first thing you would do?'

'Climb over to rescue the boy,' Gardner said.

'Hang on ...' Jake said. 'Let's not get ahead of ourselves here. A little boy is reported missing, not a fully-grown man or woman. Are you telling me this abductor was mimicking a child's voice?'

Yorke shrugged. 'Maybe. And remember, Samuel Mitchell is of way-below-average intelligence. It was also raining heavily. Even if the imitation was poor, it could still have been enough to fool him.' Yorke looked around underneath the trees. 'So, what if he stood here? Sheltering in the rain?'

They scoured the floor for a time but turned up nothing. Eventually, Yorke finished up at a cavity in a tree. He pulled out his mobile phone, switched the light on and shone it inside. '*Emma!*'

She came over and looked in. 'Yes, I see it.' She pulled some plastic gloves from her backpack and put them on. She reached into the cavity with a gloved hand and extracted a half-empty plastic water bottle. She held it up in front of Yorke.

Yorke smiled. 'The label looks as good as new, which means it hasn't been here long ... how many people do you think stray into this area around the back of the farm?' He glanced around at the empty woodland and fields. 'Not many. How much do you want to bet that this bottle belonged to our abductor?'

Gardner smiled. She loved having her former boss back.

THE ROOM THROBBED as the candleflame flickered.

Paul kept his head lowered and stared at the pool of vomit at his feet. He may have no choice but to listen to Reginald's chewing and slurping but he wasn't about to watch it too.

And there was another reason for keeping his eyes lowered. *The poor young man opposite him.*

A thin trail of blood had wound its way out from the teeth of the saw and across the table. It dripped steadily onto Paul's knee. He couldn't hear it dripping over the old man gnawing beside him but he felt it.

Every drop.

It felt warm, but that could have just been his imagination. The young man could have been dead hours for all he knew and his blood already cold.

'Cutting your nose off to spite your face, Paul,' Reginald said. 'There's nothing wrong with what has been laid in front of you. I still remember reading *The New York Times* in 1931. In the interests of research, a man called Seabrook cooked and ate human flesh. Do you want to know what he said?'

Paul shook his head to indicate that he didn't want to know. He couldn't voice his refusal though. He feared if he did so, he would either burst into tears, or vomit again.

'Let me educate you, Paul. He began by saying that it was like no other meat he'd ever tasted! Now, if that doesn't pique your curiosity nothing will.'

A spoon hovered in front of Paul. It was heaped with a pinkish meat that resembled raw mince.

'Still not convinced, eh? How about this then - "it was so nearly like good, fully developed veal that I think no person with a palate of ordinary, normal sensitiveness could distinguish it from veal." I assume, Paul, that you have an ordinary palate. Therefore, what have you to fear?'

A plate was pushed towards him. It was heaped with a charred meat.

Paul gagged but nothing came out this time. His stomach was already empty.

'And yet, Paul, you are a Ray. Your blood is our blood ... my blood. So, what repels you? In some tribal societies, deceased relatives are eaten to guide their souls into their living descendants. Have you ever heard of anything so beautiful?'

Paul looked up at the elderly man. 'Why are you doing this?'

'What do you want to hear?' The sores opened and wept on his face as he spoke. 'That I like the taste of veal? That I want to consume their souls? That I do it because I'm hungry, and cannibalism is the answer to famine? Which answer would you like?'

'The truth.'

'But the truth is too simple and will not give you the closure you want. I do this because I've always done this. I do this because it is who I am. Who we are. And you too, are part of all this, Paul.'

'No, I am not!' Paul's eyes filled with tears now.

'Exactly as I said – cutting your nose off to spite your face.' He picked up a carving knife and licked the tip. 'Now, there's an idea.'

GARDNER HAD TAKEN the evidence back to HQ in her vehicle. Yorke and Jake followed behind.

For a change, Yorke had allowed Jake the wheel.

Jake said, 'I know it doesn't happen very often when we are both in a car together, but can I just have it on the record that I prefer it this way round?'

'I agree that it is more relaxing ... sleep-inducing actually, but what happens when we have to get somewhere quickly or on time even?'

Jake laughed. 'I've missed you, mate.'

'I've missed you too, buddy. Although I only saw you last week!'

Jake slowed down as he neared a car towing a horsebox. 'Yes, I remember. You were being mildly irritating if I recall.'

'I think the word is *supportive*. Besides, I'm pretty sure I bought most of the rounds. There's no pleasing some people.'

They laughed for a moment but there was a topic looming around the corner which needed to be broached. And they both knew it.

'Could you overtake please, Jake?'

Jake sighed, but then complied.

They changed the subject until Jake took the third exit off the roundabout onto the motorway.

'So, did you put a line under it then?' Yorke said.

'Wait until I'm on the motorway before you bring that up! Do you value your life?'

But Yorke wasn't about to be fobbed off – no matter the circumstances. 'A line under it?'

'Not exactly.'

'Not exactly?'

'I'm working on it.'

'Working on it?'

'Is there a fucking echo in this car?'

'Hey look,' Yorke said, 'I'm pretty sure we spent over three hours in *the Wyndham* discussing the merits of doing the right thing in this situation. I agree, my memory of the last hour of that conversation is rather hazy, and Kenny, well into his eighties, came over to throw in his tuppence, which was an old-fashioned tuppence, and not too helpful, but I'm absolutely positive we reached an agreement by last orders.'

'Yes, we did.'

'And then you stopped by her house and slept with her after chucking out time?'

Jake's face reddened. 'How did you know?'

'Well, the *not exactly* and the *working on it* were pretty big indicators.' Yorke sighed. 'And keep your bloody eyes on the road.'

Jake looked back and continued to negotiate the slow lane. Yorke saw that he was reaching an all-time record of 55 mph. *Well,* Yorke thought, *more chance of surviving if he throws a paddy, and veers into a bollard.*

'It's your life ...' Yorke said.

'Yes, it is.'

Yorke nodded. 'Well maybe you should stop asking for advice then?'

'I will.'

A stony minute passed in silence before Jake said, 'Okay, you got me. I'm fucked. I don't know what to do.'

'We discussed—'

'*I like her,* Mike. I mean, I really, really like her.'

Yorke sighed. *'For now!* We discussed this. It's exciting, but you are reacting to the chemical explosions in your brain, and they may not last. And then what? You'll have nothing.'

'No, it's not like that. All me and Sheila do is argue. With Caroline, it's different. We just laugh.'

'You and Sheila just need to figure things out—'

'Figure things out? We've been trying for years. You, more than anyone know that. During our marriage, I wouldn't be surprised if I'd spent more time outside the bedroom than in it!'

Yorke accepted that he had a good point, but he wasn't about to concede defeat just yet. 'Think of your son, then.'

Jake turned sharply for the junction exit. He'd almost missed it. Yorke gasped. A lorry driver, forced to slow down, hit the horn. Yorke was surprised – Jake had never been that gung-ho behind the wheel before. His adrenaline was obviously high.

'Frank is all I bloody think about. The worst thing is looking into his eyes. Do you know what that feels like right now? The guilt?'

'I can only imagine.'

'You can only imagine! Is that because you, the moral and upstanding Michael Yorke would never do anything like—'

Jake was cut off by his phone ringing over the car

speakers. Yorke pressed the answer button on the control panel.

'It's me,' Gardner said. 'We have a witness.'

'Go on,' Yorke said.

'Get this address into the SatNav and head there now while I explain everything to you.'

Yorke listened and programmed the SatNav in Jake's car.

Gardner continued, 'We had a large response to our press release yesterday, but nothing like what just came in five minutes ago. A witness has reported seeing someone driving on the road behind the maze and woodland! Check your phone, Mike.'

Gardner had sent him an image from Google Maps. She'd dropped a red pin on the road running behind the woodland next to the Mitchell farm.

'It's an eight-minute walk from where we just stood under that tree,' Gardner said. 'The witness saw the driver at approximately 3 p.m. on the day Samuel Mitchell disappeared.'

'So, that would place it roughly ten minutes after the possible abduction?' Yorke said.

'Yes,' Gardner said.

'Jesus,' Jake said, 'What did this witness see?'

'The witness is a dairy farmer called Bryce Singles. While returning home in his tractor from a neighbouring farm, he says he passed a parked vehicle where I've dropped that pin. A couple of minutes later, the same vehicle was tailgating his tractor, desperately trying to get around him. Singles reports that it was lunacy. It was literally trying to run him off the road. Obviously, he pulled aside to let the maniac past.'

'Okay, so do we have vehicle details?' Yorke said.

'Yes, but that's not the best of it.'

'Go on.'

'Singles recognised the driver, Mike.'

'Bloody hell. Who was it?'

'*Another* local farmer. Robert Bennett. That's the address you're heading to now.'

'Armed response?' Jake said.

Yorke said. 'I wouldn't advise it. It's too long to wait. Both Paul and Samuel could be there and in danger now.'

'That's what I thought,' Gardner said, 'so, I've got some officers in the vicinity to come and support.'

'Good.'

'There's more.'

'Go on.'

'Singles says that Robert Bennett literally rolled his window down and hurled abuse at him. He couldn't hear what he said over the noise of the tractor, but it was clearly venomous. Bennett has eczema all over his face, Singles confirmed this.'

'So it's the grandfather who approached reception at the farm and put the fake alert out on his grandson?' Jake said.

'Let's not get ahead of ourselves,' Yorke said, 'we will discuss that later. Could Singles see anyone else in the vehicle?'

'No, but I guess Samuel could have been in the boot?' Gardner said.

'Right, we need to get there ... Jake?'

'Yes, sir.'

'You need to pull over so I can drive.'

'Now why did I get the feeling you were going to say that?'

PAUL RAY WELCOMED time away from Reginald.

He knew it was a dream, and that, back in reality, he was still with him. But he was so thankful for this break from the mean old bastard.

The chairs around the table were empty, and he breathed a sigh of relief that the mutilated young man was no longer sitting opposite him. However, every place was made, and the fine cutlery and gleaming white plates suggested that visitors were expected.

Alongside the candelabra, someone had laid out more candles. Paul had yet to see the room so illuminated.

With the absence of Reginald, and the dead young man, there were reasons to be upbeat, but there were a great many more not to be. The assortment of food laid out before him, for example. The banquet had grown. And following his conversation with Reginald, how could he not expect the worst from these dishes?

As his eyes moved from dish to dish, his fears were realised. Nausea grew, and he became aware that he was scratching a peculiar itch in his right hand. He glanced down and saw that it was red and sore.

The guests began to shuffle in. Continuing to scratch, he looked up at their faces. Some he recognised, some he didn't.

Opposite him, his father, Joe, took a seat. He winked at his son and then grabbed a napkin off his plate and tucked it under his collar to shield his shirt from food.

He recognised Lacey, his auntie. She tucked her long, blonde hair behind her ears and sat to the left of him. She placed her hand on his, leaned in and whispered in his ear, 'Never judge a book by its cover. If you look further beyond, you will see more.'

He smiled at Lacey. He'd always liked her. Yes, the

things she'd been accused of worried him, and she was a dangerous individual, but she'd always been good to him.

He felt strong hands on his shoulder and felt Lewis Ray's bristly face against his. Here was one relative who'd never been good to him. A relative who'd made him sleep with pigs, and then tried to feed him to wild boars.

'See the soul, Paul.' Lewis sat down to his right.

He noticed he was still feverishly scratching his hand. He looked down and saw that he'd drawn blood.

Then, he looked back up and saw other Rays taking their seat around the table. He recognised many of them from photographs his parents had shown him growing up. He recognised his grandparents, parents of Lacey and Joe, who'd died before he was born.

The only noticeable absence was Reginald. The head of the family.

The family then greeted one another, picked up wine glasses, clinked them together and started to prepare their plates.

His father scooped up two eyeballs, the optic nerves still trailing from the backs of them, onto his plate. He seasoned them with black pepper, and with the smaller of his forks, speared one. He got it into his mouth, closed his eyes and chewed. Paul felt his stomach turn.

After finishing, his father smiled at him. 'There is nothing that doesn't work with garlic.'

Quickly, Paul turned his attention to Lacey to distract himself, but she was also engaged in disgusting behaviour. She was working hard with her knife and fork on an ear. When she finally wrenched a piece free, she popped it into her mouth. Seconds into chewing, she spat some pieces of metal onto her plate. They looked like shotgun pellets. Paul tasted sick in his mouth.

She smiled at Paul. 'Don't you just hate it when you get one full of studs?'

He tried to shut them all out by looking down at his sore, itching hand, but that was no use, because he'd made a mess of it and some of his scratches had torn his skin.

From the corner of his eye, Paul could see Lewis scraping something from the inside of a skull. It was the top part of a skull, and he wondered if it was the piece removed from that poor young man who was sitting opposite him back in reality. Paul put a hand to his mouth; he wouldn't be able to hold back from vomiting for much longer …

The host made his entrance. Everyone stood to welcome him.

Reginald came around the table quickly. Spritely on his feet, despite his many years. He stood behind Paul, like Lewis had moments ago, and said, 'Don't stand for me, but stand for your guest of honour.'

'Hear, hear,' Joe said, raising his glass.

Lacey ruffled Paul's hair, Lewis clapped a large hand down on his shoulder.

'After all,' Reginald continued, 'they always taste better when they're one of your own!'

Everyone started to laugh, and Paul dug his nails deeper into his sore hand …

… Paul opened his eyes.

The candles still flickered, but Reginald Ray had left. The mutilated young man had now slumped forward so Paul could see directly into his empty skull.

His right hand was stinging like mad. He looked down, saw that he was scratching a bloody, bandaged stump, and screamed.

THE FARMYARD WAS MUCH SMALLER than the one they'd visited earlier, and this one was not open to the general public. Judging by the state of it, it never would be. A dishevelled farmhouse was framed by two fenced off unkempt fields. The fences, where they still stood, had rotted. Not a single animal grazed.

Yorke and Jake climbed out of the car.

'So, is this what happens if you don't turn your farm into an amusement park in the twenty-first century?' Yorke said, heading for the path to the farmhouse. 'Come on.'

'Emma told us to wait for back-up!'

'She didn't. She just said there would be back-up coming.'

Jake watched him sprint away. To the side of him, Gardner crunched to a halt in her vehicle.

She jumped out and saw Yorke, in the distance, approaching the path to the farmhouse. 'Couldn't he have waited a minute?'

Jake looked at her. 'He doesn't seem to do much by the book these days. We best catch him up. Farmers and shotguns? We've got experience in this area already.'

'With two young men missing, he wouldn't have given it much thought.' Gardner said, breaking into a run.

Yorke was banging on the door of the stone farmhouse when they caught him up.

Jake was certain he could see dust swirling down around the porch every time he pounded. 'Don't knock too hard, sir, the place might fall down.'

Yorke ignored him and hit harder. There was no letterbox to shout through, so he was probably taking his frustration out on the wooden door.

'He gets one more chance or I'm going around the back,' Yorke said.

'Is it just me, sir, or has demotion made you more edgy?' Jake said.

The door started to open. Jake pulled his badge out.

'Police,' Yorke said.

An elderly man stepped from the house. He was the man from the CCTV footage and the sketch from the forensic artist. He had a thin layer of white cream over the patches on his face.

'Mr Robert Bennett?' Yorke said.

'Yes, what is this?' His voice was muffled.

'Who is in the house with you?'

'No one. I live alone. Why?' He reached into the pocket of his jeans.

'*What are you doing?*' Yorke lifted his hands, ready to pounce if necessary.

Robert pulled out a small, purple box. 'My falsies.'

'Okay, slowly,' Yorke said, lowering his hands.

Robert opened the box and slipped in the false teeth. 'That's better. I find it so hard to talk without them in. Now why do you want me?'

'Did you find your grandson?' Jake said.

'Excuse me?'

Gardner reached over and put a hand on Jake's arm. She gave him a look to admonish him for being antagonistic. He nodded, accepting her warning.

'Can you step away from the door, Mr Bennett?' Yorke said.

'Why?'

'DS Pettman here will escort you to the vehicle, while we search your premises.'

'Again, why?'

'Because we have reason to believe that someone's life

may be in danger on this property, Mr Bennett. That is why.'

————————

Get busy living or get busy dying.

When he'd been ten years old, Paul had heard his father saying that to his mother during one of her episodes. She'd spent the entire weekend cleaning the house from top to bottom. And then from bottom to top.

Her OCD for cleanliness was unrelenting, especially when faced with extreme anxiety, and his father had been remarkably talented at bringing this turmoil into their family home. Extra-marital affairs had been his speciality.

He'd loved his father but learning about his wayward behaviours had been scarring to say the least. Would Paul have ever forgiven him? He didn't know, nor would he ever find out. Lewis Ray and his wild boars had seen to that.

So, as he stared at the bloody, bandaged stump where earlier he'd had a hand, those words came back to him. The words that his father had used on his sick mother when he couldn't stomach her irrational behaviours anymore.

Get busy living or get busy dying.

The fact that he was about to follow his father's advice after everything he'd done to his mother didn't sit right with him. But nothing could be truer than this mantra right now.

Reginald Ray, a man who had died over a hundred years ago, was alive, and eating people again. How he was alive was anybody's guess, but the fact remained ... he was eating people again.

And he had taken Paul's right hand.

Paul rose to his feet and the chair came off the floor with

him. He looked down at the chain around his ankles that snaked around the legs of the wooden chair and then looped through two wooden arches which sat underneath the cushioned seat.

The chains were so tightly wound to him that walking would be impossible. He would literally have to hop to freedom, unless ...

Get busy living.

He threw himself and the chair backwards against the wall.

The force of the blow vibrated throughout his entire body. The air was forced out of him and he heard a crunch which he prayed was wood buckling rather than his spine.

He gritted his teeth and launched himself again. This time the sound was more like a crack.

He managed two more thrusts before he had to spit out stomach acid.

Gasping for air, with bile running down his chin, and tears burning his cheeks, he went again and again ...

Get ...

It felt as if his ribs had turned to jelly but he could hear the wood splintering.

Busy ...

He screamed at the top of his lungs. The pain was excruciating.

Living.

The chair smashed against the wall, and Paul collapsed backwards into the broken wood.

Fuck you, Reginald.

YORKE AND GARDNER searched Robert Bennett's entire house. The only crime being committed here was against cleanliness. The kitchen and lounge were loaded with dirty crockery. There was a similar theme in the bedrooms, except the crockery had been substituted with piles of unwashed clothing.

Gardner looked in the bedroom wardrobe. 'Women's clothes? He said he lived alone ...'

'Maybe he lived with someone,' Yorke said. He pointed at an ashtray filled with cigarette butts. 'And they left when they'd had enough of his mess?'

'I'll grab a couple of those butts,' Gardner said. 'We can try to match the DNA on them to the bottle.'

Yorke nodded and Gardner pulled out a plastic bag.

Outside, they circled the property. They looked in an old, large shed, which was barely accessible due to the piles of old farming equipment that had been dumped in there. Some of it had toppled over and partially blocked the inward-opening door.

No Samuel Mitchell or Paul Ray.

'What has the bastard done with Samuel?' Gardner said.

'Let's go and ask him,' Yorke said as they headed back towards Jake's car. By now Jake would have read Robert his rights and installed him in the back of the car. 'And let's hope he's unsettled enough to spill his guts.'

PAUL ROLLED clear of the wood. His entire body burned, and his vision swirled.

He crawled, coughing up fluids. He hoped it was vomit but it could have been blood for all he knew. The force of those blows necessary to break the wood had been staggering.

But the bastard had taken his hand, and he'd rather die than stay and let him cut off another piece of him.

He lifted himself up onto his knees. He rocked back and forth with his head raised.

Focus, Paul, focus.

His vision swirled like mad. Was he concussed? Probably.

It was now or never.

He rose to his feet. Slowly, so as not to fall, but with determination, because now was not the time to fail.

He began to walk. Now the chain wasn't tense against the wood, it slipped free of his ankles.

He reached down and picked up a chair leg with his remaining hand. The break had left the wood sharp and pointed.

Just try and stop me, he thought, *and I'll put the stake right through your heart.*

YORKE HELD the car door open with one hand and looked down at Robert Bennett. It wasn't just the fierce skin condition which made him sick. He was bent slightly, and looked burdened, rather than angry, over his current predicament.

'Where is he, Mr Bennett?' Yorke said.

Robert sighed. 'I really don't know what you're talking about.'

'We have CCTV footage proving that you were at the Mitchell Farm at 2.48 p.m. on Wednesday. We also have a witness who saw you driving away from the property at approximately 3.00 p.m. But, more importantly, and far more pressingly, a young man called Samuel has gone missing from that property. Do you know when that young man was last seen, Mr Bennett?'

'Let me guess ... around the same time you saw me on the CCTV footage?'

'Correct. So, tell me where he is and let's end this problem before it gets even worse than it already is.'

'But you have another problem, detective.'

'And what is that, Mr Bennett?'

'It wasn't me on the CCTV footage, and it certainly wasn't me driving away from the Mitchell farm because I have been here all week. I haven't moved.' Robert reached up to scratch a patch on his face but then thought better of it and lowered his hand. 'It itches like mad when I go out.'

'What is wrong with you anyway?' Jake said from behind Yorke.

'Papillon-Lefèvre syndrome, or PLS for short. It's rare and you've probably never heard of it.'

'I haven't,' Jake said. 'It's not catching, is it?'

'No, and I've had it for as long as I can remember.' He opened his hands and showed the scaly patches on the skin of his palms. 'It's also on the soles of my feet. It affected everything holding my teeth in place. I lost them all at seventeen. As you can imagine, I've never been much of a hit with the ladies. Sometimes, I get horrendous skin infections on my face which is why I've got this gunk all over it.'

'Who do the women's clothes in the wardrobe belong to?'

'My wife. That's why you find me in this melancholy mood. Took her forty years before she decided she'd finally had enough of waking up next to *this*.' He gestured at his face.

'This is your last chance,' Yorke said. 'We need to know

where Samuel Mitchell is. If you tell us now then it will end much better for you. I can assure you of that.'

'I am seventy years old, detective. Even if I had the energy to abduct a young man, why would I?'

'Well, that's another question I hoped you would answer.'

'You are not listening to me. I don't want to say anything else until I get to the station and I have a solicitor. Your colleague here just said that was my right, and I'd like to take him up on it.'

Yorke slammed the door.

PAUL RAY STAGGERED through the house. His vision continued to swirl, and his entire body still felt as if it was being incinerated. On a number of occasions, he bumped into the walls. He had no coordination.

Stay conscious. Just stay conscious.

He banged into some furniture and something smashed on the floor behind him, but he had no idea what it was.

Ahead, in his broken vision, he saw the front door. He readied the sharp chair leg and opened it.

There was someone standing there.

He couldn't see clearly enough to tell if it was Reginald, so he didn't take any chances.

He thrust the chair leg at the figure.

4

L ACEY RAY LIVED for these moments.
Always had done, always would do.

And because she knew the importance of these moments, and knew they *defined* her, and knew if she got one wrong, it would end her, she was meticulous in planning and executing them.

She paused for a second to consider how she would feel if it did all come to an end. Not sadness, because she didn't really experience this emotion, and she was reasonably sure she'd *never* experienced it. Feelings had always been a tricky one for her.

She expected that she would feel longing. Longing for the pleasure in these moments. Yes, that was it. If they ever put her in a cage, she would feel longing. After all, she was compelled to do what she did.

She'd read enough on the subject, and around her own sociopathic condition, to know that this was probably linked to sexual gratification. But that didn't bother her. She'd traded in sex; she'd manipulated with sex; on occasion, she'd enjoyed sex. Sex was a means to an end. A means for control and pleasure.

If she took sexual gratification from killing bastards, then so be it. She smirked. There were worse things in the world.

She reached down and stroked Tobias's face. He looked up at her. He was adopted. Some would say 'stolen.' Yet, despite the biological differences, they shared so many similarities. She smiled at him.

In a greasy apartment block, they stood by the lifts on the sixth floor. They were next to the window looking out over the Port of Southampton. As was usual, the containers were piled high, and the adjacent cruise port was busy.

Tobias wasn't tall enough to see out of the window, but he was content to stand quietly and wait. Impatience was not one of Tobias's weaknesses, despite his five years.

Their backs were to the lifts. In the reflection on the glass window, she'd earlier watched the two oily bastards she was hunting emerge from the lift and shuffle past her, without paying her any attention.

Yes, it would have been easy to swoop on the two meat sacks there and then, but it was all about the moment. And that hadn't been it.

Now, over ten minutes later, she looked down at her phone screen, which was connected to a little camera in the room that the two oily men, and another of their kind, resided.

The moment was almost here. She could feel the desire building within her.

She watched the screen. There was no sound and Tobias could not see it. Not that he would have tried to sneak a peek, he was lost in his own little world, waiting for her to activate him.

The camera pointed in on their film set. *Ironic,* she thought, *how I am filming you filming.*

A young woman, mid-twenties at a guess, was tied to a metal bed which looked as if it had been stolen from a hospital. The mattress had been cast to one side and she was lying on the metal slats, wearing only her underwear.

Lacey had used a high-resolution spy-cam and so could see that the girl's mascara was running. There was a gag forced into her mouth.

She looked exhausted and had clearly given up on trying to get free of the metal bed.

Two of the meat sacks approached the bed wearing clown masks and nothing else; the other one moved in a circle around the scene with a handheld camera. He had no need to wear the mask. He wouldn't be in the movie when it hit the internet.

One of the men, who was so overweight that his belly hung over his genitalia, was holding a flick knife. The other man, marginally slimmer, stroked her face.

The woman jerked her head away. The man slapped her hard.

Lacey took a deep breath through her nose, and out through her mouth.

It was almost time for her to go.

Starting at her cheek, the fattest man ran the knife down the restrained woman's cheek and over her neck until he reached her red bra. He ran the tip of the blade over the centre of her bra, where the underwire would be, then across her breast to the strap. He cut through and threw her bra to one side.

Lacey looked away from the mobile and at her reflection in the window.

She ran a hand over her shaved head, turned her face to

one side, so she could see the head of the jaguar tattoo on her neck, which finished just below her ear. She took off her denim shirt. Underneath, she was wearing a white vest, so she could see more of the jaguar which ran down her side to her torso.

Her entire left arm was a tattoo of fire.

She looked back at the camera and saw the fattest man laying his knife on a small, metal table just behind him.

Lacey knew that eventually, when they'd finished, he'd go back for that knife. The little man spinning around the room with his camera wasn't just filming torture porn. This was a snuff movie. Lacey stroked Tobias's head. He looked up at her.

'It's time. Exactly as we discussed.'

He nodded.

She kneeled to kiss his cheek. 'While Mummy is in there, you stay out, and you do not come in until I tell you. Understand?'

He nodded again.

Tobias stroked the jaguar tattoo and sat on the floor.

'Good boy.' Lacey headed off around the corner.

RHYS PHOENIX LOWERED THE CAMERA. 'What the fuck was that?'

He was ignored. His actors continued.

There was another knock at the front door.

'Someone is at the *fucking* door. For fuck's sake, stop!' Phoenix hissed.

The men backed away, grunting. They pulled off their clown masks and scowled at Phoenix. He laid the camera on the wooden table by the knife. 'Don't make a sound. I'm going to look.'

Fortunately, the room they were filming in was shielded from the front door by a partitioned wall, so when he opened it, no one would see what was going on. He rounded the partition and then peered through the peep hole. He could see a tall, slim and heavily tattooed woman. 'What the fuck?'

Had they been too loud? Overheard?

Shit! He needed to know the answers to these questions before continuing. He opened the door. 'Yes?'

The woman had tears in her eyes and her arms crossed behind her back.

'Are you okay?' Phoenix said.

The woman didn't reply.

What was happening here? This wasn't a setup was it? He leaned forward and looked left and right. *Nobody.*

Then, an idea crept into his mind. There was no CCTV camera on this corridor. This woman could be sucked into this black hole and no one would ever be the wiser—

He saw a flash of movement and felt a stinging pain in his neck.

The woman pulled her hand away and took a step back. She was holding a syringe.

Phoenix pinned one hand against his burning neck and threw the other hand out at the bitch. He managed to grip her jacket and pull her in close before his vision started to close in. Then, it was quick. He tried to speak, but couldn't, and before he knew it, the blackness he'd wanted to offer to the woman, swallowed him instead.

Lonnie Bates wondered why it'd gone silent.

One moment Phoenix had been engaging a visitor and the next moment, there was nothing.

'Phoenix?' Lonnie said.

No reply.

'Where the fuck has he gone?'

Clive, his older brother, grimaced. 'Go and take a look!'

'You're closer to the door.'

'Fuck that, I'm naked and you're the one closer to the clothes.'

The young woman on the bed was crying. She was trying to say something through the gag.

Lonnie wandered over to the edge of the room and got dressed. Behind him, he could hear Clive talking to the young woman. 'Be quiet.'

Lonnie picked up the flick knife off the table. 'Just in case.'

'Don't go stabbing anyone in broad daylight,' Clive said.

Lonnie headed around the partitioned wall.

Phoenix was lying face-down on the floor. His legs were still in the room.

'Phoenix, man, are you okay?' Lonnie said. He moved slowly and cautiously with the knife extended. 'Is anyone there?'

No reply.

Lonnie stepped over Phoenix and out of the room. He felt a stinging sensation in the side of his head, and everything slipped away.

Lacey was surprised at how easily the heavy ice pick slid into the rapist's brain once she'd pieced the side of his head.

She let it continue slowly on its trajectory until it bumped to a halt on the other side of his skull.

She noticed the fact that she still had an inch to spare on the pick. She could probably opt for a smaller model next time; it would be easier to conceal.

It had been an easy kill. Barely a sound made in the ambush, and the bastard had been dead before he could cry out.

She stepped around the front of the dead rapist before he fell and slid her arms around his large stomach and back. She then lowered him slowly down onto the other dead man. Only when the two bodies were stable beneath her, did she pull the ice pick from his brain. She did it slowly to reduce the sucking sound.

'What's going on?' the other rapist said.

Lacey didn't respond.

'Where's Phoenix and Lonnie?' he shouted from behind the partition.

There was no way she was going draw a third out so easily.

She stepped over the bodies.

Standing behind the partition, she closed her eyes and breathed deeply. She could smell the bastard on the other side and wanted so badly to kill him.

She knocked on the false wall.

'Who's there?' The man said.

She knocked again.

'Who's there?' His voice sounded more distressed this time.

'If you lie face-down on the floor with your hands behind your head, I will let you live,' Lacey said.

There was a pause while he digested this surprising option. 'What? Who are you?'

Lacey smiled. 'Consider me a friend.'

'A friend. I don't fucking know you.'

'Not *your* friend, moron. Friend of the young lady you have tied to the bed.'

'How do you ...?'

'Look up, corner of the room, above the partition.'

'What the—'

'Is it blinking at you? Smile, you are on camera.'

'Fuck ... no ... no!'

'So, are you going to take the option?'

'The option?'

'To lie face-down on the floor with your hands behind your head?'

'Of course.' He then clearly faked sounds of movement. 'Yes, doing it now.'

'Good.' As Lacey walked to the edge of the partition, she smiled and thought, *you could have made more of a convincing attempt to lie you pathetic stain on humanity.*

When she turned around the partition, he was standing in front of the captive woman, naked.

Lacey's arms were crossed behind her back. The ice-pick was in her preferred right hand.

He sneered. 'You are an ugly looking bitch.'

'Well, that's the first time I've ever been called that,' Lacey said, 'But I guess if you are going to try a new look, you've got to be prepared for the criticism.'

'Lesbians always do talk a lot of bullshit.'

'You know what the worst thing is about you not getting down on the floor?'

'No, tell me,' he said, taking a step towards her.

'Is not the fact that I now have to kill you, I was going to do that anyway. It's more the fact that I now have to watch a morbidly fat man swinging his grotesque bollocks in my direction.'

He took another step. 'I'm going to do more than swing them at you, sweetheart.'

She revealed the ice pick. 'Even after I cut them off?'

He came quickly for a fat man, swinging an arcing roundhouse punch with his left hand. Despite having good speed and aim, Lacey was quicker and more precise and swooped to the side.

She felt his fist brushing against her cheek, but not landing. She slammed the ice pick into his side.

He groaned and slumped away from her. Blood was oozing from him, but she noted that the ice pick had not gone in as deep as she'd anticipated, probably because of his layers of fat. It had jammed to a halt in his ribs, possibly sparing his organs.

She reached out to extract the weapon and give it another go, but the bastard had sensed his opportunity and jabbed her in the face.

Her head snapped back, hitting the partition and everything flashed. She felt the full weight of him. The partition, which was brittle, came crashing down, and she crumbled with it. When she opened her eyes, she saw the eyes of the man coming towards her out of the dust and then felt strong hands around her neck.

She tried scratching his face and arms, but they must have felt like raindrops to him after being speared with the pick.

As the world around her started to fade, Lacey realised the inevitability of it all.

Living from one glorious moment to another, it could only have been a matter of time. She'd always known, as she'd reflected on earlier, that once she got one wrong, it would end her.

And tonight she had got it wrong. The ice pick had not been enough to finish an excessively fat man.

She smiled as the blackness closed in—

The hands loosened from her neck. His eyes were wide, and he looked confused. He reached up to the flick knife sticking out of his neck and then slumped off her into the rubble of the partition.

Lacey sat up and spent a few moments catching her breath before looking at Tobias. 'I thought I told you to wait outside.'

———

LACEY RAY UNTIED the young woman from the metal bed and pulled the gag from her mouth.

The woman started to scream.

Lacey placed a hand to her mouth and stroked her hair with the other hand. 'It's over.'

The scream died in the palm of Lacey's hand.

After Lacey removed her hand, the woman said, 'Are they all ...?'

'Dead? Yes.'

'How did they die?'

Lacey paused to consider how to respond. 'Violently.'

The woman's eyes widened.

'Does that bother you?'

It was the woman's turn to pause and consider how to respond. 'No ... I'm glad.'

'Thought you'd say that.'

'They tied me up ... they hurt me ...' She was tearful and the words spluttered as she spoke.

'I know,' Lacey said, 'I saw.'

'And you didn't stop them ... *before?*'

'I stopped them *before* they killed you.'

The woman took a deep breath.

'Yes. They were planning to kill you. You're not the first.'

'We need to go to the police.'

'That's not the answer.'

'What?' The woman sat up. She realised she was naked and crossed her arms over her chest.

'Going to the police will not stop the man who is doing this.'

Tobias came alongside Lacey.

'Who is this?'

'This is my son, Tobias.'

'He must only be five. How could you bring him here? *Why* would you bring him here?'

'Good question,' Lacey said. She thought of the man lying dead in the rubble. 'But I'm glad I did.'

'I don't understand.'

'It doesn't matter. What matters is that this boy's father is the reason you are here. He is the reason I am here. He hurt someone very special to me, a long while ago. Destroying his businesses, this one included, has only been the beginning.'

'I want to go home.'

'And you will do.' She stroked the woman's face. 'What is your name?'

'Claire.'

'Well, Claire, I have a place called the *Blue Room*. It is a place I visit. A place where I can enjoy many wonderful moments before I can make them a reality. A moment like today. I want to assure you of something before I go.' She leaned in and kissed Claire's forehead. 'The man who set all this up, the man who put these monsters in this room, the man who put you on the bed, has already been to my Blue Room.'

'And what did you do to him?'

'I killed him. Slowly and painfully. And it was one of the most wonderful things that I have ever felt ...'

5

YORKE WAS USUALLY a good judge of character, but even he didn't know what to make of Robert Bennett.

And when a man was drowning in this much melancholy, as Robert was, it became very difficult to sniff out falsehoods.

After taking DNA samples and submitting for analysis the water bottle they'd found behind the maze, they installed Robert in an interview room. He immediately slumped in his chair, started drumming his fingers on the table and said that he wasn't bothered about a solicitor anymore. In fact, for over twenty minutes now, he hadn't seemed that bothered about anything as an exasperated Yorke and Gardner attempted to interview him from the other side of the table.

'Why are you so miserable?' Yorke said.

'Thought I'd told you already,' Robert said. 'When you wife leaves you at age seventy, it's hard to look on the bright side.'

'Finding the bright side is the least of your worries right

now, Mr Bennett. We have evidence linking you to the abduction of a seventeen-year-old boy.'

'I thought I'd told you that already too. It's bollocks. Not that I give a shit. Put me in jail for something I didn't do, and let the real bastard keep on nicking kids.'

Before they'd come into the room, Yorke had read a potted history on Robert. He, like many farmers, had been born into privilege. His mother and father had been church-going poultry farmers, who'd given generously to the local community. Robert had left to marry at an early age, choosing to support his new wife in managing her inherited farm instead. This was one piece of land that wouldn't be passed down as Robert and his wife had never had children. Not that it mattered. The farm had fallen to ruin anyway.

In his forties, Robert had tried his hand at amateur dramatics, and had worked his way through most of Shakespeare's back catalogue in various small theatres around Wiltshire. From then, until about five years ago, he'd divided his time between the farm and his own amateur dramatic club for young wannabe actors. It had grown very popular at one point, and he'd earned many plaudits from the local council. There had even been talk of an OBE at one point.

'What is interesting about this,' Yorke had said to Gardner before this interview, 'is that it would have given him a lot of exposure to young men.'

But Robert had never been in trouble with the law and had spent the last thirty years of his life as a model citizen. However, moving through the annals of history, there were many model citizens, who'd turned out to be anything but when the big reveal had finally come.

Beside him, Gardner put a pair of glasses on, and made

some notes. Yorke was taken aback; he'd never seen her wear glasses before.

'Why did she leave you?' Gardner said.

Robert reached up to scratch a patch on his face. Some dried skin broke away and flickered in the light. 'The usual. Another man.'

Yorke hoped that this wasn't *usual*. He couldn't begin to imagine how he would feel if Patricia did that to him. 'Who was it?'

'Dunno. She left a note. Said he was younger and kinder than me.' He grinned and exposed his gleaming false teeth.

'When was this?' Gardner said.

'About a week ago.'

'And since then, you've what? Sat at home?' Yorke said.

'About the size of it, yes. Did you see the state of the place? I haven't stepped out of the house.'

'Not even for food?'

'Have you not seen the little vans Asda drive around in?'

Yorke hoped Robert interpreted the smile he responded with in the contemptuous way it was intended.

'We couldn't find a car on your property,' Gardner said.

'Correct. We had a Jag and she took it with her.'

Yorke explained that Bryce Singles had reported seeing Robert in an Audi driving past his tractor outside the Mitchell farm.

'It wasn't me. I've never owned one.'

He was telling the truth here. Yorke had already had it confirmed.

'Ever driven one?' Gardner said.

'No.'

Yorke made a note. At some point, they would run

through every known acquaintance of Robert to see if he could have borrowed the vehicle from someone else.

'Back to this reclusive lifestyle. How are you feeling, Mr Bennett, keeping yourself all cooped up like that?' Gardner said, fiddling with her glasses, clearly not used to them yet.

'Strangely liberated. People piss me off.'

'Interesting.' Yorke pointed at a brown paper file on the table. 'Because looking over this file, I'd say you have a history of being quite a people person?'

'How so?'

'Amateur dramatics? A society you ran for youngsters?'

'Long time ago now. Maybe I've just become cantankerous since then.'

No argument there, Yorke thought.

'But why did you choose to run the society just for youngsters?' Gardner said.

'Why not?' Robert scratched the palm of his hand. 'Ah ... I get it. Rather than simply wanting to help young people realise their skills, and choose Shakespeare over Celebrity Love Island, I set up a talent club to hunt?'

Yorke locked eyes with Robert for a moment. He was then calm with his response. 'Is that the case, Mr Bennett?'

Robert slumped back in his chair. 'Maybe it is time for my solicitor ...'

'Why have you changed your mind?' Gardner said. 'You didn't want one before ...'

'You lot are bloody incorrigible. The only thing I want to do is go home.'

'And stew?' Gardner said.

'Yes ... and stew. So, where is this photograph of me on a farm that I've never been to in my life?'

Yorke opened the folder and slid over the CCTV image from the Mitchell farmyard.

Yorke watched Robert carefully. His eyes widened, and the colour drained from his scaly face.

But, Yorke reminded himself, *he is a seasoned actor.* 'Something wrong, Mr Bennett?'

'This isn't me.'

'It certainly, looks like you,' Gardner said.

'Yes ... it does ... but—'

'Right down to the ... what do you call it?' Yorke looked at his notes. 'The PVS?' He reached over and tapped the eczema patches on the face of the man in the photograph.

'It's not me. I wasn't there,' Robert said and narrowed his eyes.

For the first time today, Yorke thought, *you do look bothered.*

'Forgive us, Mr Bennett, but this man is the spitting image of you,' Gardner said.

'It's someone pretending to be me.'

Yorke and Gardner looked at each other and smiled. They were moving in sync now, and they were able to feign incredulity just right. Yorke looked back at Robert. 'That's some costume—'

Robert slammed his hand on the table. 'I'm telling you, right now. It's not me. I've never been to this *fucking* farm.'

'I'd like to believe you, Mr Bennett, but without an alibi for this time, and with this CCTV picture ...' He shook his head. 'Not forgetting an eyewitness who said you hurled abuse out of the window at him. I mean why would we think otherwise?'

'Look closely. He's way thinner than me.' Robert stood up and offered his side profile. 'He obviously doesn't drink beer like I do.'

Yorke looked at the photo, but before deciding if he had a point there was a knock at the door.

Jake was gesturing Yorke to come out. He looked agitated.

As he was standing up, he realised that Gardner was the boss now. He tapped her on the shoulder, and she looked up at him. He barely recognised her with her glasses on.

She shrugged. 'No, you go.'

'Thank you, ma'am.'

Outside the room, Jake delivered some good news.

Yorke gripped him by both shoulders. '*Thank God!*'

Jake sighed. 'However, there is bad news too I'm afraid.'

Sarah Ray gripped her only son's remaining hand.

Yorke approached Paul from the other side of the hospital bed. 'How're you holding up, big guy?'

Paul lifted his freshly bandaged stump in the air. 'Well, I won't be able to bat anymore.' He slipped his remaining hand from his mother's grasp and held it up, 'but at least I can still bowl.'

Yorke offered him a sympathetic smile.

'He won't get away with this,' Jake said from alongside Yorke.

'I got off lightly.' Paul had tears in his eyes.

Sarah's hands glowed white as she took Paul's hand back and held it even more tightly; then, she started to cry. Her son leaned over and hugged her.

Yorke and Jake were already aware of most of the details. After the ambulance had brought him to the hospital over an hour ago, Paul had told local officers nearly everything he'd experienced. They'd been diligent with their note taking. While they were questioning Paul, he'd had his wound cleaned, stitched and bandaged. Tonight, the surgeons would operate on the wound, and tidy it up as best they could.

The situation was tragic. A young man was dead and mutilated in the extreme. An elderly man, who'd referred to himself as Reginald Ray, had been feeding on him. Paul had told the officers that he suspected his hand had been removed for the same purpose. 'I think he'd given up on trying to *convert* me, and just decided to have me next.'

The young man had not been identified yet, but Yorke would be very surprised if it wasn't Samuel Mitchell. They were not currently looking for any other missing young men in the area. This wasn't 1918, the year that Reginald Ray had embarked on his murderous spree in Wiltshire. And that man was long dead, regardless of what Paul's abductor had said to him. No, this body belonged to Samuel Mitchell, alright. Confirmation wasn't long off.

Gardner was already leading a major incident unit up at the crime scene. Yorke had yet to receive an update, but first responders had referred to the scene as 'the stuff of nightmares.' Yorke would head up after talking to Paul. He'd need to get a feel for the scene.

A feel for what he was dealing with.

Gardner had made it clear that it was both her and Topham that would deliver the news to Holly and Ryan Mitchell after it was confirmed.

'We told them that we'd find him,' she'd said to Yorke before. 'It's our responsibility now to give them the outcome.'

'Is Mark up to it?' Yorke had said, thinking back to the concerning things he'd been hearing about him of late.

'He'll be up to it. This situation is very sobering, don't you agree?'

Yorke and Jake waited patiently while mother and son

embraced. Eventually, Paul turned back around to speak to Yorke. 'They told me that the man I hurt is going to be fine. Is that true, Mike?'

Yorke nodded. 'He's having a couple of stitches in his arm.'

'I could barely see, and I panicked. I thought it was him again. Come back to ...' His own tears finally came.

Sarah stood up and pulled Paul's head to her chest. They all stood in silence, allowing Paul this moment.

The postman, who'd come to the door to deliver a parcel, had taken a flesh wound to the arm from a chair leg. Fortunately, he had found it easy to overpower the injured, shocked young man, before any more damage could be done. With Paul pinned to the floor, the postman had contacted the police. He never went into the farmhouse.

Good for him, Yorke thought. There were some scenes not meant for innocent human eyes. This definitely sounded like one of them.

Paul slipped from his mother's grip and winced as he straightened himself up against his pillow. 'Sorry ... my back is in agony. I almost broke it getting out of that chair. Don't worry. They've scanned me. No bleeding.'

'You did well,' Yorke said. 'You were unbelievably brave.'

'Well, not really. It was just that this time I didn't have you to come and find me.'

'You didn't need me.'

'I'm such a *fucking* idiot for burning that place down.'

'You were angry,' Sarah said. 'It's not your fault. What's happened to you, *everything that's happened to you*, is because of that family.'

Yorke didn't say anything. He agreed with Paul. Going to the old Ray farmhouse and setting it on fire was idiotic. Paul would struggle to avoid charges when all of this was done. If that was the case, Yorke would have to try and use some influence. This boy had suffered enough already.

'I know it might not be a good time for you, right now, Paul, but if you could help us over a few questions regarding the man who called himself Reginald Ray – it may put this thing to rest a lot sooner.'

'Of course.'

'Describe him to us.'

Paul described him. Yorke didn't let his expression betray his shock over the fact that the elderly man had eczema all over his face.

When Paul had finished, Yorke looked at Jake. They were both thinking the same thing.

Yorke said, 'I'm going to show you a photo now, is that okay?'

Paul nodded.

Yorke held out the photograph of Robert Bennett taken earlier at the station.

Paul flinched. 'Yes. That's him. That's Reginald Ray.'

No, it isn't, Yorke thought, *because Reginald Ray was hanged from a tree in 1918 and this man is currently in custody.*

YORKE INSTRUCTED Jake to take some downtime. It was going to be a late one and the crime scene was more than covered. Jake was hesitant at first, but then relented. He had some recent memories of how exhausting murder investigations could be.

'But go straight home,' Yorke said, '*to your wife.*'

Jake saluted and drove away, and Yorke headed to the crime scene.

Yorke couldn't believe that this was the fourth farmyard he'd been to in less than twenty-four hours. He and Patricia had been discussing the need to get out in the country more, but this was ridiculous.

This farmyard was, unlike the one belonging to Robert Bennett, well kept. The only thing it lacked right now was an owner. Widower Peter McCall harvested maize and he had several acres dedicated to this purpose. Late May, when the soil was no longer cold, was the best time to sow. It was now almost late April. Would Peter McCall be back for this duty? Yorke doubted it. He wouldn't be surprised if he was dead. Unless he was the man pretending to be Reginald Ray, but if he was, where did that leave prime suspect Robert Bennett?

Unless, Robert was telling the truth and he *was* being impersonated. Could Peter be the impersonator? *Really?* That would be some disguise.

He approached the property. It was a clear day, and the fields and farmhouse basked in some afternoon spring sunshine. If it wasn't for the major incident van, several other police vehicles and a group of officers around the perimeter, it would have been a tranquil view.

Instead, it would make a captivating front page on tomorrow's newspaper. He looked around. Thankfully, he couldn't see, or sense, the press yet.

The normally perky Gardner strode towards him with a pale face, and arms crossed.

'It's awful, then?' Yorke said.

'Way beyond that.' Gardner uncrossed her arms and reached into her pocket with a trembling hand. She shook tic-tacs into her mouth. *Her fix. Lucky her.* He could have murdered a cigarette, but she'd rip it out of his mouth before he'd even lit it.

She offered him the tic-tacs.

He took them. 'None left.'

'Sorry. Don't go in Mike. I mean it. Spare yourself that.'

'Any sign of the property owner, Peter McCall?'

'None at all. I have asked for family to be contacted to see if they can shed any light on where he might—' She took a sharp intake of breath, squeezed her eyes shut, and gripped the side of her chest.

'Are you okay, Emma?' Yorke reached out to her.

'Yes ... yes ...' Gardner said, gripping his outstretched arm. 'Just twinges now and again.'

'That looked like more than a twinge,' Yorke said. 'Let's get you sat down.'

'I'll take a breather in the van.'

'When did you last go to the doctor's?'

'This week. Stop fretting, I've had the all clear. Sharp pains in the muscles around the lung will be par for the course, I'm afraid. And stress causes it to flare up.'

'Now what have we to be stressed about?' Yorke smiled.

'I couldn't possibly imagine.' Gardner smiled back.

'Go to the van. I'm going to go in. I need a feel for it.'

'Well, okay, but just be ready. I haven't seen anything like that since Jessica Brookes.'

Yorke flinched at the name. It'd been a while since he'd heard Ewan's mother's name out loud. Jessica had been broken by a religious fanatic. Literally. That monster had taken her heart.

As Yorke approached, he noticed several large black birds circling above the farmhouse. Ravens? His knowledge of birds was such that he could not be certain, but he was fairly sure. It was a peculiar sight. Several together, hovering above the small house. Could they smell the blood inside? The death?

He quickly fastened the top two buttons on his polo shirt. A sense that the cold was clawing at his neck and the top of his chest, like a lost spirit trying to get inside him, always came to him at scenes like this.

At the blue and yellow tape, he greeted PC Sean Tyler.

'Afternoon, sir,' Tyler said, logging Yorke in the notebook. His tone of voice was too upbeat. His face was full of colour. He'd obviously not been in the house behind him.

Yorke heard a vehicle arrive. He turned around and saw a white van. A man with a camera jumped out. It looked as if they were going to get that captivating photo for the frontpage tomorrow after all.

Yorke turned back to Tyler. 'Has Price been contacted?'

Price was their Public Relations Officer.

'I don't know.'

'Get someone to check, Sean.'

'Yes, sir.'

Tyler handed him some sealed bags. He opened them and leaned against the farmhouse wall as he slipped on an over-suit. He then covered his brogues with some over-shoes.

Yorke entered the house via the open front door. Before him, in the hallway, two Scenes of Crime Officers were inspecting a smashed vase which had been knocked from a table. Apart from this, the hallway was bare. There were a few watercolours of various landscapes on the wall. A SOCO looked up at him and pointed at an open door at the end of the hallway.

Yorke nodded his appreciation and headed towards the room. As he neared, he could hear the activity in the room, and saw the flashes of a camera. So much activity. Yet all of it coming too late to save this young man.

A young man, just about to start his adult life.

Yorke imagined Robert Bennett standing before him so he could shout into his face: a*nd you didn't just take that away from him, you tore it from him.*

He marched into the room, instinctively checking, one last time, that his neck was covered.

Portable lights that worked off one main generator had been set up around the room. If the room was too dim, which this one had been, it was a necessity. Dark crime scenes were a thing of movies. Too much evidence would be missed.

Yet, right now, Yorke wished for a dark crime scene to take the edge off these atrocities.

SOCOs circled around Samuel Mitchell as if they were birds of prey, scoping for danger, and determining if there was enough left on this corpse worth swooping for.

The expletive Yorke wanted to use for such a horrendous sight didn't make it out, lodging and dying somewhere in his throat instead.

He knew Patricia was here - she was the Divisional Surgeon, after all - but he was yet to take his eyes from the poor young man, who was lying face down on the table, with his head wide open. The bloody saw beside him told a story Yorke did not want to carry with him to his dying day but knew he would have to.

He could feel Patricia's eyes on him now but he was so hesitant to meet them because he didn't want to make this a shared memory. Not that he had a choice. That moment was coming, sooner rather than later.

When Scientific Support Officer Lance Reynolds

shattered Yorke's moment of malaise with a flash from his camera, he finally met his wife's eyes.

Her eyes offered him sympathy. She knew she had a stronger constitution for this than he did. After pulling off her mask, she mouthed, 'Are you okay?'

He lied with a nod.

He looked at the body again, now being pecked at by the SOCOs. He recalled Paul's statement that the man claiming to be Reginald Ray had been 'feeding' on Samuel.

The original Reginald Ray had murdered and eaten six boys. Even worse than that, *if* there could be a worse, he'd fed them to his family too. Something *they'd* claimed to know nothing about.

Despite the connections, Yorke wasn't about to buy the idea that it was the original Reginald Ray who'd done this to Samuel. A man who swung from a branch a century ago was not a tormented demon who'd returned from the grave to continue his killing spree. He'd leave that theory for the storytellers.

Other than Paul, the only remaining Ray was Lacey. This wasn't her MO. Far from it. She'd never shown an interest in cannibalism either.

Patricia smiled at him, replaced her mask and joined the flock of SOCOs to further examine the body.

Yorke surveyed the room. It was like an old Victorian dining room you'd find in a stately home, albeit on a slightly smaller scale. The candelabra, and the range of dishes around the table suggested guests, and a lot of them. Had the man impersonating Reginald Ray been expecting guests, or was it merely a showpiece?

At the side of the room was a smashed chair, which was currently being prodded by the Exhibits Officer, Andrew Waites. Yorke thought about Paul's complaint over his bruised back and decided he was lucky not to have any internal bleeding.

As he drew his eyes away from the wreckage, over the table, he caught sight of a large bowl. The contents made him retch.

The intestines in the bowl were coiled, retaining the positioning they'd have been in when still inside Samuel.

Yorke turned away. He certainly had a feel for the place now. If he spent any longer here, he'd vomit, and contaminate the scene. Or worse still, lose his bloody mind.

Outside, Yorke leaned against the side of the farmhouse, where earlier he'd put the over-suit on.

His thoughts wandered to despair. Despite already knowing his next move, and believing, as he always believed, that they would put a stop to evil, he suddenly felt hopeless.

He rubbed his temples. How could he have any hope in humanity, when so many people were driven to such diabolic acts? And every time they stopped one of these monsters, another one sprang up from the earth like a bloody weed ...

How many weeds would they have to tear out? How many times would he have to see what he had just seen in that room?

'Sir?'

He recognised the voice and looked up at the towering figure of DI Mark Topham.

Without giving it much thought, Yorke stepped forward and embraced his old friend. At first, Topham didn't respond, possibly confused over how to respond to this sudden breach in crime scene etiquette, but he eventually returned the embrace.

Yorke took a step back, keeping hold of Topham's upper

arms. He noticed that they didn't feel as toned as they once did. Once upon a time, patting fitness freak Mark Topham's back was like patting a brick wall.

Topham had lost a lot of weight. His face was pale and gaunt. There was a darkness around his eyes which was unfitting for a man so renowned for his bright and upbeat attitude. His hair, usually trimmed and styled, hung as lifeless as his once colourful demeanour.

'I'm sorry it's been so long, Mark. I really am,' Yorke said.

'You had your reasons.'

'There's no excuse.'

'The beard suits you.'

'It's coming off,' Yorke said, running a hand over it. 'It's a hangover from my days sitting and sulking over the suspension.'

Topham sighed. He looked over at the entrance to the farmhouse for a few moments before replying. 'You had every right to sulk, sir, in my opinion.'

On the night he was suspended, and Beatrice had been born, Yorke had delivered the news to Topham that his partner, Neil, the man he desperately loved, had been murdered. He'd never heard so much anguish come from a human being before. Yorke had seen something happen behind Topham's eyes that night. Something that could be perceived, but not described. Then, after Topham had collapsed to his knees, Yorke had held his friend's head tightly to his chest as the true understanding of what had happened to Neil took root inside him and tore through his soul.

'And you have every right to be sad,' Yorke said, 'for as long as it takes.'

Topham looked away. 'It's not the time now, sir.'

'No, it isn't, Mark, I agree. However, it'll never feel like the right time to talk. But you need to, you really do.'

'I talk to Emma. I talk to my sister. All I've ever seemed to do since that day is *fucking* talk.'

'You need to talk to someone you are not close to. Someone who can really help you.'

Topham rolled his eyes.

Yorke squeezed his arm tightly. 'Yes. I know you may not want to hear this, but I kind of know how you are feeling. It took me years to get over Danielle ... get over what happened to her. But you know what helped most? Talking to someone I didn't know.'

Topham pulled his arm away.

Enough Mike, Yorke thought. *You are going in too strong.*

'I'm pleased to see you, Mike,' Topham said, 'but I can't do this right now. Not with a dead boy in that farmhouse. And not with what me and Emma have to say to his parents shortly.'

'I understand.' Yorke patted Topham's shoulder again. 'I understand. I will see you back at HQ, okay?'

Topham nodded, and approached Tyler to log in.

Yorke wanted to shout after him not to go in, to spare himself that trauma, *especially* when he was so clearly unwell.

But he didn't. He'd done enough damage for one evening.

———

JAKE DIDN'T GO HOME to his wife. Instead, he went around to Caroline's house.

It wasn't the first time they'd had sex this week, and he'd be lying if he said it'd be the last.

Afterwards, he lay beside her, sweating, and wondering if what Yorke had said to him was true.

Was this just a series of chemical explosions in my brain?

He looked over at her naked figure. She was facing towards him, smiling. His eyes ran the length of her body. She perspired, and glistened.

Yes, she looks perfect, Jake thought. *But so does Sheila.*

He'd once told Sheila that he could never find anyone as attractive as he found her. He hadn't been lying. Even now, he was sure the statement remained true.

Caroline continued to smile.

But that smile, Jake thought. *God, that smile. When was the last time Sheila smiled at me like that?*

Caroline reached down and pulled the blanket up and over them before they grew cold. As it covered Jake, he suddenly felt weighted by guilt.

When was the last time I smiled at Sheila like that?

He wondered if Sheila was spending the afternoon in bed with someone else.

Well, no, she wouldn't be. She would be too busy taking care of their son.

6

L ACEY RAY WATCHED Frank Pettman.
He was particularly daring for a boy of his age
and managed to scale a climbing wall which was surely
meant for older children. After reaching the summit of the
wall, he scurried into a treehouse shaped like a mushroom.

Lacey glanced at Sheila Pettman, who was staring up,
wide-eyed, at her son.

Keeping you on your toes, Lacey thought. *Just like his
father does.*

Frank launched himself from the treehouse like a
cannonball, sprinted over the rope bridge, forcing an older
child to turn to his side to avoid being taken out, and
nosedived down the slide. With a smile, Lacey watched
Sheila running over the rubberised playground surface in
her faux-leather trousers with a leopard-print cardigan
billowing around her. Other mothers, of which there were
many, looked on.

You certainly bring some glamour to Mummy Club,
Lacey thought.

At the bottom of the slide, another young boy waited.

He was of a similar age, but of a different temperament. He stood, still and silent with his hands in his pockets, and stared at Frank.

When Sheila reached the bottom of the slide, she was out of breath. *'Careful, Frank!'*

But there was no need to worry because Frank's wellies had created enough friction against the slide to slow him before he reached the end.

Sheila picked up Frank, and then looked down at the boy standing at the bottom of the slide. 'Sorry, young man.'

He looked up but didn't reply.

'Maybe you should stand away from the slide? It's safer,' Sheila said.

Lacey smiled. *Sheila meet Tobias.*

An awkward moment passed between Sheila and Tobias. Tobias was not one for communicating. Never really had been.

'Where's your mummy?' Sheila said.

Tobias turned in the direction of the park bench where Lacey was currently sitting. The typical behaviour at this point would have been to point Lacey out. Lacey smiled again. Her boy was anything but typical.

The park bench wasn't too far away, hence the reason Lacey could overhear everything Sheila said.

'Why don't you go along to your mummy?' Sheila said.

Tobias remained still.

THE YOUNG BOY's mother looked familiar to Sheila. She couldn't recall meeting anyone with so striking an appearance since her last visit to Whitby during the famous Goth Festival. Tattoos reached up the woman's neck on both sides. Her head was shaved, and she had thick black eyeliner and lipstick on. She wore a black T-shirt with a blood-stained silver cross on the front, tight black jeans, and knee-high laced Goth boots.

The boy, who had simply stood there as Frank flew down the slide towards him, was not making any effort to return to his mother.

Not that I really blame him, Sheila thought, *she doesn't look that approachable.*

'Is that your mummy?' Sheila said.

The boy didn't reply but continued to stare over at the woman.

The woman stood and raised a hand. 'Tobias?' She had a strong Southern American accent. 'Come over here!' She spoke slowly and with a drawl. 'I told you before about staring!'

Sheila felt Frank tighten his grip around her and burrow his face into her neck. He was clearly unnerved by the woman and this, in turn, made Sheila feel very sympathetic towards Tobias.

'He wasn't doing any harm,' Sheila said. 'I just didn't want him to get hit at the bottom of the slide.'

The woman took a couple of steps forward. 'Personal space is an unknown to my Tobias. You have to forgive him.'

Sheila recognised several other mothers, wandering past and rubbernecking. In a few minutes, they'd be gossiping about Sheila and her peculiar new friend in the park. Not that she cared. She was way above that.

The woman had drawn in close now, and Sheila could see that she'd applied some white foundation to accentuate her pale complexion. The woman held out her hand. 'I'm Millie Radford.'

'Sheila.' She shook her hand.

'And this little man is Tobias.' She kneeled behind him and kissed him on the cheek. 'He ain't like other children as you could probably tell. God put him so far on the spectrum, he almost fell off the other side!'

Sheila was stunned by the way Millie was speaking about her son while he was in earshot. She looked down in case her expression betrayed her unease.

'You know. We come over to Salisbury to see our people. The first time, mind, he's ever seen his people. And do you know what he says to them all?'

Sheila looked back up and shook her head. Frank gripped tighter.

'Not a thing! It don't matter how much I egg him on, he just refuses. You know, I'm going out of my mind. Continues like this, I'm going to have to give him a whupping.'

Sheila's eyes widened.

'Gee - sorry! Don't look so torn up, I was just joking. He's my ragdoll. I wouldn't harm a hair on his head, even if he does put me through hell.'

She reached over and touched Frank on the shoulder. 'What's your name little one?'

Frank jerked away. Sheila supported him by taking a step back. Something felt very wrong here.

Millie's smile dropped away and her hands fell to Tobias's shoulders. He was staring up at Sheila and Frank. He was not smiling. In fact, his face looked rather barren. As if he wasn't really connected with the situation evolving around him. *Poor boy.*

'Y'all not as friendly here as back home. Is this how you always treat outsiders?' Millie said.

'I'm not sure what you mean,' Sheila took another step back, 'but we really have to go.'

'Back to your husband?'

'Yes ...'

'What's his name?'

'I'm sorry, but we've *really* got to go.' Sheila turned to walk away and didn't look back.

Yorke sat alone in the incident room, staring at a blood-stained souvenir from the last case involving the Ray family.

It was a photograph that had been recovered from the corpse of Thomas Ray after his son Lewis had murdered him. The vicious killer had pinned it to his father's leg.

Yorke wasn't sure there were any answers in this photograph, but his memory needed refreshing and signing it out from the evidence room hadn't cost him much in the way of time.

The photograph had been taken in 1944 at the Ray Pig Farm, eighty years before Paul Ray would arrive to burn it to the ground and get himself kidnapped for a second time. Dotted on and around a fence were that era's crop of Rays.

He looked first at a young boy and girl dangling a small child by his legs. The small child had been Thomas Ray. The young boy holding him was Ritchie Ray, father of Lacey Ray, and Paul's grandfather. Ritchie spent a lot of his youth institutionalised after being suspected of murdering his sister – the girl holding Thomas's other leg.

Yorke sighed. Ritchie and Thomas. Chunks of badness in a very bad family.

He moved onto the next chunk. Andrew Ray, Thomas's father. A heavy-set man with a nasal bone that had been broken so many times, it lay flat against his face and snaked in all different directions. Chunks of badness didn't get any worse than Andrew. A man who'd become so obsessed with the existence of aliens that he'd established a depraved cult and started recruiting from the local area.

'Pray for the Rays,' Yorke said.

That was the phrase which many local people used as Andrew's cult marched, riotously, through town, vandalising local churches who refused to support them in their misguided beliefs.

On the photograph, Gladys Ray, Reginald's widow, stood alongside the family. She had a distant look in her eyes as if she were remembering happier times gone past. A time prior to 1918 perhaps. The year that she discovered her beloved Reginald was a serial killer who'd been feeding the local children to them in their Sunday lunch.

Gladys and Reginald's daughter, Dorothy, was also on the photograph. She'd died not long after this photograph was taken during the great influenza epidemic.

Yorke took a deep breath. There was a grainy image of someone in the pig pen in the background. He couldn't remember noticing that during the last investigation. He went down the corridor and borrowed a magnifying glass from Wendy, a Management Support Assistant. She gave him a stare over the rim of her glasses. 'Pleased to have you back, sir.'

'You don't look pleased!' Yorke smiled.

'I am, really. It's just when you're here the workload tends to increase.'

Yorke gestured over at her tea station and winked. 'Just giving you something to do - I noticed that you'd worked your way through that monster pack of teabags I gave you before I went on leave.'

'Behave, sir!' She broke her pretence and smiled.

'I'll be back later with this.' He left, holding up the magnifying glass.

'No, you won't,' she called after him. 'You'll leave it lying around and I'll have to come and find it!'

Back in the incident room, Yorke used the magnifying glass on the grainy image. It was of a young girl cleaning up in the pig pen.

Now who is that?

They'd been through the process of tracing the whole family tree during the last investigation; and, as far as Yorke knew, there were no other relatives at this point.

Yorke estimated from the poor image that this girl was between ten and thirteen-years-old. *Maybe she just worked there? A farmhand?*

He'd touch base with Gardner about it on the way home, and get it flagged up at briefing tomorrow.

PC Collette Willows appeared at the door. He liked Willows because she always looked so eager. Whenever he was flagging, he always felt a burst of motivation in her presence.

'Sir, you are not going to believe this!'

'I probably will, Collette. I am getting to that stage of my career where nothing much surprises me. I take it you got it then?'

'Yes, wasn't hard to dig up the old crime reports on the Reginald Ray murders. After all, he did terrorise Devizes.'

Yorke took the brown folder off her. 'Bedtime reading.'

'Bloody hell, sir. Could you sleep after reading through that?'

'I'll let you know tomorrow morning.'

'You probably know it all already, I guess.'

'Most of it, yes, but a refresher course for tomorrow's

briefing wouldn't go amiss. So, go on, Collette, what won't I believe?'

'Open it up and look at the photograph of Reginald.'

Yorke did just that. He then looked up at Willows. 'I stand corrected, Collette. You were right. I don't believe it.'

JAKE WAS in Caroline's bathroom, freshening himself up before the journey home. He stared at himself in the mirror and saw the lies on his face. They were practically carved in. How would others not notice them too?

These days, whenever Sheila looked at him, he avoided her eyes. It was probably the most obvious sign that something was wrong. Despite knowing this, he couldn't help himself. How many times could he make up reasons for looking away?

I've had a dreadful day ... my head is pounding and I'm just going to lie down.

He didn't have a whole lot of choices in this situation. If he properly engaged with her, he'd trip himself up or she'd see through his bullshit. But, if he continued to avoid her, she'd soon put two and two together ...

Jake ran his hand over his shaved head and thought, *there is only one choice, just end this sodding affair.*

His phone rang. He took it out of his pocket and saw that the number was withheld.

'Hello?' Jake said.

Nothing.

'Hello?'

Still nothing. He was about to hang up when—

'Guess who?'

Jake steadied himself against the sink. *No, no ...*

'Guessed yet?'

Jake took a sharp inhalation through his nose. *Not again...*

'Anyone would think you didn't want to talk to me, Jakey—'

'*Talk to you?*' He hissed his answer. 'Last time I *talked* to you, Lacey, you had me handcuffed me to a chair, and threatened to cut pieces off.'

'*Jesus*, Jakey, you are so sensitive. Yes, I was pissed off, but I thought we'd moved on from that. I seem to remember a rather intimate moment. Don't tell me you've forgotten?'

'*You* kissed me while I was chained up. Nothing intimate about that.'

'Wasn't it just yummy?'

'Not really.'

She sighed. 'Do I really repulse you that much, lover?'

'What do you want?' He really wanted to shout but bringing Caroline running in wouldn't help matters.

'To put all of this behind us. We were close once, a long time ago. We can be close again.'

'We were close before I knew you were a sociopath. Before you started killing people.'

Lacey laughed.

'*What?*'

'Well ... how can you be so sure you came *before*?'

Jake groaned. 'Tell me what you want, Lacey.'

'I wanted to talk to you, first and foremost, about being a bad boy.'

'What do you mean?'

'Where are you now Jakey?'

'Home.'

'Liar.'

'Why would I lie?'

'Well, you're lying to your wife and child, so why wouldn't you lie to me?'

Jake put his forehead to the mirror. *She knows. Fuck. She knows.*

'I'm assuming by the sudden silence that I have your attention?'

'You always have my attention, Lacey. You seem to be very skilled at that.'

'Nice of you to say so. So now, the million-dollar question ... do you love your wife, Jake?'

Jake tapped his forehead on the glass. Not hard enough to hurt, but hard enough to wake him up should he be lucky enough to be asleep. 'I *really* don't want to have this conversation.'

'I'll take that as a *no* then. To be fair, I'd struggle to love anyone wearing those faux leather trousers! Mind you, I struggle to love full stop. Saying all that though, I did like the leopard skin cardigan.'

Jake felt the blood rush to his temples.

'She dotes on your little boy. I like that in a mother.'

Jake felt his throat closing in.

'You scored yourself a right yummy mummy there, Jake. No question.'

'*You stay the fuck—*'

'*Careful, Jake.* You know how I respond to aggression. Especially from wannabe alpha males like your good self. It's always been my weakness.'

Jake closed his eyes and rolled his forehead over the glass.

'Listen, Jake, I could help you out here. After all, Sheila is a burden now, isn't she? I can make her go away. *Both* go away if you—'

'*Where are they?*' Jake had given up trying to keep his voice down now.

'We're all in the park together.'

Everything started to spin. Jake closed his eyes. 'Please ...'

'Quit it, Jake. You don't have to beg. I've always been very accommodating with you.'

There was a knock at the bathroom door. 'Are you okay in there?' Caroline said.

'Yes,' Jake said, covering the mic on the phone. 'Just on the phone to work.'

'Okay, cup of tea?'

'Yes, please.'

He waited a few seconds and then put the phone back to his ear. 'Which park?'

Lacey said, 'Ah, isn't Caroline sweet? She's worried about you.'

'*Which park?*'

Lacey told him. 'And all four of us are having a great time.'

'Four?'

'Oh, sorry, didn't you know? I'm a mummy now.'

'*What? ... How?*'

Lacey laughed. 'Come on now, Jake. I'm sure I don't have to explain all that to you! You've got me blushing now.'

'*Whatever ... I don't care*, just don't hurt Frank and Sheila.' He paused, suddenly remembering something. 'I don't understand though ... Sheila *knows* you. You threatened her before. Why would she talk with you?'

'She didn't recognise me. She's only met Millie from South Carolina.' She turned on a South American drawl. 'Anyway, you can stop worrying. She's left. I think she found me a little intimidating.'

It was music to Jake's ears. He sighed. 'Thank God ... Lacey, what do you want from me?'

'Would you believe me if I said I wanted you to come and meet my son, Tobias?'

'No, I wouldn't believe that.'

'Well, you best had, because I do. I need your help.'

Jake shook his head. 'After everything you've done to me, you want my help?'

'Yes.'

'And if I told you to fuck off?'

'Do you really want the answer to that question?'

Jake didn't have to think about it for very long. 'No.'

'Come and meet me in the park now. There are three benches, see if you can work out which mummy I am.'

'Out in the open? Not like you. Last time, you dragged me to a secluded workshop. Are you mellowing in motherhood?'

'I wish that was the case, Jakey boy. If anything, it's going the other way of late. Come and find me. If you bring your colleagues with you, I'll use my one phone call from jail to contact Sheila and tell her all about Caroline.'

Jake gritted his teeth.

'It's a gamble on my part, Jake, because you may do the right thing. You could arrest me and then go and tell Sheila the truth anyway. But I've met Sheila. She's feisty. I love a gamble, and I bet you can't cope with Sheila knowing the truth. I suspect she'll do even worse things to you than I would ...'

He wasn't sure how to respond.

'See you soon, Jakey. Give my love to Caroline.'

The phone went dead.

Jake had a decision to make, but first he had to throw up in the toilet.

As Yorke drove home, his eyes kept wandering over to the brown folder on his passenger seat.

The photograph of Reginald Ray, taken in 1916 when he was sixty, had him spooked. He was the spitting image of prime suspect Robert Bennett, right down to the red patches on his face.

But, despite being unnerved, Yorke wouldn't succumb to any wild theories. The explanation was obvious. He'd discussed it already with Gardner on the phone, and it would be unleashed on the team in tomorrow's briefing.

Robert had to be a direct descendent of Reginald.

Just like Lewis, Thomas Ray's son, had tumbled from the family tree so, too, had Robert. The next step, tomorrow, would be to find out where and when that tumble had occurred.

CROWN had earlier confirmed that they had enough evidence to move to trial, especially if the test results came through in the morning indicating that Robert's DNA was on the water bottle Yorke had found in the tree behind the Mitchell farm. However, one thing was still really bothering Yorke about Robert's involvement.

Earlier, he'd spent time looking at Google Maps. Then, he'd also made an awkward phone call to Samuel's auntie. Finally, he went back to the Mitchell farm to trace Robert's supposed route from the front of the farm to the back of it.

The timeline suggested that the following occurred in only five minutes: Robert reported his made-up Grandson missing, walked out of the farm to the carpark and was caught on CCTV, drove around to the back of the farm, walked through the trees and across the fields to the back of the maze, and abducted Samuel.

Yorke's research showed that it would take fifteen minutes in total.

There was no way Samuel would have taken fifteen minutes to reach the perimeter of a maze he probably knew like the back of his hand. In the same way that it was highly unlikely that he would have lingered there for thirteen or so minutes on the off chance a missing kid might just materialise. No. Samuel must have been abducted within five minutes. Robert could not have made that journey in such a short space of time.

Yorke chewed his bottom lip. *What if Robert wasn't working alone?*

The DNA result tomorrow may just confirm this. Everyone was expecting it to be Robert's, but what if it wasn't? *Who would be the second kidnapper? Would the DNA sample throw up a match in their database?*

And then there was the dairy farmer, Bryce Singles, in his tractor, to consider. He'd *seen* Robert overtaking him, and then had been subjected to a mouthful of abuse from their number one suspect. So, if Robert wasn't alone, where had the second kidnapper been hiding? The one who'd actually grabbed Samuel from the perimeter and dragged him across the field and woodland?

Had this second kidnapper been in a second car which followed later? Or, had he been lying low on Robert's backseat, with poor Samuel potentially stuffed in the boot?

His phone went. It was Gardner.

'Ma'am?'

'As you suspected, Mike. The owner of the property, Peter McCall, is dead. I went back after speaking to Samuel's parents. They've just been scooping his body parts out of the septic tank around the back. SOCO have got one hell of a night ahead of them.'

They discussed this horrendous turn of events for a couple of minutes, before Yorke unleashed his theory surrounding the timeline.

Gardner sighed. It spoke volumes. She agreed with him.

'And I thought we were about to put this case to bed,' Gardner said.

'No, you didn't, Emma. If you'd had thought that, why would you have gone back to the crime scene?'

Gardner sighed a second time. 'I guess you're right.'

'I'd go home and get an early night. It was such a shame that there were no fingerprints recovered from the bottle, as that would have thrown up a faster result. But we'll get the DNA results on it first thing, and then I suspect it'll be all go again.'

'Yes.' She sounded tearful.

'Are you okay Emma?'

'Yes ... kind of. Telling Samuel's parents was one of the worst experiences of my life. They knew as soon as they saw us at the door. I've seen anguish before, but I've never seen anything like this. Ryan was down on his knees and Holly just screamed and screamed. It took all three of us, Mark, me and Bryan, to calm them down.'

Bryan was the Family Liaison Officer, there to support them through this experience and discover more information about the victim.

'Has Bryan called in some extra support for this evening?' Yorke said.

'Yes.'

It was Yorke's turn to sigh. 'I respect you for doing that yourself, Emma. It's never been the job's most glamourous responsibility. Many would have passed it on. It's bloody hard enough when they lose someone in an accident but when it's murder, it brings a new level of anxiety. The

123

ambiguity, the lack of closure ... the sodding senselessness ... it can cause extreme reactions. I've been there, Emma. You need to go home, be with your family, and get some rest.'

'I will, sir ...'

Yorke laughed. 'There you go again.'

'That's because it's your job. No one I've ever met can do this job like you. I'm not going to stomach being an imposter too much longer.'

'Goodnight, Emma.'

'Goodnight, Mike.'

———

IT WAS GETTING LATE, and the park was quietening down. Jake stood at the entrance, looking from bench to bench, confused.

Only one bench was occupied. By a woman with her head shaved, wearing black clothing. There was no child with her, but there was a little boy sitting on a swing in front of her bench. He was too young to operate it properly, so it just teetered back and forth in the wind.

Surely not ...

As he approached, she didn't look up at him, but that didn't prove it wasn't her. After all, she'd be game playing. That was all she ever did.

When she looked up at the young boy on the swing, Jake saw that her eyes and lips were caked in black make-up and she'd opted for tattoos that reached up her neck to her face.

It made sense. She wanted to lose the heat her recent exploits had brought down upon her while still being a complete exhibitionist.

He stood in front of her. 'Millie from South Carolina?'

'You bet ya!' Lacey used the Southern American drawl she'd introduced earlier on the phone.

He sat down beside her. She smiled and pointed at his shaved head. 'Wow, when did you do that? You look totally different.'

Jake shrugged.

'You know,' Lacey said, returning to her normal west-country accent, 'I regret this choice of venue now, because I just want to kiss you all over. And I can't,' she pointed over at two teenagers on a seesaw, 'not in front of the children.'

'Well, at least there are other things you won't do to me either.'

'Come on now Jake! Can't we let bygones be bygones? If I was going to kill you, don't you think I would have done it already? As long as you remain interesting to me, I prefer you in the world.'

'Thanks, Lacey,' Jake said and sneered.

'At least tell me I look good?'

Jake shook his head. 'You're not my type.'

'Shit ... don't say that! I did this for you.'

Jake sighed loudly. 'Why are you back, Lacey?'

'I like it Jake. Straight to business.' She patted his thigh. 'Before I ask for your help, I'm going to help you.'

Jake shook his head. 'I don't need your help.'

Lacey started to rustle in her backpack at her feet. Jake glanced at her. *What was she doing?* He remembered facing off against her secateurs several years ago in that car workshop. His heart started to beat faster.

From the corner of his eye, he noticed the young boy teetering on the swing, staring at him. His face was pale and blank.

'That's Tobias, my little boy or *my ragdoll,* as I call him back in South Carolina.' She pulled an A4 brown envelope from her backpack.

'Funny that, because last time I saw you, you had no children, and he must be about five?'

Lacey shrugged. 'Always so suspicious, huh? We will get to Tobias in a minute, but first I need to help you.' She held out the envelope. When he reached to grab it, she pulled it back. 'But first, promise to help me, if I help you.'

'No—'

'Okay, then no help.'

'*When have I ever asked for your fucking help?*'

'You haven't. But you need it. Believe me, you *really* need it.'

'Fucking ridiculous, as usual!'

Lacey began to slip the envelope in her backpack. 'Fine by me. Live in ignorance. Continue with Caroline until ... until ... until ...'

'*Until* what?'

She blew Jake a kiss. 'You die.'

Jake held his hand out. 'Give me the envelope!'

'And ...?'

'And what?'

'And you promise to help me?'

'Whatever. I promise to help you. Now give me the bloody envelope.'

'Good boy.'

Lacey waved Tobias over. He stepped off the swing and walked slowly over. She handed Jake the envelope.

'Sit on my knee, darling,' Lacey said.

Tobias hopped on her knee and she folded her arms around him.

'What did she tell you she did for a living, Jake?'

'She's a beauty therapist.' Jake pulled out some photographs.

'Uh oh, the first lie. Look at the top photograph.'

The top photograph was of a tall, suited man. He had a waxed side-parting. Attached to his arm, wearing a glamourous red dress, was Caroline.

'Ex-boyfriend?' Jake said.

'Our survey says *no*. That's her husband, David Hewitt. He works with Simon Young. Heard of him?'

'No.'

'You would have done if you worked in Southampton.'

'Why?'

'Simon is CEO of Young Properties, or at least that's his front. Really,' Lacey took her hands from around Tobias's waist and made a symbol of a gun with her hands, 'he's a hot shot gangster.' She pretended to shoot. 'Pow pow.'

'I don't understand ...' The colour started to drain from Jake's face.

'Well, start with this. She doesn't have to work as a beauty therapist because she's absolutely loaded. She's married to Simon Young's Lieutenant, David Hewitt.'

'I don't believe any of what you are telling me.'

'You really do have trust issues, don't you? Let's move to photograph number two.'

Jake looked at the next photograph of Young and Hewitt eating a meal together in a restaurant.

'Things have been getting a little bit hot in Southampton for Mr Simon Young of late. Someone has been interfering with his enterprise.' She tapped her chin and faked being deep in thought. 'Oh yeah, that would be me! I think this is the meeting they had about a year ago when Simon told David to be more vigilant. That someone, *yes that's me*, was messing with his empire and on occasion, hurting and killing certain members of his staff. That was about the time that sweet little Caroline moved to Salisbury. Or was sent to Salisbury rather. Out of harm's way.'

Jake felt his heart bashing against his ribs. 'These are just words and images ...'

Lacey kissed Tobias's head. He stared straight ahead. He showed no response to Lacey's display of affection. *He probably realises how false it is,* thought Jake.

Lacey continued, 'Look at the next photo, Jake, and then maybe, you'll give me the benefit of the doubt.'

Jake looked at the next photo. He wasn't expecting it, and he flinched. It was a photo of a man and woman with their arms around each other. Both of their throats had been slit.

Across their laps was a dead child.

'Ah shit.' He put his hand to his mouth.

'You know what I'm going to say next Jake, don't you?'

He nodded.

'I'm going to say that this is a picture of the last man Caroline had an affair with. That poor woman next to him is his innocent wife. And the dead child across their laps is their four-year-old son.'

If Jake hadn't already thrown up earlier at Caroline's, he probably would have thrown up right now.

'Yes, David and Simon are very bad men, Jake. And the worst thing is, they're on their way to Salisbury now.'

Jake looked at her. 'How do you know?'

'Two reasons.' She stroked Tobias's hair. 'Firstly, this beautiful little man is Simon's son, and he wants him back.'

She rubbed her nose against the back of Tobias's head. He still offered no facial expressions.

'And the second reason?'

'Well ... I invited them, of course.'

She stared off over Jake's shoulder. He turned to see what she was looking at.

Outside the park, over the street, there was a man watching them. Lacey waved to him, and the man turned away.

EACH TIME SIMON YOUNG watched the recording his breathing quickened slightly.

The psychotic bitch had only filmed the events inside the room. Most of her kills, two in fact, took place off-camera at the front door.

This was disappointing. He wanted to see every blow this vicious whore struck against his people. *Every blow.*

Every time she struck, *every time*, she emailed a video file. Her assault on his businesses around Southampton had been unrelenting. But business wasn't the only thing she'd taken from him, was it? She'd taken something far more important too.

He watched as Clive Bates threw his obscene carcass at her, only to miss and receive an ice pick in his side. At least he got a blow in; and after, when he was on top of her, he managed to squeeze some of the life out of the blood-sucking slag.

Young's breathing continued to quicken. How he wished, *desperately wished*, that it was his hands around her neck.

'They will be one day, Lacey,' he told the video recording. 'You can be certain of that.'

The next moment on the video was one that clouded the purity of his rage with another emotion.

He watched a young boy bury a knife into Clive's neck.

His son.

Tobias.

So, with rage, came another emotion. One he wasn't really used to. Despair.

He'd always known that he would get his son back one day. He'd never doubted it. Not for a second. But this boy on the video ... was this really his son?

He looked so different ... so cold ... so empty ...

Where was the child he'd lost? The joyful little man he used to snuggle with, read stories to, build Lego farms with?

So, today, now, he felt real despair, because she'd taken his son over two years ago, and it looked as if he was never going to get him back. Not the one he lost. Not the boy he loved.

With traces of tears in his eyes, he restarted the video, only to be interrupted by his phone.

'It's Johnny, Mr Young.'

'Go on, Johnny.'

'She came back. Exactly how you described her to us. Tattoos, shaved head. She stopped first at her dead brother's cottage in Salisbury. One of my men was positioned there and he clocked her looking the place up and down. It's unoccupied as the remaining family have moved to Wilton. I thought she might just break in and use it as a place to lay low, but she bottled it.'

Young rose to his feet. He was still breathing quickly.

'Are you okay, Mr Young?'

'I'm fine, Johnny. But know this, she didn't bottle it. She went there because she knew we'd be there. She's inviting me to come out and play.'

'Okay, Mr Young. We know where she is right now. The cheeky bitch just waved right at me. What would you like us to do?'

'Nothing, Johnny. You do nothing.'

There was a pause. 'Really? I don't understand. Why?'

'Because I am accepting the invitation. I'm going to come out and play.'

After hanging up, he noticed that his breathing had returned to normal.

7

YORKE HAD PARKED the shitstorm that was Operation Bookmark to the back of his mind ten minutes ago. Now, he was turning his attention to something that mattered no less.

Ewan. His adopted son.

What a horrible thing to do to someone, he thought, *to call them an orphan.*

Yorke didn't bother asking the question – what makes people do such horrible things? There was no point. He knew people did horrible things. Far more horrible things, in fact, than calling someone an orphan. He also knew that treating the cause of the problem wasn't the final solution. That the problem always returned.

It was the same when Yorke and his team put a stop to evil. They stopped Robert Lock, only for Christian Severance to crawl from the shadows a year later.

You had to accept that it would never end. You had to learn to live with the existence of evil and just learn to deal with it every time it reared its ugly head.

So, how was he going to explain this to a thirteen-year-old?

Well, he'd have to make it clear that there would always be people out there who would try to hurt him. The answer was not to succumb to it. And knowing that it would come back again and again built resilience.

Yorke grimaced. Not only was he going to have to broach this now, but he was also going to have to admit that he'd stolen a look at Ewan's mobile phone. Invaded his privacy. And had not behaved like a good father. A worried one, yes, but not a good one.

He rehearsed what he was going to say in his head.

'Until you, and Beatrice, I didn't have much experience of taking care of anybody. Even now, I don't have much experience. Bea has only just come along, and you, Ewan, not that long before. I want to be the best I can be, I really do, but I think it's going to take time, and I'm bound to make some mistakes along the way ...'

He imagined putting a hand on Ewan's shoulder at this point.

'We are not here to replace your parents. And we would never dream of trying. You will always have them in your life, Ewan, regardless of what anyone says. You may not be able to see them anymore, but that does not mean they are completely gone. Never believe that. Never believe those that say such things to you.

'Since you came to us, our lives have never been better, Ewan. We do not ever want to replace your most special people, but we cannot help but think of you as our son now. We love you so much, and I only did what I did because I was so, so worried. And I made a mistake, because I openly admit I'm a fool who is learning as he goes ...'

Yorke wiped tears away and parked his car in his

driveway.

He saw the lights were on in the kitchen. He turned the car engine off.

And then decided to run through his apology one last time before he went into the house.

MARK TOPHAM WAS three drinks in and making eye contact with a handsome young man on the other side of the bar.

He then turned back to the barman and ordered a fourth Gin and Tonic.

Three drinks hadn't quite taken the edge off an evening in which he'd just had to tell Holly and Ryan Mitchell that their son was dead.

However, the fourth drink, especially when he drank so quickly began to make his senses blur.

And it was more than welcome.

He didn't have to order his fifth drink. The handsome young man had now stepped alongside him and ordered for them both.

WHEN PATRICIA'S MOTHER, Jeanette, stopped him at the entrance, Yorke was taken aback. Not by her being there, because Patricia had already alerted him to the fact that Jeanette was taking care of Ewan and Beatrice while she worked the crime scene at the farmyard, but because she practically manhandled him into the living room.

'Okay.' Yorke closed the door behind them. 'I'm guessing this isn't going to be good news.'

'I have to tell you something,' Jeanette said. 'Patricia already knows because she found out before she was called away, but she knew she wouldn't have chance to talk to you at work.'

'Go on.'

'Ewan was sent home from school today.'

'Okay, why?'

Jeanette sighed. She brushed white hair over her ears. She took her glasses off and hung them from her cardigan. She seemed to be doing everything but get to the point ...

'Jeanette?'

'He beat the living daylights out of someone.'

'What? Ewan? ... no way.'

'He put them in hospital. Fractured the lad's cheek and nose.'

Yorke started to move towards the door. He didn't know if he was worried or angry. He assumed it was a mixture of both.

Jeanette's hand shot out and grabbed Yorke's arm. 'Oi Mister, you just calm it.'

Yorke stopped, looked at her and took a deep breath. 'I'm starting to see where Patricia gets her edge from.'

'You better believe it! So, before you charge off, you need the full story.' She took her hand away.

'Okay.'

'Ewan has admitted it, and he has been excluded for a couple of days. He's already told me why he did it.'

'I think I can hazard a guess. Did it involve the word *orphan* by any chance?'

Jeanette nodded. 'Among other things.'

'What other things?'

'In the changing room, they started to laugh at his scar.'

'For pity's sake,' Yorke said, wondering whether to add,

135

well they had it coming then, before he realised that it'd be the anger talking, and that he didn't genuinely believe that. 'Is nothing off-limits?'

Yorke heard the living room door open. He turned. Ewan stood there with a black eye and a cut lip.

Yorke glanced back at Jeanette, and then walked over to Ewan. 'Did he hit you first?'

'No. His mates did this to me. Afterwards. While they were pulling me away.'

Yorke went over and put his hands on Ewan's shoulders. 'This is not the answer. Not to anything. It never is.'

'What is the answer then, Uncle Mike?'

Yorke shook his head. At this moment, he genuinely didn't know. And the worse thing about it all was that everything he'd rehearsed on the journey home had disappeared out of his head.

JAKE LOOKED in his rear-view mirror at Tobias. He was perched on one of Frank's booster seats. 'Just let me do all the talking, okay?'

Tobias stared ahead with a blank expression. Jake figured that he had nothing to worry about there.

He gripped the steering wheel tightly and sweated. *What the hell am I doing?*

For a start, he was taking Lacey at her word. Shouldn't he be verifying the existence of David Hewitt first? Was Jake really conducting an illicit affair with the wife of a gangster?

But as Lacey had pointed out: 'Do you really have time to confirm everything I've said while you and your family are in grave danger?'

Her proposal had been simple. 'I've been dancing for a long time now, and Simon Young is moving too close to my dancefloor. I'm going to end this and, lucky for you, Jakey, that means an end to David Hewitt. But I need your help.'

Jake had scoffed. 'Or I could *just* take you down to the station and get my colleagues involved?'

'You could, Jakey, but it's not a gamble I would advise. If Simon has even half the power and influence he has over the constabulary back in Southampton, I'd say you might find things moving a little too slowly for our tastes – especially when we have loved ones in danger.'

'So, what would you expect me to do?'

'The easy part. Kick back. I want you and Sheila to take care of Tobias while I trap the spiders.'

At this point, Jake had looked at Tobias. 'Easy? Kick back? He looks as dangerous as you are.'

'He is.' Lacey had smiled. 'Don't you just love him for it?'

Jake had shaken his head, clueless of how to respond.

'But you'll be safe. Believe me. In fact, he may even protect you. Imagine that, a five-year-old child looking after an alpha male like you?'

At first, he'd been in disbelief that as a policeman he'd actually listened to the proposal. Now, as he turned his car into the driveway, looking at a five-year-old boy who was dead behind the eyes, he was in complete disbelief that he'd actually accepted it.

Yet, his choices had been limited. If he'd refused, and marched into the station with her, he'd have alerted the big dogs of Wiltshire Constabulary. Yorke had already filled him in on his suspicions that there was corruption in the police following his recent experiences. What if he came up against that corruption now? Was it a risk worth taking?

His second phone, the one he hid from Sheila, was ringing again. *Caroline*. She was the only one who used this number. She'd called three times since his meeting with Lacey, and he was yet to answer any of them.

He couldn't really ignore her a fourth time. It might start to raise suspicions. He checked first that Sheila wasn't looking out of the kitchen window, and then answered. 'Hello, Caroline. I'm at home, so I can't talk long.'

There was a pause before she replied. 'That was a rather abrasive way of answering the phone!'

Shit ... 'Sorry, I just get a little bit jumpy when I'm so close to home.'

'I see ... I'm not surprised after everything you've told me about Sheila.'

Jake felt a wave of guilt crash over him. This was his wife. The woman he was supposed to love. *Did* love. And he was criticising her to someone he was having an affair with.

'Well, you best go and play househusband, I just wanted to hear your voice before I turned in. Will I see you tomorrow?'

'I'll ring when I get chance.'

'Okay, goodnight lover.'

'Goodnight.'

And then he knew. *Lacey had been telling the truth.*

To Caroline, he was nothing more than a plaything, a welcome escape for the trial-laden life of being married to a bad man. If he wasn't, how would she be able to stomach him going home to his wife every night? After all this time, wouldn't she be demanded that he ended the marriage and come to be with her? The subject had never even been broached.

Before, at the park, Jake had demanded that Caroline

not be harmed by Lacey. Lacey had nodded in agreement, but she'd not passed comment, as she so liked to do. So, Jake had suspected she may have been lying. Part of him had wanted to warn Caroline, but now he was so glad he hadn't made that mistake.

If Caroline had had an affair before, and sat back as a family were murdered, only to go out and do it all over again, didn't that make her evil too?

Jake ran his hand over his shaved head. He suddenly felt like he was surrounded by monsters, and he suddenly felt used.

YORKE SAT with the file open on his lap and looked at the photograph of Reginald Ray hanging from a tree.

In 1918, the party line had been that Reginald had hanged himself. No longer able to cope with a skin disease and a murderous appetite, he'd opted for suicide. Yorke was surprised that the police had managed to get the theory of suicide to stick. Reginald hung a fair distance from the ground. He must have had some help. Yet, all those involved sold the same story; the police, his wife Gladys, the farm boy that worked for them. And it was bought, despite everyone in Wiltshire suspecting the truth that Reginald had been executed by six soldiers.

Different times. It was amazing to think that these lawmakers of Wiltshire could opt to avoid justice because these soldiers had already been to hell and back. Not just in the trenches but in Little Horton where their children had been stolen and eaten by the Ray family.

So, despite everyone in Wiltshire suspecting, *knowing even*, that the parents of the murdered children had killed

Reginald, nobody questioned it. Public enemy number one had gone, and these soldiers had suffered enough for King and country and deserved to be left in peace.

In fact, the only information pertaining to the actual events was at the back of the file. It came from the last remaining soldier, William Walsh. On his death bed in 1960, he described in detail the events of that evening in 1918.

William hadn't wanted to die with the knowledge 'that the evil bastard, Reginald Ray, wasn't given an easy exit from God's green earth.'

Yorke read the statement William had dictated to his wife.

The events were written into local history and had been even before this statement came to light, but in a more modern era, where the world had seen its fair share of monsters with murderous desire, some of this information took on a new clarity. After his own experiences, Yorke felt he could read it with fresh eyes.

After looking at the photograph and reading William's reference to the moment Reginald called his own face 'a piece of rotten fruit,' Yorke reasoned that Reginald, too, suffered from PVS. The same condition that Robert Bennett, who looked like Reginald's twin, suffered from. Robert was a descendent. Of that, there was no longer any doubt.

But it was the other things Reginald said that resonated with Yorke right now. He'd bemoaned to William, and the other soldiers, that he wasn't able to find sexual partners when he was a young man. Despite not remembering Reginald's exact words, William had said that 'he talked about sex like an animal. He even licked his lips at one point.' Modern thinking considered sexual deviancy, and sexual motivation, large triggers in serial killing. According to William, he also showed no remorse and was flippant with his admissions of murder. More trademarks.

To Yorke and his colleagues, Robert had, so far, not revealed any of this. Not that this was conclusive. Another trademark of the sociopath is how well they lie and mask desires.

According to William, Gladys had known nothing. Yorke believed this. Reginald had possessed this much younger woman like an object. Abused her. Controlled her. Her ignorance was certainly believable.

He compared this to Robert's marital situation. His wife had upped and left him. Another sharp contrast. Unless he'd murdered her, of course.

But it was the twisted, maladaptive thinking which really struck a chord with Yorke. He'd seen it before in Terrence Lock and Christian Severance. Reginald had eaten the children because he wanted 'their youth, their freshness, *their health*' inside him.

Yorke wasn't surprised that William could remember this part word for word. Who could forget such an utterance?

Had that been Reginald's motive? The belief that eating children would regenerate a decaying appearance?

William had told Reginald that it hadn't worked. Reginald had disagreed.

Looking at the photographs, Yorke leaned more towards William's viewpoint.

Was Robert Bennett now doing the same thing? Did he also harbour the delusional belief that he could somehow improve his appearance by preying on young victims? The victims weren't as young as Reginald's had been, but they were young, nonetheless.

Yorke heard the front door open.

Patricia.

He put the file down.

She came into the lounge. 'Part-time, my backside. How many times they going to murder my day off?'

'It's your fault for being so good at your job. Surely, they could have pulled someone else in for an emergency?'

'No. Apparently there's stuff going on in Southampton, and the other full-time option was busy. And what a scene to have dropped on me! I've got a strong constitution, but tonight was something else.'

Yorke nodded.

'They were still pulling pieces of him out of the septic tank when I left.'

Yorke sighed.

'Yes, sorry.' They had strong guidelines for avoiding discussions about work in the house. The sigh was the cue to change the subject.

Unfortunately, the subject they changed to came loaded with its own fair share of anxiety.

Ewan.

———

SHEILA WAS onto her third menthol cigarette. Her blood was boiling, and she was trying to cool herself down.

She smoked out of an open window, so as not to put at risk the lungs of Frank, who was upstairs in bed, and Tobias, who was in the lounge probably staring at a wall. *Although,* Jake thought, *smoking was the least of that poor boy's worries.*

Jake realised his lie was elaborate and understood that

Sheila may see through it at any point. But what was the alternative? *Okay, Sheila, I am having an affair with someone who is married to a killer who works for the Al Capone of Southampton. Said killer is on their way to Salisbury for a reunion with his wife, who currently has one of my suits hanging in her wardrobe. Did I mention that this killer doesn't mind murdering the children of those who sleep with his wife? Yes, I know. Staggering, isn't it? Anyway, not to worry, as Lacey is back. You just bumped into her in the park dressed like Marilyn Manson and speaking with a South Carolina accent. Well, her son, you know the one who doesn't do facial expressions? Yes, him in the lounge! Lacey has said that if we babysit him for a few days, she will execute all the bad men, and life can return to normal ...*

If he told her the truth, then she would be out the door, and at her mother's house within the hour. She would also call the police, and then put everyone at risk.

Earlier, when Jake had arrived at the front door with Tobias, Sheila's eyes had widened and she'd said, 'I don't understand ... this boy, Tobias, I met him earlier.' She then explained her experience with Millie at the park.

Jake let her talk. He'd learned about this encounter from Lacey already, but he acted like this was the first he'd heard about it.

'Millie,' Jake said, 'kidnapped this young boy. She's a dangerous woman.' *At least that bit was true ...*

'We picked Millie up. Turns out that not only is she dangerous but the people she took the boy from are dangerous too.' *Sort of true too ... but the next bit? Not so much ...* 'You know I can't explain the ins and outs of an operation we're on, Sheila, but I can tell you this: the young boy, Tobias, is in danger. I have volunteered to keep this boy safe, until we can take into custody those who want this boy back.'

Sheila creased her face. 'That doesn't sound like any kind of procedure I've ever heard of.'

And she was right, of course.

'Yes, but sometimes situations require creative thinking, and this was the best we could come up with.' *Or the best lie I could come up with in next to no time.*

'It's bollocks.'

Jake shrugged. *Yes, I know.*

'Why you? Why couldn't someone else do it? Why couldn't the great Michael Yorke have stepped in?'

'Come on, Sheila. It's his first day back ...'

'Emma, then?'

'Her husband has flu.' Jake pictured himself as half-spider, spinning a web around himself.

The conversation bounced back and forth like this for quite some time, until they put CBeebies on for Tobias in the lounge and retreated into the kitchen to continue the discussion.

Sheila dropped her third menthol cigarette into the sink. It sizzled. 'You've put us in danger.'

It's kind of the opposite, Jake thought. *I've given us the best shot.* 'Not at all, the dangerous person, her husband, has no idea Millie is in custody. We need to keep the pretence that she is still at large with Tobias to draw him back out. As soon as he arrives, we'll collar him, and poor Tobias will go into the system. With that in mind, maybe we should offer Tobias a happy couple of days? He won't be allowed back with his real parents for similar reasons. The poor lad hasn't got long left before he ends up in care.'

'Why couldn't he have gone into the system now? His father wouldn't have known?'

'I can't answer that question.' *Which was true. He had no idea of how to justify this.* 'I'm really not allowed to. You are going to have to trust me, you really are.'

And that is the final word on the matter, Jake thought.

Fortunately, for once, Sheila seemed to agree. Although, she did have this to say on the way out of the room. 'Two days. Any longer and I'll drive him back to the station myself. I understand he's a young boy and I'm not a monster, but you have brought work home with you. It isn't safe. You're not safe. You and Tobias can sleep wherever you want. I'm taking Frank into our room with me and moving a table in front of the door. Good night.'

With that, she stormed out, leaving Jake to feel like shit.

After they discussed Ewan for half an hour, Yorke and Patricia decided that they were still none the wiser about what to do next and so made love instead.

They moved slowly, and compassionately, with each other. They were both emotionally fragile following Ewan's exclusion and a particularly horrific working day, and just needed affection and tenderness, rather than frenetic passion.

Afterwards, Patricia laid her head on Yorke's chest and he ran his fingers gently though her hair.

Yorke felt revived by the experience and offered a solution to the Ewan problem. 'I'll contact Helen tomorrow.'

Dr Helen Saunders was the child psychologist that Ewan had met with for over a year following the death of his parents. After being discharged, his local doctor had applied for more sessions, but this was proving to be a long waiting game. It was time to go private.

'Do you think she'll be able to get him in soon?' Patricia said.

'At over a hundred pound a session, I'm sure she'll give it a go.'

'Don't be cynical – she was amazing.'

'Yes, I know, hence the hundred pounds! It's not the money I'm bothered about though. It's Ewan's reaction to it.'

Patricia turned her head to kiss Yorke's shoulder. 'I doubt it'll be positive.'

When they had applied for more sessions a couple of months ago, Ewan had tried to talk them out of it. He was ready, he said, to put it all behind him and get on with his life. They went ahead and applied anyway, knowing it would be quite some time before the sessions materialised. Now, they were about to hit the fast-forward button.

'He'll see it as a setback,' Yorke said. 'But we have to make him see that it isn't. This is part of the whole thing. He's going to have to learn to deal with the insensitivity of others because that, I'm afraid, will never go away. Are you going into work tomorrow?'

'Yep. Too many tests to report on. I've spoken to Mum; she'll spend the day here with Ewan.'

'Okay, we'll talk to him tomorrow night then.'

After Patricia had drifted off to sleep, and turned her back to him, he stroked the scars on her back, and lay awake most of the night. His thoughts plagued by cannibalistic farmers, troubled teenagers and corrupt police officers.

The only advantage to his insomnia was that he was alert and ready for Beatrice at an ungodly hour, sparing his beloved wife a poor night's sleep.

8

T HIS WASN'T THE first time Mark Topham had
been in this situation, and it certainly wouldn't be the
last.

It was frightening to think that the whole experience
had developed its own little routine.

Flirtatious behaviour at a bar; copious amounts of
alcohol to mask his depression; unprotected sex available at
a higher cost; a sudden comedown from an alcohol-induced
sexual frenzy; and an awkward moment when he asked the
prostitute to leave the hotel room.

Cue the prostitute's moment of indignation. Because no
one really liked to be used, even if it was in the job
description.

'You know, it's kind of late. I could stay over. It wouldn't
cost any more,' James said.

Just like Bobby, the prostitute from the evening before,
James was pleading for more time.

And isn't that bizarre? Topham thought. *Shouldn't it be
me, the customer, pleading for more time?*

But that just showed how truly malignant this whole

situation was. Everyone was lonely. James, in his loveless life, being treated like a piece of meat every day. And Topham, because someone had murdered his fiancé.

Topham wiped tears from his eyes. 'I'd like you to leave.' He felt James's hand on his back, and he jerked away.

'You opened up to me back at the bar.'

'I don't remember.'

'I was a good listener then; I can be a good listener now.'

Topham felt the hand on his back again and he flipped over. '*I won't ask you again.*'

And then came the moment of indignation. James jumped out of the bed, naked, and pointed down at Topham. 'Please don't talk to me like this. Show me some respect.'

'Why?' Topham grinned, despite not feeling amused in anyway.

'Because I'm not some object.'

'Aren't you?'

Topham could hear himself talking as if he was merely an observer. It shocked him. Horrified him, even. He would be the first to admit that with all the alcohol abuse, and sleepless nights, he wasn't completely in control of himself. 'Just leave ... please. You really don't understand.'

'I understand well enough,' James said, grabbing his trousers from the floor. 'That last fella you told me about at the bar? The one that left you broken-hearted? He had a lucky escape. I understand *that*!'

Topham sat up. '*Enough!*'

James pulled on his trousers. 'Enough? The meter has run out, darling. I don't have to do what you tell me to do anymore. I'll decide when enough is enough.' He fastened his belt. 'Yes, that last fella was so lucky. What was his name?' He clicked his fingers. '*Neil*! That's it! Well, this

Neil must have seen through you.' James turned his back to Topham and knelt over a chair at the end of the bed to grab his shirt.

Topham swung his legs off the bed. 'That's not what happened.' He rose to his feet.

'So, you do want to talk now?' James pulled his shirt on and turned around. He flinched when he saw Topham standing a metre in front of him.

'How many times do I have to ask you to fucking leave?'

James began fastening the buttons on his shirt. 'What do you think I'm doing? I'm leaving, just like everyone else in your life has left you. Just like Neil did.'

Topham clenched a fist. 'Do not say his name again.'

'Why?'

'Because he's dead, *that's why.*'

James's eyes widened.

Topham closed his eyes. He could feel his heart bashing against his ribcage. In his mind, he could see the words written on a card by Christian Severance, a mute man who had seen Neil's corpse: *There were bits of him everywhere, Mark. He'd been stabbed thousands of times.*

He felt a hand on his shoulder.

'Hey ... I'm sorry.'

Topham reached up to touch the hand. 'Neil? Is that you?'

Then, in his mind, he could see the words written on the second card by Christian Severance: *And she was still doing it when I left. Stabbing him. Again and again.*

He opened his eyes. Of course, the man in front of him was not Neil. He was just someone else in the way. In the way of everything.

Topham struck James on the side of the head. It was a crushing shot, and the young man went down to his knees.

Topham threw another arcing punch. This time James's nose cracked, and he fell sideways to the ground.

Topham looked down at his groaning victim. Blood was streaming out of his nose and over his mouth and chin. He knew he should walk away. Right now. James posed no threat, and Topham was behaving dangerously out of character.

But, the release! He ached to feel again what he'd felt with the last two blows.

He lowered himself down over the young man and drove his fist into his chin. James's head snapped back so hard that it would surely leave a mark on the parquet floor. Blood was running up his face now and into his eyes.

'Please ... please ... I can't see!'

Inside, Topham pleaded with himself. *Stop ... stop ... stop!*

He hit him twice more and then, breathless, rolled off him.

Barely a minute later, Topham glanced over at James, and started to cry.

PAUL RAY LOOKED DOWN at his right hand.

He knew it was a dream, but he was glad to have it back again, if only for a short while. Life without it was going to be tough.

Above him, a raven swooped from the blackness of the treetops into the moonlight. Paul followed its path with his eyes. It turned him all the way around and he stared with both wonder, and horror, at the restored Ray farmhouse. *Was he here to burn it down again?* He realised that nothing would give him greater pleasure.

He felt a hand on his shoulder. 'Son?'

He turned to face his father, but instead faced another raven, hovering several metres in front of him. 'Dad?'

The raven squawked and rose higher into the air, turned, and flew away from Paul. It glided slowly. It wanted to be followed. Paul obliged.

As he neared the twisted tree where Reginald Ray currently fought for air at the end of a rope, Paul increased his pace. He wasn't sure why he was doing this because, dream or no dream, he wasn't about to save the life of this vicious killer.

Paul drew up alongside the six men. He assumed these were the soldiers who had executed his ancestor. He knew the tale well enough. The woman with them must have been Gladys, Reginald's young wife.

Starved of oxygen, Reginald was now going into a desperate frenzy.

Despite knowing what his great-great-grandfather had done, watching him die gave Paul no pleasure. Because he was a relative? *No,* that had *absolutely* nothing to do with it. It was the fact that he knew that this death, this moment, did not close off the vile atrocities wrought by his diseased line. They had continued and, even now, might be continuing through his auntie, Lacey.

And, back in reality, who was the man pretending to be Reginald? The one who had taken his hand? Was he, too, another descendent of his grim family? Surely, to look so like this hanging man, he must be.

After Reginald had died, the raven swooped for his protruding tongue. Paul looked away in disgust and noticed that all the soldiers had disappeared. He was completely alone again.

When he looked back at Reginald, he saw that his body

was covered in ravens, head-to-toe. *The birds were consuming him.*

Paul closed his eyes. *I am ready to wake up now, I really am ...*

He opened his eyes and gasped. An empty noose swung from the branch. He felt someone tapping him on the shoulder.

'Son?'

'Dad?' Paul turned, feeling relief swell through his body.

But it wasn't his dad. It was Reginald Ray.

His eyes had been pecked out, his ears had been chewed into little stumps of flesh and most of the skin had been stripped from his face. He was a mess of blood and bone.

Reginald wrapped his arms around Paul and pulled him in close. He rubbed his wet, exposed flesh against Paul's face. 'We are blood, Paul. We are blood.'

Paul tried to pull away, but he felt locked in.

'We are blood ...'

Paul opened his eyes, and saw his mother sleeping in the hospital bed adjacent to him. She'd paid for them to share a room overnight.

She was awake and sat up when she saw he was disorientated. 'Paul, are you okay?'

'Can we go home tomorrow?'

'Well ... I'm not sure ... the doctors wanted to observe you for a few days—'

'Please Mum ... I need to get on with my life. Put this behind me.'

Paul already knew what the answer would be. His mother would do anything for him. He loved her dearly for it. Whatever was wrong in his life, she was the antithesis of that. She made everything so much better.

'I'll speak to them in the morning,' Sarah said.

Paul lay back, smiling. 'I love you Mum.'

'And I love you so much, Paul.'

Paul was soon asleep again. And this time, he didn't dream.

It was another late one for Gardner. This was her routine. Three nights a week. She waited until Barry and Anabelle were asleep, drank a glass of wine to slow her racing thoughts, and slid her notebook out from behind one of the kitchen cabinets.

She had no real need to hide this notebook. Barry knew about it and vowed never to read it. He was true to his word about everything which was one of the reasons she'd hooked up with him in the first place. Anabelle wasn't a worry either; she was far too young to be perusing her mother's CBT diary.

But still, these were her thoughts, and they felt incredibly private to her. More private even than her own body, which she was happy to share with her husband. But not these thoughts. No. Not these. So, she kept it hidden, regardless.

I think, therefore I am was written across the front of the notebook. It was the words of the great philosopher, Descartes.

Gardner had written underneath the proposition: *I am what I think.*

She always smiled when she saw that. *I'd give these philosophers a run for their money.*

She ran her hand down the front of the diary. *This is me in this diary. If I choose what to think, then I choose what I am.*

She opened to a page from earlier in the year:

By shooting Robert Lock, I saved an innocent boy's life. If I'd lowered that weapon, refused to commit this act, an eleven-year-old boy would never have grown up. This is unacceptable for me as a mother and is unacceptable for me as a police officer. If I'd spared his life, they would have tried to treat him, help him. But at what cost? The life of a young boy. Unacceptable. And if I'd shot him in the arm, or leg, and maimed him, I'd have given him chance to finish what he'd started with Ewan Brookes.

She wiped tears from her eyes. It had been a tough time, but she now believed, wholeheartedly, every word on the page. Every one of those new thoughts.

She ran her finger down the maladaptive thoughts, of which they were many: *you could have handed the gun to someone else ... you could have tried again to calm him down...*

Each one came with an alternative thought now, but she didn't need to read them. She *knew* the new thought. Not just off by heart, but just through *believing* it, and thinking it.

She moved forward to a later date, following the near fatal attempt on her life.

It was someone else's decision to stab me. I didn't choose to be stabbed. Therefore, it is not my fault. I have chosen a job to help people, and my intentions that day, as they are every day, were to help. I wanted to help someone whose life was in danger. I was not sacrificing my life, I was not choosing to leave my daughter without a mother, I was simply choosing to be altruistic. I would do this again, and my husband would support me in this decision.

She moved forward in the book until she reached a blank page.

She wrote down a couple of thoughts that she'd had today which caused her anxiety levels to rocket.

What if I'm ever in the same situation as Holly and Ryan Mitchell? Sitting there while someone explains that my child's body has been found? If I wasn't so bloody busy all the time, would I be able to offer Anabelle more time and safety? Would this prevent such terrible things ever becoming a reality?

She wrote down a list of emotions each of these thoughts made her feel: paranoia, guilt, terror etc.

Then, she started to write down more palatable thoughts: *Statistically, the chances of your child being murdered are extremely slim. No parent can watch their child twenty-four hours a day.*

Her phone started to ring. The screen indicated that it was Topham.

'Mark?'

'Shit, Emma. I need to come over. I need to talk to you.'

She looked down at her CBT diary, and then thought about her family in bed. 'What's happened? Can't it wait until tomorrow?'

Topham explained what he'd done. She was on her feet before he'd finished.

'Is he okay?'

'Yes. I think so. Black eyes. Bloody lips and nose. I gave him a lot of money. You think that'll keep him quiet?'

'I don't know.' She wanted to scream down the phone at him, but she kept the edge out of her voice.

'I want to come and stay there, Emma. I'm afraid. I lost control.'

Which is precisely why I can't have you here, Gardner thought. *I'm not bringing violence anywhere near my family, no matter how much I care about you Mark.*

'I went blank. I felt nothing. It's scared me.'

'Where are you now?'

'In the hotel room. I don't want to be alone, Emma.'

'Listen to me, Mark. Where's your car?'

'At home.'

'Well, at least you're not driving pissed again. Right, you put on your clothes, and you get yourself home. I'll meet you there. You need to put distance between yourself and that place immediately. Chances are he won't go to the station. He's a prostitute. It's not good for business. But the longer you stay there, the more chance those that run the hotel might put in an emergency call. Do you understand? How pissed are you?'

'I sobered up quickly. Please meet me at home.'

'I will Mark.'

'I'm afraid.'

'I know you are, Mark. Now, do as I say.'

After she hung up, she returned her diary to its hiding place, and phoned for a taxi because she'd had too much to drink.

As she sat there, waiting, she tried to think up ways of helping Mark, but she was at a loss. She didn't think a diary like hers would cut it right now.

He was spiralling out of control.

9

THE NEXT DAY, Yorke was first through the door of Wiltshire HQ, and so was the first to receive an update on the DNA recovered from the water bottle found around the back of the maze at the Mitchell farmyard.

It was Louise Tenor from the lab.

'In plain English,' Yorke said down the phone.

'Do I ever give it to you in any other way?'

'No, you don't. That's why I always come to you first.'

'You're too kind, Mike. It's good to have you back. Here it is, in plain English. We ran the DNA against the DNA we have in the database for the deceased Lewis Ray. They are related. We also have a match between the same trace and Robert Bennett's DNA.'

Yorke took a deep breath.

'Are you okay? It's as you expected, isn't it?'

'Not sure. I was starting to change my mind.'

'Really?'

'I guess that this match is certain?'

'Unless he has a twin brother, yes, I—'

'*Come again?*'

'Twin brother.'

'Wouldn't the DNA be different?'

'Yes ... but let me explain. Originally, we were taught that the DNA in identical twins would be the same. But things have moved on since then. Traditionally, we only compared parts of the DNA sequences – the elements we know to be particularly variable from person to person. We still do this in most cases. That's why you get your results so quick! However, there have been some cases where identical twins have been suspects and we've had to sequence the entire genome of each to look for subtle differences that come from genetic mutations and environmental influences. It is expensive and time-consuming. They've got more tests on the way that can pick up these epigenetic changes quicker, but we haven't got access to them just now. But I guess the chances of there being a twin involved in this case are slim anyway?'

Nothing would surprise Yorke right now. Especially considering the peculiar time discrepancy between Robert Bennett walking out of the entrance of the Mitchell farm, and then kidnapping Samuel five minutes later from the back of it. 'I would like to get the DNA to a lab that has access to this faster testing. Is that okay?'

'Well, it will be expensive, so you will need it signing off.'

'It'll be done, Louise.'

It was DCI Emma Gardner's incident room. All eyes were on her.

Yorke knew there was nothing to worry about. She could handle it. Yorke had given her enough experience of leading cases when he was DCI. Today, he could watch her with pride.

Yes, she looked worn out, but wasn't that true of all effective leaders working in the world of law enforcement? She steered the ship every second of the day on a case like this, simply because every second counted.

How did the old saying go? You can sleep when you're dead. Or in the case of a murder investigation, you can sleep when no one else is in danger of becoming dead.

He smiled at her and she smiled back. He'd be lying if he said he wasn't worried about her but, God, was he ever so proud?

As she addressed her audience, and weaved from image to image on the whiteboard, Jeremy Dawson from HOLMES 2, the Home Office Large Major Enquiry System, struck the keys on his laptop rapidly; the shiny layer of sweat on his face was testament to his dedication to not missing a single beat in this investigation.

Yorke liked Jeremy and was pleased to see that he looked as if he was finally growing up, and no longer appeared like a sixteen-year-old on work experience. Gardner had told him earlier that things were getting serious between him and another HOLMES 2 operative who had assisted on the Christian Severance case nine months previously.

Yorke looked around for Topham but couldn't see him. He remembered their little chat at the crime scene yesterday. He hoped that he'd finally decided to take some time off and grieve.

His eyes settled on Jake, who was gulping back coffee, desperately trying to pump some life back into himself. Was anyone sleeping around here?

He was far less happy to see DC Luke Parkinson. The

man had been persistently disruptive during the Severance investigation, and Yorke had reacted inappropriately by launching his phone out of the window in this very room. Their relationship had soured further when Parkinson had attended Yorke's arrest outside the brewery, and they'd come to blows. Parkinson sneered at him.

In a way, Yorke thought, *he's probably glad to see me. It gives him chance to gloat.*

Gardner finished her recap of the previous day with the identity of the victim in the septic tank at the Crime Scene. Once she'd been through the grisly details of how someone had worked long hours with a saw to reduce fifty-eight-year-old Peter McCall to tiny parts, she unleashed some information that Yorke had only heard ten minutes previous when Gardner had greeted him at the incident room door. 'After Peter McCall's family in Southampton was informed of the widower's demise, interesting information came to light. He is descended from a man called Lionel McCall.'

Looks passed between officers. Yorke knew that every single one of them would be trying to recall where they'd heard that name before.

Gardner relieved their frustrations. 'Lionel McCall is one of the six soldiers who executed Reginald Ray in 1918. Peter was his great-grandson.'

The looks continued and Yorke noticed that more than a few faces had lost their colour.

'It could be coincidence but the first thing we will be doing this morning is compiling a list of every living descendent of these six murderers, or *heroes*, as some folk believe. We then must contact every single one. I have put three officers on this task. You will find the assignments taped to the whiteboard as per usual.'

At this point, Gardner had planned to let Yorke

introduce the Ray angle. He moved to the front of the room. It was a long while since he'd addressed the team he used to lead regularly.

Less than a sentence in, it felt like he'd never been away. 'I spent most of last night buried in the Reginald Ray investigation. If turning a blind eye could be called an investigation.'

There was laughter from some of the officers, but not Parkinson, or the cronies that gathered around him like moth flies around a drain. Yorke was *still* his superior officer and could still dress him down if he so wished, but that was one wound he wanted to avoid reopening if at all possible.

'We know Reginald Ray was a cannibal, and we know that Samuel Mitchell's killer was behaving in a similar fashion.' Yorke didn't feel the need to elaborate – they were all very much aware that the murdering bastard had feasted on the poor young man. 'So, I was looking for motive.'

He nodded at Willows, who went around the room, handing out copies of the statement delivered by William Walsh on his deathbed in 1960. He'd highlighted appropriate sections in yellow before it'd hit the colour photocopier.

One of the officers beside Parkinson read out the first highlighted piece of information as Willows finished handing them out. 'I don't want to die with the knowledge that the evil bastard, Reginald Ray, wasn't given an easy exit from God's green earth.'

'I don't blame him,' Parkinson said. 'Although I disagree that hanging is a hard way out. It's far too quick. This bastard should have been made to pay for longer.'

His cronies nodded. Yorke noticed a malignant look in Parkinson's eyes. *Part of your true nature slipping out, Parkinson?*

'Face like rotten fruit?' Jake said. 'Nice.'

'And who can we link that to, DS Pettman?' Yorke said.

Jake's eyes widened. 'Robert Bennett? With his PVS?'

'Precisely, prepare for this.'

Yorke nodded at Tyler, who then went around the room handing out photographs of Reginald Ray. There were audible gasps. Someone said, 'Impossible.' Another said, 'No question, Bennett is a bloody Ray then.'

Once the photographs had been distributed, Yorke said, 'We've also linked Bennett's DNA to the Ray family tree. You can see that he's inherited the PVS.'

'He's inherited the entire bloody look!' Jake said.

'Yes, there is more than a striking resemblance,' Willows said.

'Fucking supernatural if you ask me,' Parkinson said and grunted.

'So, back to motive,' Yorke said. 'Please look back at the statement from William Walsh. I've highlighted, ten-lines from the bottom, the reasons Reginald gave for killing and eating six local children.'

Their youth, their freshness, their health.

'Jesus,' Willows said. 'Has there ever been such a crazy family?'

'So, I'm throwing it out there for your consideration. Did Reginald really believe he could reverse his illness, his PVS, by feeding on these poor youngsters?'

'Well, if he did, it didn't bloody work!' Parkinson said, stabbing his copy of the photograph with his finger.

'William Walsh made precisely the same comment,' Yorke said. 'Maybe, in Reginald's twisted mind, he thought it was working? I don't know. But that was the motive he gave. So, could Bennett, or whoever is *actually* responsible, be eating these young men for the same reason?'

Parkinson was halfway out of his chair. 'Why did you say, "whoever is responsible"? We know it's Bennett! He's disfigured in exactly the same way for pity's sake.'

'I'll get to the reason I have doubts in a moment, but first let's stick with this idea of motive. The children that Reginald targeted were younger than Samuel Mitchell, but he is still rather young, and so could still fit this philosophy of *youth, freshness and health*.'

Yorke noticed that all eyes were wide and firmly fixed on him. The suggestion that he'd had second thoughts about Robert Bennett's guilt had thrown them into disarray. The thought of a cannibal still at large, even though they doubted it immensely, would be too much to bear.

Yorke pointed at a photograph of the bottle recovered from behind the Mitchell farm. 'The DNA in the bottle *is* Bennett's. He didn't leave fingerprints and was probably wearing gloves, but he left saliva for us to sample.'

Some of the officers looked confused. Some shrugged.

'That proves that it is him then, doesn't it?' Jake said.

Yorke pointed at a photograph of the bloody saw from last night's crime scene. 'SOCO have recovered more DNA from this saw. It is also a match for Bennett's. The blood on the saw shows that it has been used on both Samuel Mitchell, and Peter McCall.'

Gardner looked nervous. She widened her eyes at Yorke. She was instructing him to get to the point before Parkinson and his cronies piped up.

'But despite this overwhelming evidence, the timeline just doesn't work,' Yorke said.

At this point, Superintendent Joan Madden walked in. She walked slowly to the back of the room. Nobody spoke, so Yorke could hear every footstep. Once she reached the wall, she turned and leaned against it with her arms crossed, listening.

To say she looked intimidating would be an understatement. At least it may shut Parkinson up for a moment.

Yorke took them through the problem. There was no way that Robert could have got from the front of the farm *to* the back of the farm, behind the maze, in such a short time frame.

'Could someone have the time wrong?' Jake said.

'The CCTV footage of Bennett leaving puts a stamp on the time. He'd literally just reported his made-up grandson missing, so Samuel would have been straight into that maze. Doesn't matter how many times I trace the route on Google Maps, or drive it myself, you cannot do that route in less than fifteen minutes. And he can't have gone back through the farm because he isn't caught on CCTV again.'

Madden coughed. 'Okay, this seems indisputable. So, the options, DI Yorke?'

'The most obvious option would be that Bennett scoped the area at an earlier time, or date. He left the water bottle there at that point, but he wasn't the one behind the maze on the day of the abduction.'

'So, you are suggesting,' Madden said, 'that he was not working alone?'

There were murmurs from the crowd.

'The farmer who saw him. Bryce Singles? Could it be him?' Jake said.

'It's possible,' Yorke said, 'But would he really have come forward to report Bennett shouting abuse at him if he was involved?'

'But there's no harm in pulling him in for more questioning,' Madden said.

'Agreed,' Gardner said. 'That duty has been assigned to DC Parkinson.'

Yorke noticed Parkinson's eyes narrow. He'd consider this lead a non-starter. Mind you, he grumbled about most tasks, so it didn't matter too much which they gave him.

Yorke said, 'The more I run through this, the more I am convinced that someone else working with Bennett grabbed Samuel. And, if everyone here spends some time digesting this on HOLMES following the briefing, I know that you will all reach the same conclusion.'

'Could Bryce Singles be framing Bennett?' Willows said. 'He could have made that false report about seeing him. He could have easily planted Bennett's bottle.'

'But how would he have got Samuel into the maze at that exact time without Bennett's help? And why would Bennett be in there reporting his fictional grandson missing?' Jake said.

Willows face went red. 'Yes ... you're right.'

'Okay,' Madden said. 'There are two of them. So, who is the second if not Singles?'

Yorke paused and looked at Gardner. She looked down. She knew what he was going to say next and was nervous.

'Someone who looks exactly like Bennett *and* Reginald Ray.'

Some officers shook their head, some exchanged glances. Parkinson just went right ahead and guffawed.

Yorke realised that because of his recent suspension, he'd lost some respect in this room.

Madden said, '*Silence, everyone*! We want to hear this theory.'

'Dr Tenor informed me earlier that although the DNA from the bottle matches Bennett's, it is not a hundred percent conclusive. There is a longer test which will look for subtle differences in DNA as a result of different environmental influences over a subject's life. I've submitted our sample for this test. Look, we didn't expect another Ray to crawl out of the woodwork as it is. I think we need to be open-minded here. What if there are two of them? What if they are twins?'

'It makes no sense,' Parkinson said.

Gardner said, 'No, DC Parkinson, it makes perfect sense. Bennett sets up the trap for Samuel. Five minutes later, at a time when Bennett couldn't have been around the back of the maze, Samuel is abducted by Bennett's twin brother, also a dead ringer for Reginald, and also suffering from PVS. It is the twin brother that Bryce Singles received a mouthful of abuse from.'

Parkinson and his fanbase were shaking their heads.

Madden started to walk towards the exit. Yorke listened to her footsteps again.

At the door, she turned and addressed the room. 'Right now, as far as we know, there is no one missing or in immediate danger. You have the luxury of exploring DI Yorke's theory. Yes, it's far-fetched but I'd ask most of you to spend some time reading over old cases. History is littered with the far-fetched. Well done DCI Gardner and DI Yorke for finding a theory that supports the timeline and I know that the team around the room will support you in ruling it in or out. Good morning, everyone.'

She turned to leave the room.

Yorke exchanged eye contact with Gardner. There was a ghost of a smile on her lips. If there hadn't of been a cannibal, or two, on the loose, Yorke may just have cheered.

'DI Yorke is going to be following up Bennett's heritage. We need to know at what point Bennett tumbled out of the family tree and, just as importantly, who with. If it does, as

DI Yorke suspects, involve a twin, I think this can quickly be put to bed. DS Pettman and I will take another crack at Bennett with this new theory to see if we can jar something loose. Which takes me to another element, that I almost forgot to cover. Despite the best efforts of PC Hammond and DC Willows, we have not managed to locate Bennett's wife, Sandra. Bennett claims that she has run off with another man, but we are no closer to finding out who this elusive person is.'

'Because it's a lie,' Parkinson said. Several officers around him murmured their agreement.

'Well, PolSA are scouring Bennett *and* McCall's property again today,' Gardner said. 'If there's foul play here, I've no doubt we'll turn something up.'

After everyone had left, Yorke, Jake and Gardner hung back in the incident room.

'Went well I thought,' Jake said. 'Do me a favour though, sir? Next time, you decide to throw Parkinson's phone out of a window, could you throw him out instead?'

Yorke clapped Jake's big shoulder. 'I was going to ask the muscle to do that. He's too heavy for me.'

'You were always the best at delegating.' Gardner smiled.

Yorke addressed Gardner. 'Mark?'

'Phoned in sick. Migraine.' She looked away.

Yorke nodded and glanced at Jake. 'You look shattered.'

'The usual. The sofa bed.' Jake looked away too.

Yorke left the room feeling miserable. His two closest friends had blatantly just lied to him again.

10

ROBERT BENNETT'S MOTHER, Elysia, had died five years earlier, and the father had died several years prior to that. Yorke had looked at photographs of them already and there was no PVS and certainly no family resemblance to the Rays. Yes, they could be descended from Reginald, but he doubted it. Up until the arrest of Robert yesterday, the Bennetts had been churchgoing, respectable farmers for the best part of a century.

There had already been some local outrage following the press coverage of Robert's arrest. Several phone calls from irritated Devizes' residents who referred to the Bennett family as the 'best of the best' and as 'altruistic as they come.'

If they knew he was really part of the Ray family, they wouldn't be making those phone calls. No chance. The Rays were magnets for violence and tragedy and no matter how well they hid, they weren't ever going to escape that legacy.

So, if Robert was not a Bennett and was, in fact, a Ray,

how had Wiltshire's family of the century inherited a descendent of that psychotic lineage?

Other than Robert and his wife, Sandra, no Bennett was still alive. Wiltshire Council clarified this. They also clarified that a birth certificate did exist for Robert, dated 1945.

Yorke followed his instincts to Charlotte Wilson; an 83-year-old who had placed four phone calls regarding the 'disgusting' treatment of Robert by a society built on the 'bedrock of the farming community' of which the 'members of the Bennett family had been the most wonderful ambassadors.' Yorke figured that anyone that put that amount of effort into glorifying chicken farmers must know them and their history very well.

Charlotte Wilson was widowed and lived with her daughter, Lucy, in an apartment at Spire View. As Yorke journeyed into the industrial eyesore on the outskirts of the medieval heart of Salisbury, he wondered how a woman who'd spent most of her existence in the 'bedrock of the farming community' was coping with city life.

Not that well, Yorke reasoned, if she was finding time to put in phone calls like the ones yesterday.

Yorke had phoned ahead to warn Charlotte and Lucy of his arrival. Charlotte was more than happy to see him. She was probably ready to put the world to rights over Wiltshire Police's miscarriage of justice.

After parking up, he rang the doorbell labelled Lucy Wilson. It was Lucy that answered.

'Hello ... it's Detective Inspector Michael Yorke. I phoned ahead earlier to speak to your mother.'

'I'll buzz you up but you're going to be disappointed I'm afraid.'

Yorke considered asking her what she meant before

realising she'd already rung off. The buzzer sounded and he entered.

Two boys were squabbling over a bike in the stairwell. One must have been about fifteen, the other several years younger.

'Everything alright?' Yorke said as he approached the stairs.

'Fine,' the older boy said, 'he's my brother.'

Yorke looked at the younger boy, whose face was red and blotchy. 'Is that the case?'

The younger boy nodded.

The older boy snatched the bike from his brother and started wheeling it towards the exit. 'He's going to be lending me his bike for a bit, the little retard.'

For a moment, Yorke imagined Ewan in that changing room with a boy pointing at the scars on his chest saying *'Orphan.'*

'Hey, get out of my way,' the older boy said to Yorke.

Yorke had stepped in front of him. 'Which flat are your parents in?'

'What's it to you?'

Yorke took a deep breath. *Control yourself, you are dealing with a petulant child, not an armed thug.*

Ewan's experiences really did have him wound up.

The door opened behind the two boys and a wide, squat man with a squashed looking face trudged out. The polo shirt he had on was too small for him and Yorke was surprised it didn't tear. He also wondered if the reason that his face looked so squashed was because he'd squeezed it through such a narrow collar.

'Dad, this man is in my way,' the older boy said.

The man started to growl so Yorke flashed his badge.

'Come here, Todd,' the man said.

'And give your brother his bike back,' Yorke said.

Todd wheeled the bike back to his younger brother. The tearful boy smiled.

'Sorry.' The man took Todd by the shoulder. 'They're always falling out.'

As Yorke walked upstairs, he listened to Todd being led into his apartment for a rollicking. He glanced over his shoulder and saw the younger brother disappear out of the door for a bike ride and smiled.

Lucy Wilson, who looked youthful for sixty, was waiting for him at the apartment door. She had a short-sleeved shirt on, exposing interlocking flowers tattooed up and down her arms. It made Yorke think of his grandmother's wallpaper in the house he frequented regularly back in the early eighties, while his mother was binging on drugs and alcohol.

'My mother took a turn and is asleep now, detective. It'll be hours before she'll be up again.' She sighed. 'They're getting more and more regular now.'

'I'm sorry to hear that.'

'Thanks. It's better if it's almost her time. Not for me, you understand, I love her, and I'll do anything for her. But she can't get used to this life I've brought her into and everyone else she's ever known has gone. Besides you wouldn't have got much out of her about the Bennetts. She has them on a pedestal. As you probably found out yesterday evening before I pried the phone off her!' She smiled and showed bleached white teeth. 'To be honest, you might be best speaking to me. I know about the Bennetts - warts and all.'

Yorke felt his heart rate quicken. 'That would be great.'

'Come in then and I'll put the kettle on.'

LACEY RAY WONDERED what would have happened if she'd been loved as a child.

These days, she often gazed on young families who were *so contentedly* lost in each other and wondered if things would have turned out differently if she'd also had this.

She would watch as the young mother would kneel before her darling child to teach them to look right, then left, before crossing. She would stare at the young father who would hoist his little cherub up onto his shoulders.

And all the time she wondered.

Just wondered.

Her father, Richie Ray, had been a cold man, who'd murdered his sister in a fit of madness, and spent most of his life institutionalised. Her mother, Mary-Ann Ray, had been a drug addict lost in a kaleidoscope that turned her in and out of reality.

Her mother had never taught her the Green Cross Code and her father had never held her up to see the world from high.

So she had punished them.

Tampered with their car so they died in fire and tangled metal.

And now, she stood here wondering if things really could have been any different.

For as long as she could remember, she'd felt perennially bored and in need of stimulation. But even when presented with stimulation, arousal of any kind had been hard to come by. She had rarely, if ever, felt happy. She had struggled to care about the feelings of others, unless they were being unjustly treated in some way. Even anger would only manifest itself as a form of mild irritation.

Very recently though, in the face of all this numbing monotony, she'd managed to find a sparkle. Tobias. She'd discovered a capacity in herself to worry, and potentially, care for someone.

Was it love? She doubted it. But she hoped. And hope was also something new she was experiencing.

Many years ago, the doctors, who genuinely believed that they could categorise every thought process and put every individual into a box, had called her a *malignant narcissist*.

It would be quite an achievement to prove them wrong. Yes, they were probably right about her psychological need for power. After all, she was about to go into Caroline's house and assert her authority over her. They were probably also right about her sense of grandiosity. She was boastful of the fact that many of her actions had positive outcomes. She struggled to recall a single victim who'd been any good for society when they were alive.

But the absence of conscience?

She felt that they were wrong about this. If something bad happened to Tobias, she would blame herself for that. She just knew she would.

Worry, hope, a conscience?

Were these signs that things were changing for her? Was it so wrong to wonder if things would have been different if she'd been given love? Would she have been *taught* how to love?

She watched a young lady leave Caroline's house. Caroline waved goodbye at the door and closed it.

The woman was all alone.

Lacey walked over the street, so she passed alongside

the young lady. She had a striking figure, and jet-black hair pulled back tight into a ponytail. She had a tan, and thick, fresh microbladed eyebrows.

Was that lust I felt? Lacey smiled. *Add that to your list doctors!*

'Nice job.' Lacey winked.

The young lady avoided eye contact. Her tan was too dark for Lacey to determine if she'd blushed or not.

Lacey reached the curb and stepped up onto the pavement. She turned and watched the beautiful woman climb into a red Audi Convertible. She took long deep breaths.

Yes, that's most definitely lust.

She turned back, walked down the path and rang the doorbell.

Caroline opened the door.

Another lady with a fine figure, Lacey thought. *Is there a chance I'm sexually frustrated here?*

She spent a moment trying to recall her last sexual encounter, but her train of thought was interrupted by Caroline. 'Can I help you?'

'Yes, you can,' Lacey said.

She hadn't come wearing goth clothing, and instead stood in a brown leather jacket, and some tight jeans.

'I came across this.' Lacey held up Caroline's business card. 'And I really need your help. Not with this ...' She ran a hand over her shaved head. 'But with these.' She touched her right eyebrow and then her left.

Caroline scrunched up her forehead. 'That's not really how this works. You need to phone ahead for an appointment. My next appointment is in thirty minutes I'm afraid, and after that I was planning on finishing for the day. So, there's nothing I can really do at such short notice.'

'I thought you'd say that and until my girlfriend woke up this morning and pointed out her dislike for them, eyebrows were the last thing on my mind also! Which is why I brought this.' Lacey pulled a wad of twenty-pound notes out from the inside of a leather jacket.

Caroline raised her eyebrows. 'This seems rather—'

'—unorthodox?'

'Yes.'

'Well, I'm desperate. My girlfriend is a soap actress and I really don't want to mess this one up. If I tell you who she is, you'll see my predicament. No price is too high to keep this fire burning. So, there's a thousand pounds here. If you ring ahead and cancel your appointment, we can get on with it.'

'A thousand pounds, *really?*'

'She's paying,' Lacey said. 'Drop in the ocean for her.'

Caroline nodded. 'I guess I can make an exception. Come in, Ms ...?'

'Ms Ray, but you can call me Lacey.'

There was no recognition over the name but why would there be? Caroline was from Southampton; the legacy of the Rays would not be in her memory bank.

'Okay, Lacey, come in.'

She stepped into the house.

'And do tell me, who is this soap actress?' Caroline said, closing the door.

As YORKE TOOK a mouthful of tea, he listened to the muffled shouting coming from the apartment beneath them.

Lucy looked down and sighed.

'Sorry, I may have caused a little family argument on the way in,' Yorke said.

'Don't blame yourself. Those arguments are an hourly occurrence.'

'It's not good. I was brought up in a similar household. It'll get to those boys eventually.'

She looked at him sympathetically. 'Well, it's the opposite for me, there were no arguments in my household. Didn't make it any less trying, nonetheless. We were the *perfect* family.' She made quotation marks with her fingers over the word *perfect*. 'You see, when you are *perfect*, impression is everything. God forbid anyone should think you're not *perfect*.'

'I can imagine,' Yorke said. 'Strict then?'

'Very. As children, we were seen and not heard. My father used to shake my brother by the hand rather than hug him. You get the picture. Cold, it was. But *perfect*.' She guffawed and took a drink. 'Mother remembers but she'll never admit it. It was a form of abuse in its own right.'

It was Yorke's turn to offer her a sympathetic look. 'Ms Wilson, what do you know about the Bennett family?'

'Another *perfect* family!'

'You disagree then?'

She smiled. 'You know they kept their boy, Robert, practically hidden away?'

Yorke put his cup of tea down on the coffee table and leaned forward. 'No, I did not.'

'He was home schooled. Not that I would have seen him at school anyway, he was ten years older than me. But some of my older friends remember daring each other to go onto the farm and stare at the mysterious boy's face through the window.'

'Really? And what did they see?'

'A boy with horrendous eczema and bald patches on his head. Poor kid.' She sighed. 'Glad to say I wasn't old enough to be part of that crowd. They treated him like a freak. No wonder he never came out. I wouldn't have done either. Mind you, that wasn't the real reason he never came out. It was because his parents were ashamed of him.'

Yorke sighed. 'Who looked after Robert when they were out being pillars of the community?'

She brushed her hand back and forth over her floral-tattooed arm. 'He festered at home with a live-in maid.'

'Live-in maid?'

'Yes, I suppose it wasn't uncommon back then. A lot of wealthy farmers, such as the Bennetts, had live-in maids and farmhands. No doubt this woman raised him. She certainly home schooled him. I bumped into her a few times in town. She was a very quiet lady. Polite enough but never really spoke to anyone.'

'Was she elderly?'

'Not really,' Lucy said. 'She was probably middle-aged when I was about fifteen.'

Yorke did a quick calculation in his head. 'A strange question I know, but do you think that this could have been his real mother?'

She shrugged. 'Dunno. But it's not actually a strange question. The rumour always was that Robert Bennett had been adopted.'

'Why?'

'Because prior to the arrival of baby Robert, Elysia and her husband had no children and were apparently unable to conceive. You see, the father had served in the war and had picked up a horrendous shrapnel injury.' She pointed downwards at her own crotch.

'Just rumours?'

177

'Everything was rumour then, Detective Yorke. Everything was Chinese whispers. I do know this though ...' She paused to smile. 'If you were interviewing my mother, you wouldn't be getting any of this!'

'Did she not know about these things?'

'*Of course she did!* But she would not spoil the *perfect* picture to an outsider like you!'

Yorke smiled.

They talked for a few more minutes before a tingling bell interrupted their conversation.

'She's awake, I have to go,' Lucy said. 'It will take her about twenty minutes for her to completely come round. Would you like to wait?'

Yorke declined. He felt that he had more than enough to go on right now.

As he left Spire View, the bullied young boy from earlier pulled a wheelie on his bike as he passed. Yorke thought of the damage labels such as 'retard' or 'orphan' did to kids. Then, he thought about Robert sitting by the window as the children from his village pointed in, laughing, and wondered what damage that had caused him.

AFTER GARDNER and Jake had taken another crack at interviewing Robert Bennett and had made no progress, they stood by the coffee machine bemoaning the state of the latte it churned out.

Gardner's phone rang. It was Yorke.

After several minutes of listening to Yorke and making notes, Gardner grabbed Jake's arm. 'We're going back in.'

'Want to tell me why?'

'No time. You'll find out in there.'

They sat down opposite Robert. He was handcuffed and an officer stood close behind him. He had thick splotches of cream all over his face, hiding his aggravated patches. He looked like a circus clown that had been hit with a cream pie.

Gardner put on her new glasses and looked down at her notepad. She could sense Jake leaning over her trying to read her notes. She threw him a stare; he shrugged and sat back.

'Some new information has come to light, Robert,' Gardner said.

'Robert? First name terms, are we now?'

'Well, as I'm the only person still standing in the way of a life sentence for you, I thought we could drop the formalities.'

He shrugged.

'I understand both of your parents are dead, which I'm very sorry about.'

A wry smile spread across Robert's face.

'And we have something very important to ask you.'

Robert nodded but didn't reply.

'Is the maid who took care of you as a child still alive?'

His smile fell away and his eyes widened. 'Who told you about that?'

'That's not relevant. The only thing that is relevant is whether she is alive or not.'

'She's alive but it's a dead angle for you. She had a stroke a few years back and her brain stem has been damaged which means she cannot move.'

'Locked-in syndrome,' Jake said.

'Yes.'

'I've heard of it. They still have consciousness but can only communicate with eye movement?'

'About the size of it,' Robert said. 'But she stopped communicating long ago.'

'What's her name? Where is she?' Gardner said.

'And if I refuse to tell you?'

'Then we will end all discussion. I will deem you a hostile suspect and proceed with charging you. When your court date arrives, your complete refusal to cooperate will be taken into account. Or, you could just do yourself a favour, give me the information and let us try to help you.'

He grunted. 'Her name is Hayley Willborough. But it won't help any. I'd leave it alone.'

'Thank you. Just a few more questions, Robert.'

He didn't respond.

'When did you leave home?'

'When I was twenty-five. I met my wife and she finally got me out of that house.'

'What was wrong in that house?'

'Well, I take it you already know after walking in here with such purpose!' Robert snorted. 'I was treated like a prisoner. Didn't go to school with the other kids and when I grew up, the only friend I ever made was my wife. She helped on the farm. If she hadn't have started working there, I'd probably never have left that bloody place.'

'And now she's gone and left you,' Jake said.

'Thanks for reminding me, detective.'

'Did you stay in touch with your parents after you finally left?'

'Of course! They were my parents after all! Even if they did treat me like a leper.'

'And Hayley Willborough too?' Gardner asked.

Robert looked down. 'Yes. She was the only one who ever treated me with kindness. Apart from my wife when we first met.'

'Can we ask about a rumour we've heard?'

Robert smiled. 'That I'm adopted?'

Gardner nodded.

'How would I know? They'd never have told me if I was.'

'Apparently, your dad was wounded badly in the war.'

'Yep. Shrapnel made a right mess of his family jewels. Even worse than my own face I might add. Yet, he still could go out all the time while I stayed at home. Harder to keep my disfigurement hidden away I suppose.'

'So, he may not have fathered you?'

'My parents were popular. They could have asked another male farmer for a sperm donation for all I know. Once again, these are questions I've never been able to answer so I can't really answer them now, can I?'

'How about Hayley Willborough? Could she be your real mum?'

Robert took a deep breath. His eyes wandered up and away. There was a long moment of silence before he answered. 'Who knows? Like I said she was the only one who ever treated me like a son.'

'Did you still see her? In the home?'

'Yes, every week.'

'Would you please tell us where Hayley is now?'

Robert sighed and wrote down the address.

11

LACEY PROWLED THE lounge while Caroline prepared her treatment room following her last appointment with the stunning, dark-haired woman she'd passed in the street.

She was taking a long time. What had the previous customer opted for? A full body wax?

She sipped on chamomile tea, which had been provided by Caroline, along with the endorsement, 'It will bring a healthy shine to your skin.'

The room was kitted out with expensive gear. There was a leather chaise longue opposite a top-of-the-range TV screen and sound system.

Being married to a gangster and running a beauty business from home clearly had massive financial benefits. Lacey had taken a large gamble with the thousand pounds on the doorstep. Was money really an object to Caroline?

Not that it really mattered. Lacey would have wrestled Caroline into her own house if she'd needed too. But subtlety was always the best option. Boring, yet safe.

Caroline was taking too long, and Lacey decided it was

time to act. She placed her cup down on the mantlepiece beside a silver-framed photograph of two young children on the deck of a yacht. From the inside pocket of her leather jacket, she took a souvenir from her adventure into the Southampton snuff-porn industry.

The flick-knife.

'My nieces,' Caroline said from behind her.

'They look like you.' Lacey slipped the flick-knife back into her pocket. 'I assumed they were your children.'

'The treatment room is ready now if you'd like to follow me.'

Lacey turned and nodded. 'No photos of any men?'

There was an awkward pause. 'That's right.'

Lacey smiled. 'I assumed you'd be married.'

'Why would you assume that?'

Lacey shrugged. 'It's a good question. I have a problem with making assumptions.'

Caroline scrunched her forehead, just like she'd done at the front door earlier.

I confuse you, don't I? Lacey thought. 'So, you're not married then?'

'No, but why the sudden interest?'

Lying bitch. 'Just making small talk.'

Caroline led her through to the treatment room, and Lacey was pleased to see the lighting in this place was blue. It reminded her of her own room, the Blue Room. A place of harmony and judgement. She went there often with her victims, just before she physically met with them, and ended their lives.

She'd not been to the Blue Room with Caroline. This was unfortunate because Caroline was suitable. She was a homewrecker. More than that, she preyed on the innocent. Caroline knew that, eventually, fire and fury would arrive in

Salisbury in the form of her homicidal husband, and Jake would pay the ultimate price.

The death of his wife and an innocent young boy no older than her own beautiful Tobias.

Caroline was not her usual gender, but she was *more than suitable* for her Blue Room.

But, alas, the promise had been made to Jake. She wasn't to kill Caroline. And Jake had done her a significant favour this time.

However, nothing had been said about inflicting some pain ...

'I like this room,' Lacey said. 'Especially the lighting.'

'I chose blue because it's a calming colour.'

'Yes. It's my favourite colour. The Chinese use it to soothe pain ... am I going to feel pain today, Caroline?'

'No, I will use a numbing ointment.'

The room was small. It consisted of a bed, covered in towelling, and a light, which resembled something from the dentist's, coming down from the ceiling. The room was laid out with equipment.

'If you'd like to take a seat on the bed, I'll talk you through the process.'

'All in good time, Caroline. I'd like to talk to you about something else on my mind first.'

With satisfaction, Lacey watched the colour drain from Caroline's face. *She knows she's about to be rumbled ...*

'Ever since you've come into my house,' Caroline said, 'you've been behaving oddly.'

Lacey smiled. 'Yes, it's often remarked on.' *I'm a malignant narcissist, don't you know?*

'I'd like you to leave, please?'

'For being different? Did your husband never teach you to be accepting of everyone – no matter their eccentricities?'

Lacey put her hand to her mouth. 'Ah, sorry, my mistake, you're not married, are you?'

The colour had well and truly disappeared from Caroline's face now.

'I'm going to guess what you're thinking ... You're thinking that I am here because of Jake. You know I'm not his wife, Sheila, because you will have seen photographs of her, so you are assuming I'm a family friend here to put the shitters up you?'

Caroline didn't respond.

'Well, you're wrong. I'm not really a family friend. I mean, me and Jake have history but not in the way that you're thinking ...'

'Do you realise what my husband will do if he finds out about all of this?' Caroline said. 'Do you realise how dangerous he is?'

'Yes, I do. I know all about David, and his boss, Simon.'

'*Who are you?*'

'I told you at the door. Unlike you, I didn't lie today. Well ... maybe about the soap star, but some embellishment never goes amiss. The fact of the matter is, Caroline, you are not going to die today because I made Jake a promise. However, this isn't the case for David and Simon, I'm afraid.'

'But they're in Southampton,' Caroline said.

Lacey noticed her glancing at the open door – she was preparing to make a run for it.

Lacey shook her head. 'I'm afraid not. They're on their way to Salisbury and their first stop will be here. I have no doubt.'

Caroline ran. Lacey was quick. She hoisted the gangster's wife backwards and curled an arm around her neck. She squeezed until the beautician went limp in her arms.

YORKE ALWAYS THOUGHT that nursing homes tried so hard to look welcoming without actually being welcoming. This one was no exception.

The Orchard Care Home filled the outer garden with an orchard. Wandering in through a decorative display of apple, apricot, blueberry, hazelnut and fig trees did nothing to disguise the reality. An abundant garden of colour and life just seemed like an obvious trick to Yorke. People were not put here to thrive like this garden, they were put here to die.

After Yorke had received Gardner's update and headed to the Orchard Care Home, he'd called ahead to say that he would like to speak to Hayley Willborough. The manager had sounded genuinely surprised. She hadn't communicated in a long while. Yorke had said he still wanted to try.

So, after he'd signed himself in with the same manager, the nurse led him down a white corridor. It was ridiculously clean, and ridiculously long. But what unnerved Yorke about the corridor most was its sheer length. He tried to make small talk with the nurse, but she was uninterested, and the three-minute journey seemed painfully longer than it was.

Eventually, they entered a sterile white room, which was a far cry from the colourful and fruitful orchard.

Hayley Willborough, propped up on several pillows, was the size of a young child. She had a breathing tube in the centre of her neck. He noticed her eyes following him around the side of the bed.

He took her hand in his. Only afterwards, did he realise that he'd done this instinctually. There was no hidden agenda behind his display of sympathy for this poor woman. He suddenly felt immensely guilty over the fact that he was about to broach subjects that would be very painful to her.

The nurse came around the other side of the bed. She took Hayley's other hand. 'Hello, Ms Willborough, are you enjoying *Deal or No Deal?*'

There was no response from Hayley. During the initial phone call, the manager had informed Yorke that Hayley had stopped responding over a year ago. 'She used to be able to use a computer programme where she could generate speech with different movements of her eyes but not anymore unfortunately.'

Yorke looked up at the television suspended from the ceiling. Noel Edmonds was on his black phone to the banker while a contestant sweated over a red box.

'Is it okay if we turn the volume down for a moment please Ms Willborough?' The nurse said.

No response again.

The nurse picked up the remote control and turned the volume down.

Earlier in the car, Yorke had asked the manager by telephone whether Hayley knew about Robert Bennett's arrest. It had made it onto the news and was hard to avoid. Yorke had been informed that she was unaware and that the only things she watched on television were soap operas and quiz shows, and whether she understood them anymore was anybody's guess.

Yorke sat beside Hayley still holding her hand. 'Ms Willborough, my name is DI Michael Yorke and I'm so sorry to come to your home and disturb you like this. There is nothing I dislike more than having my viewing pleasure interrupted but it is very important.' He paused to smile, and gently stroked her hand.

Yorke took a deep breath. He felt truly dreadful. 'I'm here about Robert Bennett.'

He paused to see if she reacted. She didn't.

'Healthwise he is fine so please don't worry about that. However,' he took another deep breath, trying to frame this right, 'he's got himself into a spot of bother ...'

Spot of bother? He thought, inwardly mocking himself.

'... and he could do with some help getting out of it.'

He waited for any sign that she was listening to him. Nothing happened. He looked up at the nurse. She shrugged.

'Many years ago, you were a maid to Elysia Bennett and her husband. Is that correct?'

Nothing. It was frustrating but he didn't let it show. He owed this poor lady more than that.

'I know you are very close to Robert, Hayley. People we have spoken to suggested he was like a son to you.'

And then Yorke detected some movement. The tiniest flicker across her eyes. Maybe he was mistaken?

'Was he like a son to you, Hayley?'

No, he wasn't mistaken! There it was again.

He looked up at the nurse. She suddenly looked interested for the first time since he'd walked into the Orchard Care Home.

'People have told me that you practically raised Robert. That he was home schooled, and his parents kept him as a virtual reclusive.'

More movement. She was responding. He was getting somewhere.

'Is this true, Ms Willborough?'

She blinked once.

'*Yes!*' the nurse said, and her eyes widened. '*That means yes!*'

Yorke felt adrenaline whipping through him. 'Did you love him?'

Another blink.

'Do you still love him?'

Blink.

'Ms Willborough, are you Robert's mother?'

Nothing.

'Ms Willborough, are you his mother?'

Still nothing.

Yorke felt like sighing but held back. He looked up at the nurse, showed her a disappointed face and then looked down again.

He wasn't sure if this was worth it. Damn it, he wasn't sure if this was even ethical!

Maybe he should call it a day?

And then Hayley blinked.

SHEILA WATCHED from the lounge door as Frank attempted to play with Tobias.

God, she loved Jake despite everything. She'd spent years getting past the fact that he was consumed by his job and had little time for her and Frank. She'd even got past the fact that his sociopathic ex-girlfriend had threatened to kill her in the street several years ago.

But this? This was a whole new level!

Tobias sat at a little desk that had been set up for Frank. He didn't move. Just stared. Not unlike yesterday when she'd first come across him and his annoying mother, Millie. If anything, he'd appeared to grow paler and stiller overnight.

He watched Frank rustling around in a box of Duplo before wandering over with handfuls of the plastic bricks. Her son was ever so kind. He was laying the Duplo in front of the older child, trying to help him, engage him. But he was failing. And it was concerning for Sheila.

She felt sympathy for the boy, she really did, but she couldn't help wondering what Jake had brought into her house.

It was at this point that she decided that, as soon as this boy had been returned to his mother, she would leave Jake once and for all.

'Frank,' she said.

Her son looked up at her.

'Come and help Mummy get lunch ready for everyone.'

Frank, her good little boy, toddled from the room, leaving Tobias to stare, vacantly, at the Duplo bricks.

YORKE PRESSED on with his questions but only some were answered. Anything that related to Robert stimulated a response. Questions revolving around her caring for him, educating him and wanting him with her now were all met with a solitary blink. Yorke was yet to see a double blink.

'When he left to be with his wife, did you miss Robert?'

Blink.

'Were you happy for him though?'

Blink.

'Did you give permission to the Bennetts to adopt your son?'

No response.

'Did you like the Bennetts?'

No response.

'Would you like to see Robert again?'

Blink.

'Did you know, before today, that Robert was in trouble?'

Her first double blink.

Yorke rustled in his pocket and brought out a photograph taken of the Rays in 1944. He slid it out of its small plastic bag. 'Do you know who these people are, Ms Willborough?'

She didn't blink, but Yorke was certain that he could see something in her eyes. Something that resembled fear.

'Do you want to help Robert?'

Blink.

'Then, you must help me. Do you know these people?'

Blink.

Yorke pointed to the young girl cleaning the pig pen. The one that he'd examined earlier with Wendy's magnifying glass. 'I don't know if you can see this clearly, Ms Willborough, but there is a young girl, maybe thirteen years old, cleaning up the pig pen behind the Ray family. Is that you, Ms Willborough?'

Pause. Nothing.

'Please, Ms Willborough ... is that you?'

Blink.

Yorke's heart thrashed in his chest. Pieces were coming together.

'Is Robert's father on that picture?'

Pause. *Come on, come on,* Yorke thought.

Blink.

Yorke pointed at the young man holding the toddler Thomas Ray in the air. 'Was it Richie Ray?'

Double blink.

Thomas was too young, so that left ... 'Was it Andrew Ray?'

Nothing.

'Andrew Ray is Robert's father, isn't he?'

She blinked and a tear ran down her face.

'Does Robert know?'

Double blink.

'Did you have twins, Ms Willborough? Does Robert have a twin brother?'

Blink.

Yorke stood up. He couldn't help it. His adrenaline was sky-high. 'Just to confirm, he had a twin brother?'

Blink.

Yorke ran a hand over head, down over his forehead and over his beard. *This is it*, he thought. *She has all the answers. She may know the location of Robert's brother. Yet, she cannot communicate ... unless ...*

'Ms Willborough, you used to communicate with a computer. Can you still do that if I get you the equipment?'

Double blink.

Shit ... shit ...

'Ms Willborough, have you ever recorded these events? A diary perhaps? Some information which will help us find your other son, and help us end a situation that is out of control?'

Blink.

Okay ... okay ... think ... Mike, think!

'Will it be at the Bennett farm?'

Double blink.

'Is it here? In the hospital?'

Blink.

'Okay ... did you record your story using the computer when you were stronger?'

Blink.

He looked up at the nurse. She shrugged.

'So, who has this information?' Yorke said.

'I have it,' someone said from the door.

Yorke turned. It was the manager he'd signed in with. 'She recorded her story three years ago and asked me to take care of it for her.'

The nurse backed away and allowed the manager to take her position at Hayley's bedside.

She stroked Hayley's head. 'Hayley, you told me that you never wanted it to see the light of day. You said you only shared it with me because you didn't want to die with the story untold. I'll ask you now, and I'll only ask you once.' She paused to look up at Yorke. 'Only once, detective.'

Yorke nodded.

She looked back down. 'Do you want me to share the story with the police, Hayley?'

The wait for the response was agonising. Yorke chewed his bottom lip. He stared down at Hayley, pleading with his eyes.

She blinked.

12

NOW THE EXISTENCE of the twin brother had been confirmed, Yorke contacted HQ to initiate a trawl through Wiltshire's medical records. It felt like the most obvious route. It stood to reason that Robert's identical twin would also have the rare disorder of PVS. He was confident they could draw up a list of potential suspects.

Hayley Willborough's story, provided by the manager of the nursing home, wasn't long. It had, after all, been told by the eye movements of an elderly woman. But the short length did not reflect the depth of the tragedy, which was bottomless.

Yorke ate fast food as he read. At times, the tale was so engrossing, he forgot to eat. It wasn't long before he was shovelling cold fries into his mouth.

Hayley had worked on the Ray family farm in 1944. The picture of her shovelling pig shit in the background was taken when she was fifteen. It would have been fortunate that she didn't live with the Rays and only worked for them, if it wasn't for the fact that her own family, the Willboroughs, were abusive bastards too.

Because of this, indoctrination was a simple task. Andrew Ray's cult seemed to offer the promise of a far safer and more secure life.

Unfortunately, as is the case with many cults, this promise was broken.

In 1952, when Hayley was 23, Andrew Ray made his claim that he'd been abducted by aliens. The only evidence that this had happened was a large bloody cross carved into his chest. A wound which everyone, apart from members of his growing cult, believed he'd inflicted on himself. 'It's where they cut me open. It's where they went in to explore my insides.'

The philosophy behind Andrew's cult was a simple one. The aliens were investigating human bodies, *working them out*, so when they returned in fifty years (apparently, the aliens *had* told him this), they could wipe them out with relative ease.

Andrew found people, such as Hayley, from all around the local area. He looked for troubled individuals. Individuals who could not find solace in religion in this god-fearing time and were drawn to sanctuary on his farm.

Andrew formed an army of twenty people to listen to him preach about the coming of aliens and the only requirement for entry was to have a cross carved into your chest by him.

Perks of the job? Thought Yorke. *You twisted bastard ...*

His members soon began to look dishevelled. They had given all their finances to Andrew and nothing was left over for clothes and haircuts. He started to lead them in rallies outside churches and in town centres, warning about the coming of aliens.

But most people spat in their direction and many others

muttered, 'Say a prayer for the Rays,' as they passed these beleaguered individuals.

Eventually, the group dropped to nineteen when one of Andrew's flock, Alan, broke a fundamental rule. Hayley was lucky because she'd also broken the same rule, but it seemed Andrew had a soft spot for her.

The rule was simple. All women, of which there were twelve, could only copulate with Andrew. The men, of which there were seven, had to practise abstinence. It was necessary, Andrew said, to keep their strength at a maximum should the aliens make an early appearance. These creatures may have been aware of a rising army and would be keen, at an unexpected moment, to descend and put a stop to it. Therefore, there could be no forging of sexual relationships, and the army would grow only through Andrew impregnating his flock.

Despite Hayley claiming that it was only actually her who became pregnant, Yorke felt a sudden surge of panic. *Please God! Don't let there be more of this vile offspring out wandering Devizes!*

On more than one occasion, Hayley and Alan had found real hope in one another that things could be better, rather than the false hope offered by Andrew and his cult. They'd planned to run away together.

At this point, in Hayley's account, she'd focused long and hard on her regret that it hadn't been Alan who had fathered her children. For many years, she had forced herself to believe that he had, until the skin rashes had appeared on Robert's face and shattered her illusions. Her offspring were the true descendants of Reginald Ray.

The day that Andrew discovered the illicit affair, he imprisoned Hayley in an old barn for three nights. During these nights, Alan was left outside, tied to a tree with the cross on his chest carved back open.

Hayley didn't know how long it had taken Alan to die but the animals had almost picked him clean on the day she emerged from that old barn. In her story, she recalled this as the worst moment of her life. Down on her knees, she screamed at anyone who would listen that this was the death of all hope. Andrew responded to these screams by dragging her away to his room and raping her.

When Hayley discovered that she was pregnant a month later, she fled the farm and found safety in a church she'd once picketed outside.

Andrew never found her. As far as Hayley was aware, he never even tried to. He died not long after from cancer. Yorke recalled Andrew's final words to his son, recorded in Thomas Ray's case file. 'It's through this same door in fifty years, they will come back for you, they told me so. And remember, those creatures can come in human or animal form.' Yorke paused for a deep breath. It was the warning that would lead to the death of Dawn Butler, his best friend's wife.

As Yorke read the next part of the tale, his heart quickened.

Eight months after her escape, Hayley gave birth to two identical baby boys. Hayley wanted, desperately, to keep them, but she was convinced by the church that they stood a better chance with a good family and that such an adoption could be arranged.

'Besides,' she was told, 'do you want them growing up with the legacy that you bring to their lives or would you rather they started afresh?'

The children were taken to the church-owned Orphanage of Salvation. Three months later, Hayley finally resigned herself to never seeing her children again and was about to commit her life to the church when a funny thing happened.

Elysia Bennett came to the church and asked to speak to Hayley. She was an affluent, influential member of the community who had been unable to conceive. She'd recently adopted a baby boy from the Orphanage of Salvation and had called him Robert.

Elysia was a god-fearing woman and she believed that it was her duty to thank the person who had given her the ultimate gift of a son. She'd contacted the orphanage and used her power and influence to acquire the mother's name. So, Elysia thanked Hayley and then asked her if there was anything she could do in return.

Hayley asked to be the Bennett's live-in maid. She promised to never divulge the truth behind Robert's parentage and would be content to just serve him and the rest of the Bennett family in any way she could.

The rest of Hayley's document gave a potted history of the happiest parts of her life up until the stroke that left her paralysed. She had been content to be with her son and care for him without him ever really knowing the truth. The fact that she had ended up raising him due to his skin disorder was a bittersweet bonus. She'd come to terms with the tragedy of never seeing her other son again, simply because she'd been given this second chance at happiness and couldn't risk ruining it.

She often described Robert as a 'gentle' person without a 'bad bone in his body' unlike his 'natural father.' She described the moment Robert found happiness with his wife as 'the first real moment in her life when she realised that her existence, and great suffering, had been worthwhile.'

Yorke finished his cold fries.

Feeling emotional, he contacted Gardner and relayed the salient parts of the story.

There was a moment of silence before Gardner said, 'Are you alright, Mike?'

'I don't know. I *really* don't. There was so much pain and suffering in that story. And I just can't stop thinking about Robert, isolated in his house, mocked by the other children. Despite what he's involved with. I just can't get that image out of my head.'

'Maybe, you should take an hour off?' Gardner said.

'Not a chance. I've got to find out what happened to the other brother at the Orphanage of Salvation. And you and Jake have got to get back in with Robert. Tell him everything, although I suspect he already knows most of it. Tell him, the game is up. If he doesn't tell us where his brother is quick smart, he's going back into isolation. For good.'

CAROLINE LAY on the bed in her treatment room. She was still unconscious after having the oxygen restricted to her brain by Lacey's headlock.

Lacey hoped that she hadn't squeezed too hard. If she'd accidently thrown her into a coma, she would struggle with the next stage of her plan.

This concern reminded her of 'To a Mouse', the Scottish poem by Robert Burns she'd read at school. She recalled the line, 'The best laid schemes o'mice an' men gang aft a-gley,' which translated as 'the best-laid plans of mice and men often go awry.'

She thought back to her last plan at the snuff house in

Southampton in which she had lost control of the situation, leaving poor Tobias to bale her out in a bloody manner.

She smiled. Sometimes it was good when plans went slightly wrong. It brought excitement. Stimulation. Something she so desperately craved.

Caroline opened her eyes. She stared up at Lacey and gasped.

'Don't move,' Lacey said.

Caroline's eyes widened.

'I have a needle against your neck. It contains a poison. You will not die in pain, but you *will* die.'

Caroline lowered her eyes to try and see the needle pressing against her neck. 'Okay.'

'Before you tried to run, I told you that it's not you that has to die today. I made a promise to your stallion that I wouldn't kill you.'

'Jake?'

'Do you have more than one stallion?'

'He wouldn't have anything to do with this!'

'Do you trust a man cheating on his wife?'

'*What do you want?*'

There was knock at the front door.

'Sounds like you're about to find out.'

After Gardner and Jake had told Robert Bennett everything, they waited for a response.

They were waiting a long time.

'How much did you know of that already?' Gardner asked, trying to move the conversation along.

Robert sighed. 'Knew some of it, suspected some of it. Who cares? It's all irrelevant. Changes nothing.'

Gardner, feeling a surge of frustration, hit the palm of her hand on the table. She could sense Jake staring at her. She didn't care if he was shocked. Enough was enough. 'What do you mean changes nothing? Wake up, for pity's sake! We know there are two of you. One of you spun the story at the reception at the Mitchell farm, the other kidnapped the boy from the back of the maze. And then you *both* ate him.'

Robert pointed at Gardner. 'Listen you, I ate no one. I had nothing to do with that. I may look like a fucking monster but I ain't one.'

'Did your brother eat him?'

'Please don't call him that!'

'So, you have a brother?' Jake said.

'Can't deny the evidence, can I?'

'Do you admit you're involved?' Gardner said.

Robert took a deep breath and drummed his fingers on the table. 'You've got DNA, camera footage, God knows what else. There's no point in us dancing over the same old ground forever.'

Gardner and Jake exchanged glances, both feeling relief over the fact that they were finally getting somewhere.

'Where's your brother then?' Gardner said.

'If you call him that one more time, I'll cut my own tongue out rather than talk to you again.'

'Okay, where is the other man that looks like you?' Jake said.

Robert glared at Jake. 'I don't know. I don't know who he is. I don't even know where he is.'

'When did you make this plan together?'

'I can't tell you that.'

It was Jake's turn to slam his hand on the table. Gardner

took her glasses off and rubbed her forehead instead; she felt the beginnings of a headache.

'You're happy to let others die?' Jake said.

'Of course not. I just can't tell you anything else. I'm sorry.'

'Well, at least you're sorry,' Gardner said, 'I do believe that this is the first time that you've shown any remorse.'

Robert narrowed his eyes. 'Actually, detective, I feel remorse. A lot of it. But I do not feel the need to display it to you. After all, you and the other detective, are just two of the many people that walk this horrible earth showing no remorse over the way you treat others. There are only two people in my life that have ever shown me kindness. My mother, who is suffering in a home, and my wife, who ...' He paused.

'Who left you?' Jake said.

There was a knock at the door. Willows was looking in.

'I'll go,' Jake said.

While Jake was outside, Gardner and Robert stared at each other. Robert now had tears in his eyes. She thought back to Yorke's words on the phone earlier, 'I just can't stop thinking about Robert, isolated in his house, mocked by the other children.'

'I do feel sympathy with everything that has happened to you,' Gardner said. 'I really do. No one should experience what you experienced, but we weren't there to stop it. We are only here now to stop *this* situation getting any worse. We are here and you are too.'

Robert shook his head. 'You don't understand.'

The door opened. Jake stood there ashen faced. Gardner and Robert both stared up at him.

'What is it Jake?' Gardner said.

Jake looked at the guard standing behind Robert and

gave him a little nod. Gardner suspected he was warning him that there could be a reaction. The guard nodded back.

'What?' Robert said.

'I'm sorry, Mr Bennett ...'

Robert started to rise to his feet.

The guard put his hands on his shoulders. 'Please sit down, Mr Bennett.'

'*What is it?*' Robert refused to sit down. The guard pressed him down hard into his seat.

'We've recovered another body at the McCall farm, buried in the field behind the house ...'

'*Who?*' Robert said, trying to rise again, but failing due to the guard's firm grip.

'We have reason to believe that it is your wife, Robert. I am so, so sorry.'

'NO!' He writhed under the guard's hands. 'NO! NO!'

The guard was really having to dig in to hold him down now. Jake ran around the table to give assistance.

'HE FUCKING LIED!' He pounded his feet on the floor and tried to rise again. Jake pinned his arms to his legs, while the guard continued to press down from above. 'HE LIED. HE FUCKING LIED!'

'Who lied?' Gardner said.

'HE FUCKING LIED!'

'Who? Let's put a stop to this now. For Samuel, for your wife, for anyone in danger. Tell us and put a stop to this right now!'

13

D I MARK TOPHAM winced as he opened and closed his fists. His knuckles were raw.

Standing at the island in his kitchen, he stared at an unopened bottle of Southern Comfort. He'd turned the music up high in the background to try and drown out James's voice in his head. *No ... no ... please ...*

It wasn't working. He could still hear the young man pleading for his life as he hit him again and again.

He ran a hand over his tangled mop of hair. He used to take such good care of his appearance. Used to care so much about the way he looked.

Used to.

As he unscrewed the cap on the Southern Comfort, he imagined Gardner sitting at the kitchen table, where she had been sitting the previous night when she'd come to his aid. He pictured her wagging a finger, scrunching up her face and delivering the words, 'Mark, remember that drinking is what got you into trouble in the first place.'

'But it's the only thing that helps me to forget. It's the only thing that drowns out the voices. Severance describing what he saw ... describing Neil's body. And now James's voice, pleading for his life as I beat him. It's not James I was seeing though, Emma. It was Mayers. The Conduit. The bastard responsible for Neil's death. It is his fucking face I keep seeing ...'

After Topham had retrieved himself from the darkness of his imagination, he saw that he'd poured himself a glass of Southern Comfort.

Just one, he thought, *just one to help me forget for a few hours. Drown it all out for a time ...*

He swallowed the brownish liquid, felt it burn his mouth, throat, chest then stomach. He stood there with his eyes closed until his thoughts began to blur.

He opened his eyes and saw Neil sitting at the kitchen table wearing his 'Pink Freud' T-Shirt. He typed away on his laptop, pausing every now and again to stroke his goatee, and mutter, 'I see.'

'A breakthrough?' Topham said and smiled.

'Kind of,' Neil said. 'I really think I know now what's eating this guy.'

'Do tell.'

Neil looked at his watch. 'What about the after-six ban on work talk?'

'Good point, but you do realise that also involves putting the laptop away?'

Neil smiled and closed the laptop. 'Let's end the week how we started it.'

'With a takeaway?'

Topham closed his eyes, and when he opened them, he stared at an empty chair.

He could hear the Conduit whispering in his head. His voice grew louder by the second.

Topham reached for the Southern Comfort, unscrewed the cap and started to drink from the bottle.

YORKE CONTACTED the council and spoke to the department in charge of LAC - Looked After Children. Lauren Miller was fascinated by the request. She happily told Yorke that once upon a time, there had been many homes such as the Orphanage of Salvation but now very few remained. Record numbers of children were being placed with foster families. As happy as this made him, and her obviously, it wasn't moving the case forward, so he politely steered her back to his enquiry.

It didn't take her long to rustle through her archives. They were now all computerised.

The news wasn't what he'd expected.

Yes, Robert had been adopted at three months of age by the Bennetts, but Christopher, his brother, had *never* been adopted. In fact, Christopher had died from influenza at the orphanage less than a month after Robert's adoption.

He pleaded with Lauren, told her that it couldn't be true, because he knew *with absolute certainty* that his twin brother was still alive. She apologised for being unable to help him any further.

Until the PVS medical trawl threw something up, Yorke realised that there was only one avenue left.

The church which had taken Hayley Willborough under its wing.

After entering the church into his SatNav, he took a call from Gardner. She informed him about the death of Robert's wife. 'Her death was different from the other deaths in this case. Less savage. There was no cutting, or dismemberment. It seems she died from a blow to the back of her head. Patricia seems to think it was from a fall backwards, but obviously that's not conclusive yet.'

Gardner then relayed the entire interview with Robert, warts and all. Yorke absorbed it all as he followed the SatNav to the church.

It had taken a while for Jake and Gardner to get Robert to communicate again. He'd been inconsolable, and had simply muttered the words, 'Liar ... fucking liar ...' repeatedly. When the truth had finally spilled out, it had come fast and furious ...

'Sandra didn't leave me. *Obviously.* She loved me. She's the only person who ever gave two shits about me apart from my mother. My *real* mother, that is.'

Jake released Robert's arms and the guard lifted his hands from his shoulders.

'He *came* to me ... the bastard. He marched right up to my bloody door. I thought I was dreaming and when I realised that I wasn't, I thought I'd gone mad. He looked *exactly* the same as me. Even down to this.' He pointed at his blotchy face. '*Imagine that?* It took me a while to even speak properly and when I finally did, he was sitting in my kitchen drinking tea. He said his name was Reginald Ray. I know! Bollocks, right? I told him I knew the history of the Rays and that they were all gone. I remember his laugh at that point. It was horrendous, like the sound of a blocked pipe or something. He had false teeth too, but they didn't fit quite as well as my own and they clattered as the creep cackled. He repeated his belief that he was Reginald Ray. He said they'd hanged him from a tree, but the last laugh had been on them bastard soldiers because he'd come back! Took the body of a descendent. He said that the funniest thing was that I was his twin brother and if I looked closely at his face, how could I deny it? But what he said next shook me even more. I felt his words sink into my bones and my soul. He told me I was Reginald too! *We are Reginald*, he said. You may not know it yet, brother, but *we are Reginald*.

'The bastard then claimed that because we were Reginald, we could do something about our appearance. He talked through the idea that we could absorb the youth and freshness of a victim through consuming them and start reversing the damage our condition was doing to us. This man was completely insane! It was at that point that I was on my feet and reaching for the phone. Then, he asked me where my wife was.' Robert buried his head in his hands and cried. Jake and Gardner respected these few minutes of despair, before he continued. 'I told him that she was at work. He smiled and said: *the butcher's? In town?* And then I knew. Knew that this man, my brother, wasn't just insane, he was dangerous. I phoned Roland, the owner of the butcher's, and discovered that she'd never turned up for work that day. Then, I flew for the bastard. Two old men, rolling around on the floor, I'm surprised neither of us walked away with broken bones. When we'd worn ourselves out, he gave me an ultimatum: if you want to see your wife alive again, you will do as I say.' He rubbed tears from his eyes. 'And I did. Everything he said. To the letter. And he lied. I'm never going to see her again, am I?'

Gardner finished recounting Robert's experience of meeting his twin brother, and Yorke listened to her grow tearful on the other end of the phone.

'Poor man,' Yorke said. 'We had him wrong.'

'When I left him, he was inconsolable.'

Yorke sighed. 'Well, he's still guilty of assisting. I get the pressure he was under, but he remains partly responsible for the death of Samuel Mitchell.'

'Yes, and he provided those details. Robert admits to setting up Samuel Mitchell by going into that reception and issuing an alert on his missing grandson, Jordan. As you were suspecting, Mike, it was the insidious brother who stole him from the back of that maze and drove him away in the car. He probably drugged him, slung him in the boot, so Bryce Singles didn't see him when he passed his tractor. When Robert went to the McCall farmhouse to retrieve his wife, he was met by his brother feeding on the poor boy. He was challenged to do the same. Robert claims to have wanted no part in it. He just wanted his wife back. His brother gave him an ultimatum. Unless Robert joined him heart and soul, in this act of cannibalism, the whereabouts of his wife would not be revealed. He was told to go home and think about it and return the next day prepared to do as he was asked. Of course, there was no next day. At that point, Robert was taken into custody as our prime suspect. It's easy to say this, but I think if it was me, I'd have come clean at that point and given us a chance to save his wife.'

'Yes, Emma, that's easy to say. We haven't met this bastard yet. Robert must have genuinely believed that if he assisted in our investigation, his wife would perish in a similar fashion to that poor boy. Terror affects people in different ways. We've seen it before.'

'You're right. She didn't perish in the same way though, did she? A fatal blow to the back of the head? A fall? Could it be that she tried to escape and died in the attempt?'

'There's only one way we're going to know for sure. We must find him, before he moves again. I'm continuing with this lead – it's all we've got right now unless something comes out of the medical records. Can you continue with Robert? Keep going over the story with him until something jumps out.'

'It sounds like you're giving the orders again, Mike.'

'Yeah, sorry ...'

'Don't be. I like it.'

REGINALD RAY WATCHED the bartender pick up some empty glasses. He liked the way he moved. *Really liked it.* It reminded him of his own youth when he was quick and agile. Of course, he'd never had the fresh face this young man had, but he'd had that bounce in his step.

Reginald sat in the corner of the pub. It was a dimly lit tavern. An appropriate choice. His face did seem to be much better after gorging on Samuel Mitchell these last couple of days, but it would still stun and shock most people, especially under bright lights.

The glass collector couldn't have been older than eighteen. He had long black hair and wore jeans that were too tight for him. *How the hell do you get into them, young man?* He thought to himself. *Such dexterity, strength and ... flamboyance.* He licked his lips.

He was disappointed, but not saddened, by his brother Robert's refusal to join him in this adventure. His wife's death had been an accident. Sandra had attempted to flee the barn at the Ray farm, and she had tripped and smashed the back of her head on an old pig-feeding trough. He didn't feel bad about this. Not in any way. She was always going to die. Just not by his hand, but by the hand of his brother, when he'd eventually seen sense.

But, alas, Robert had not come round to his way of thinking and for a reason completely unknown to Reginald, the police had caught up with him! This didn't worry

Reginald. He'd been incredibly careful. His brother would not be able to point out his whereabouts.

His thoughts turned to Paul Ray. This did sadden him somewhat. He'd stumbled on him completely by chance on the night Robert's wife had died. Reginald had been heading back to the Ray farmhouse to retrieve some old artwork he suspected was still on the property. He'd worn a bag over his head to protect his sores from the bitter winds. When he'd arrived, he found Paul burning the farmhouse down! He'd been too late to stop this, and so had simply knocked him unconscious with one of his tools and took him back to the farmhouse where he was keeping Samuel. Paul Ray, his beautiful descendent, had fire in his belly, and Reginald had been so sure that he'd get through to him. But then he'd just upped and left... No worries. He knew where he lived. He would be picking at that thread later.

Reginald took a mouthful of his pint as the only other drinker in the pub wandered over. He looked older than Reginald and swayed slightly while he walked. It clearly hadn't been his first pint of the day. Judging by the absence of any other clientele in this place, he was probably keeping this place afloat.

As he passed the bartender, he handed him an empty pint glass. The bartender pulled out an earphone so he could hear the old man.

'That pint of Crop Circle just rocked my world, Steve.' He had a thick Irish slur. 'If you continue to churn them out as nicely as that fella, it's going to become my usual.'

'Come on now, Kenny! In place of the Lightning?'

'Aye buddy. In place of the Lightning.'

Kenny wandered over to Reginald's table. He paused, looked down at him and squinted.

'Horrified by my appearance, old man?' Reginald said.

'No, sir. If there's one thing my old mother taught me before she departed these sweet climes was to never judge a book by a cover. Appearance doesn't matter to me one bit. Nor does shape, size or colour. I was just trying to remember your name ... Robert Bennett! That's it! You know, I never forget a name. I don't believe I've ever seen you in one of Salisbury's public houses before, have I?'

Reginald took a mouthful of beer. 'Not that I recall. Probably should have come sooner. The beer tastes good.'

'To die for.'

Reginald smiled. 'Interesting choice of words. Truth is my wife died recently.'

'I'm sorry to hear that, buddy, and I'm sorry for my play on words. My wife died a long time ago. Must be fifteen years since. I know exactly how you feel. But I want to tell you something.' He tapped his head. 'She's always with me. I hear her in here. Everywhere I go, everything I do, I can still communicate with her. Sometimes she nags at me, but more often than that, she keeps me company and I still love her for it.'

Reginald smiled again. 'It's funny you should say that. I can hear those that have long gone in here too.' He tapped his own head.

'They're never truly gone!' Kenny said, smiling back.

'You are so right. Soon, hopefully, my late wife can join in the conversation.'

'Aye, she will. If she's anything like my wife, you won't keep her quiet for long.' Kenny looked at his watch. 'But I'm running late now to meet some buddies. I'm heading to *The Cloisters*. Feel free to join us when you're done here.'

'I'll think about it,' Reginald said. 'Goodbye old man.'

After Kenny had left and Reginald had finished his pint, he waved Steve over. The bartender came but he barely seemed to notice Reginald's appearance. Surprising really, considering the mess his face was in. It was probably the earphones lodged in the young man's ears which were distracting him. He bobbed his head up and down.

As Steve reached down for the glass, Reginald stroked the back of the young man's hand. He pulled away.

'Sorry.' Reginald held the palms of his hands up.

It was at this point that Steve noticed Reginald's face. Reginald knew this because it was the same reaction that he'd seen countless times before. A quick flickering of the eyebrows to show surprise, a slight scrunching of the cheeks to demonstrate disgust, before a chewing of the bottom lip to reveal embarrassment over the inappropriate response.

The bartender took his earphones out. 'No bother.' Again, he reached down to take the glass and again, Reginald stroked his hand. 'Hey man!' he said, jerking away.

'Sorry, again.' Reginald put his hands up a second time. 'You needn't worry though; you won't catch it.'

Steve's face reddened as he chewed his bottom lip again. 'It's not that.' He shook his head, thought for a moment, and then swooped for the glass a third time. Reginald's hand darted out and he sighed as he brushed against the young skin. Steve took a step back. 'I'm going to have to ask you to leave.'

'And why is that, *Steve*?'

The bartender creased his forehead. He was surely wondering how he knew his name. It took a moment for him to recall the fact that Kenny had used it. 'Just leave, sir, please.' He took another step back.

'An old man touches your skin, wants to feel your freshness ... and you won't let him?' Reginald shook his head. 'Well, they say the youth of today are selfish, but I had no idea that it was this bad.'

Steve looked around the pub.

'Yes, we are all alone.' Reginald rose to his feet. 'It's still quite early. I had to wait for the Irish dribbler to leave before I could talk to you.' He kept himself hunched over slightly. 'You have to excuse me, young man, the muscles aren't what they once were.' He put his fists in the centre of his back and pushed his shoulders back. There was a cracking sound. He moaned, feigning discomfort and reached down for the Tesco bag-for-life on the chair beside him.

'So, you're leaving?' Steve said.

'All in good time, son, all in good time.' Reginald hobbled around the table. He acknowledged that pretending to be old and frail, and moving this slowly, was actually more tiring than moving at his normal speed. 'I'm just going to make one more visit to the bar.'

'Then, I'll go out the back and phone the police.'

'Will you do that, son? Will you deny an old man a last drink just because he wanted to lay his hands on a fine young thing? The modern world beggar's belief sometimes, it really does.' He hobbled towards Steve and stopped inches from him.

'Maybe I should just escort you out myself.'

'Do please,' Reginald said. 'If there's one thing I enjoy more than touching youth, it is being touched by it.'

Steve raised his hands.

Good, Reginald thought, *the pretence is working. He thinks I am weak and vulnerable. Oh, you overconfident young man. To be young and full of spunk! How I miss it. How I crave it.* 'Go on, *Steve,* make an old man's day.'

Steve huffed. 'That's it. I'm calling the police. It's not

my place to manhandle an old man. Something goes wrong, I'll be the one that ends up in court.'

Steve turned and marched to the bar. He didn't bother lifting the hatch, he just swooped under it.

Ah, there it is again, Reginald thought, *the agility of the youngster*.

Steve bypassed a shelf of spirits and disappeared through a doorway.

Reginald stretched out fully, suddenly feeling more alive. He reached into the bag-for-life and his hand settled on the handle of his claw hammer. He grinned and let the bag fall to the ground.

He held the hammer up in front of his face and turned it. Despite the lack of lighting in the public house, the stainless-steel head and its claw sparkled.

Oh Steve! The old man that you think you left standing out here isn't as vulnerable as you think.

He chuckled and strolled to the bar. Like Steve, he didn't bother with the hatch, and ducked underneath it.

Not bad for a seventy-year old man, eh? I have the energy of a sixteen-year-old boy coursing through my veins. Literally. Bless you, Samuel.

Raising the claw hammer again, Reginald bypassed the shelf of spirits and turned to face the open doorway. Steve's back was to him.

Steve had a mobile phone to his ear. 'Fucking reception,' he hissed.

'You could always try outside, Steve?' Reginald said.

Steve nearly jumped out of his skin. His phone fell to the floor. 'Shit! Now look what you made me do!' He turned.

Reginald swung and buried the claw into Steve's

forehead. He let go of the handle, and the claw stayed rooted. 'You are a lovely young thing, Steve.'

The claw hammer slipped free and fell. Reginald hopped back so it didn't hit him on the foot.

Steve stared at him for a few moments, swaying slightly. Blood spewed out of the hole on his forehead and streamed down his face. He opened his mouth to try to speak but nothing came out.

Then, his face started to twitch. His top lip curled right up as if he was sneering, and then he plunged backwards to the ground. There, he convulsed a few moments, before finally growing still.

Reginald took off his T-shirt and jeans and laid them on the bar. He closed the door behind him and Steve. Then, he knelt and licked the blood from the young man's face.

He leaned backwards, letting the blood slide down his throat, and took a long, deep breath.

It feels wonderful.

Reginald fell onto Steve and started to feed.

14

T HE CONTRAST BETWEEN boss, Simon Young, and his loyal lieutenant, David Hewitt, was striking.

Simon Young was a very short individual, who should not have been able to hold court over people, but did, with great success, due to a set of stony eyes, which seemed to bore through any person held by them. Whereas, David Hewitt, was a hulking man, who had long features and a lazy eye, and was renowned for being a difficult conversationalist. He was good at giving orders, because if you ignored them, he would crush you to dust, but he couldn't hold a room with a simple, menacing look like his boss.

The only similarity they shared were the silenced pistols they pointed at Lacey.

'I used to watch a programme called Little and Large when I was younger,' Lacey said to the two new occupants of the treatment room. 'Do you remember it?'

Young didn't respond. He just continued trying, unsuccessfully, to chisel away at Lacey with an icy stare. Hewitt did look confused for a moment, but he quickly returned to his go-to angry stare. His wife was in danger, after all. She had a primed needle filled with a deadly chemical pressed to her neck.

'Guess not,' Lacey said. 'How about the Krankies? Kids' entertainers? One dressed as an adult, the other as a little boy. Remember? They were actually man and wife. It was a bit worrying that it was the wife playing the little boy—'

'You really don't give a fuck about anything, do you?' Young said. 'We are about to put holes in you.'

Lacey smiled. 'On the contrary, Simon, I do give a fuck. *Dangerously* so by the looks of it. I gave a fuck when you killed someone very close to me back in Southampton and, for that, I took Tobias from you and destroyed your businesses.' She paused to relish the twitch that had suddenly flared up in Young's top lip. She looked at Hewitt. 'And David. I gave a fuck when your wife decided to get involved with a friend of mine, despite her knowing what would happen to him and his family—'

'That's *bullshit*,' Caroline said.

'*Shut up, bitch*,' Lacey said, applying pressure to the needle against her neck.

'*Okay ... okay ...*'

Lacey continued, 'Now, where was I? Oh, yes ... Caroline got involved with him despite knowing what would happen to him and his family, and so, for that, I want her to watch her husband die.'

Silence settled over the room for a moment.

And so, Lacey thought, *begins my best laid plan.*

Young burst into laughter. He looked at Hewitt, who was now as white as a ghost, and nodded to signal it was okay. Hewitt started to laugh too but it was obviously forced. Caroline didn't laugh.

'You really are *fucking* crazy, aren't you?' Young said.

'Jesus,' Lacey said. 'How many times do I have to go through this with people? Crazy is far too general. I have a label! I'm a malignant narcissist. I crave power, I have a sense of grandiosity – as I hope you are starting to realise – and I have sociopathic tendencies. Unlucky for Mr and Mrs Hewitt here, I do not have a conscience. So, when he dies, I will feel no remorse.'

Young laughed again. Hewitt forced out a chuckle for his boss. Caroline remained stoic.

After they had stopped laughing, Lacey said, 'How is it that only Caroline is taking this seriously? Have you watched the films I sent you, Simon?'

'Oh, I watched them alright,' Young said, the gun shaking in his trembling grip, 'I know what you're capable of. That's why there will be a hole in your forehead, the moment that needle pierces her skin. Good luck pushing the plunger.'

She removed the needle from Caroline's neck, placed it on the floor and with the sole of her shoe rolled it forward. It stopped at Young's feet. 'Go on, have it. I can't kill her anyway. More's the pity. I made a promise to a friend of mine.'

Caroline sat up and grabbed Lacey's shoulder. 'Bitch!'

'GET THE FUCK OFF HER!' Young said.

Caroline let go of Lacey's shoulder, scrambled off the bed and over to her husband. He wrapped an arm around her, while keeping the gun pointing at Lacey.

'Where's my son?' Young said.

Lacey clicked her fingers. 'And there it is! The reason.'

'The reason *you* will die,' Hewitt said.

'No, David, the reason that *you* will die,' Lacey said.

Young stamped a foot. '*Enough of this*! Where is he?'

'Last night, after myself and Tobias gave your man the slip, I took him somewhere very special.'

'Where?' Young said.

'Somewhere far from prying eyes like yours, Simon. But the thing is, I have no conscience, as I explained before. I thought to myself, if I can't have him, then you can't have him, so I put him in a little black box …'

'*No,*' Young said, taking a step towards her. The gun shaking hard now. 'You're fucking lying.'

'Calm yourself Simon. He's still alive, for now. I put Tobias into his little black box, and I screwed the lid down tight. If you check my bag, which I left in the lounge, you will find the screwdriver I used. If we get to him, then we can open it up, quickly – no need for us to scramble around for one that fits. Yes, we still must dig him up first, I buried him quite deep, but after that, we can open …'

Young had taken another few steps and now had the silencer on the pistol pressed against her forehead.

She smiled. 'What time is it Simon?'

Young now had tears in his eyes. 'I'm going to fucking kill—'

'*What time is it?*'

Hewitt shouted out the time.

'Shit,' Lacey said, still smiling. 'It's a little bit later than expected. He should have enough oxygen left for the rest of the day, but you can never be too sure. You use it up quicker when you panic—'

'YOU COLD-HEARTED BITCH.'

'Yes, precisely,' Lacey said. 'And, if you think about it, right now, in this situation, there's no better type of person to be … so, let's stop fucking about … *get on with it.*' She moved her eyes to gesture his lieutenant behind him.

'You'll break if I put a bullet in your leg,' Young said.

'No, I won't. I'll just sit here and bleed to death. Tick-tock. Tick-tock.'

'I'll pull your nails and teeth out.'

'Yes, you could do that. Except I don't really feel fear and I can always retreat into my Blue Room if it gets too painful.'

'Blue what?'

'Meditation. Come on Simon. Tick Tock. Tick Tock.'

'What do you expect me to do?'

With a word per tick, she clicked her finger from side to side like a metronome. 'Shoot ... David ... Hewitt ... in ... his ... head.'

She could see Young thinking. Calculating a way out of this mess. When he realised there wasn't one, he turned back to look at Hewitt.

The colour drained from Hewitt's face. 'Hey, you can't be serious.'

'Of course not,' Young said.

Hewitt sighed in relief.

Caroline's expression didn't change though. She knew what was coming. 'David—'

There was an explosion. The white walls of the treatment room were spray-painted red. Caroline clawed at the blood and brain in her eyes, screaming. Hewitt fell forward and what was left of his head bounced off the bed frame with a sickening clunk.

Young turned back to Lacey. 'Now my son. As you promised.'

'Easy tiger. Just one more thing,' she pointed at Caroline. 'Pick up that needle and put it in her neck. Once you do that, I'll take you straight to your son. No tricks.'

Young looked back at Caroline. Her wide eyes shone white through the mask of blood. 'No, no ...'

'Go on, I'd do it,' Lacey said, 'but I made a promise. The only person who could tolerate her in this room is dead, so you'll be doing us all a favour.'

Young knelt and picked up the syringe.

Lacey recalled the line of her favourite poem: *the best-laid plans of mice and men often go awry.*

To be honest, she thought, *there's nothing awry about any of this so far.*

'IS EWAN OKAY NOW?' Yorke said down the phone to Patricia.

'Not sure. He's in his room. I took him in a glass of water, but he didn't even look in my direction.'

Yorke stared up at St. Francis Catholic Church. It wasn't particularly large and hulking, like most churches, but it still maintained an impressive presence due to it being the only building for several acres. There was a small rectory alongside it that Yorke walked towards now.

Patricia had called him after she'd returned home from the McCall farm where Robert Bennett's deceased wife had been unearthed. Her mum, Jeanette, had been taking care of Ewan during his suspension from school. When Patricia had arrived back, there was a smashed glass in the kitchen, and Jeannette had been crying on the sofa. She'd told Patricia, 'He just lost it, *completely.* Started saying no one really understood and then just threw his glass across the kitchen. He went upstairs but hasn't been down yet and he won't talk to me through the door.'

'Give him a bit longer to cool off,' Yorke said, 'I'll try and make it back as early as I can, but I'm on to something here.'

Patricia sighed. 'Okay. Love you.'

'Love you too.'

Yorke knocked on the rectory door and was admitted by Father William. He was ninety-years old, and despite being in impressive health for his age, he still accepted Yorke's offer of a supportive arm.

'I could manage it myself, young man, but you'd be waiting all day for me to hobble to the lounge.'

'It's no bother, Father,' Yorke said, helping him all the way to his sofa, 'but if I could just record you calling me "young", I can play it back to my wife later who has started to ridicule my grey hairs.'

'Be my pleasure,' Father William said with a chuckle. 'She's a spicy one then?'

'If she was on a menu, she'd have three red chilli peppers by her name.'

Father William laughed again.

Yorke sat down on the sofa beside him.

'I'd offer you a cup of tea, but you'd be sitting alone a fair old while,' Father William said.

'Don't worry, Father. There's nothing I'd like more than to share a cup of tea with you right now, but I have some really pressing issues ...'

'Yes, I know you have, son. I know you have.' He sighed. 'I'm glad you called ahead. It gave me time to focus. My mind is not what it once was. It also gave me time to come to terms with the information I'm about to share with you because I have never shared it with anyone before.' He sighed again.

'We appreciate it, Father. And it may ensure no more harm comes to anyone.'

'You are going to wonder why I'm not presenting you with documents, but I'll tell you in advance that there aren't any, son. We're going back to a time I miss greatly. A far kinder time.

A time not dressed up in red-tape and bureaucracy. A time that doesn't fail people because they do not tick certain boxes or delays things unnecessarily to the detriment of those involved.'

Yorke disagreed. This bureaucracy was necessary. It was there to protect people and help people. To stop things going badly wrong.

'The event you want to know about came after Robert Bennett was adopted and spirited away to safety and happiness,' Father William said.

Yorke thought about that reclusive boy, staring out of the window. Happiness didn't seem like the best word to describe his life with the Bennetts.

'A rumour got out. I don't know how. Maybe one of Ray's cult members saw Hayley in the church grounds, pregnant. Maybe someone else told the cult members. Although, why anybody would share information with *that* lot would be anyone's guess. So, after Robert had left, Andrew Ray visited the Orphanage of Salvation looking for Hayley and her child. Fortunately, he had no idea that there was a second child so we could keep our story simple. Hayley's child had died in childbirth.'

'Do you know how he responded? Is there any record at all of the meeting?'

'No record. Although I know how he responded alright.'

'How come?'

'Because it was me, son. I was the one who lied to him.' He paused to sign the cross on his chest. 'And I ask for forgiveness for my sin of deceit, but I believe that this was the only option available to me. Andrew Ray believed my lie. I told him he could come back and see the documents the following day if he wanted evidence, and I even went about forging them that evening.' He crossed his chest again. 'But he never returned. He died not long after I believe. Cancer.'

'Did he want to know where Hayley was?'

'I told him she'd disappeared into the ether. No, he didn't press this. And I still, to this day, do not know why.'

Probably, Yorke thought, *he knew he was dying, and didn't want his name sullied by the truth that he'd murdered someone within the cult. If he let her be, to live her life, she might keep the secret. If he started to hunt her, she might have revealed the truth.*

'So, the second child?'

'Christopher Steele.'

Yorke felt his nerve-ends tingle. He swooped into his pocket for his notepad and wrote the name down frantically as if it might suddenly evaporate from his brain as quickly as it had come into it.

'The Steeles were a good family. They were connected to the church and I asked them for this favour. They had no children and were happy to raise him. I asked them to move away and change churches so there was no connection to the Orphanage of Salvation. Just in case. I knew Andrew Ray was dying but there were more Rays, as I'm sure you well know, and a clean break was necessary for Christopher.'

But that clean break hasn't worked out, I'm afraid, Yorke thought, feeling despair bubbling like acid indigestion in his stomach. 'And apart from the false record of Christopher dying in infancy, you are certain none of this is written down?'

'Not a thing, son, like I said before, there was no pressure for paperwork. It wasn't a time of bureaucracy. It was simply a time of compassion.'

Except, Yorke thought, *that act of compassion may have delayed this investigation.*

Father William told Yorke all he knew about the Steele family. They were a charitable, middle-aged couple who had farmed most of their lives. 'They will probably have passed by now. They were older than me at the time. But as to where they went and what became of them, I cannot say, detective. That boy was away from the Rays and that was all that mattered. All that mattered.'

Yorke thanked Father William, told him not to get up, and left the rectory.

His phone rang before he had the chance to update Gardner on the news. It was from HQ and turned out to be Gardner anyway.

Yorke sighed when he heard Gardner's news and wished that Father William had opted for bureaucracy rather than compassion way back then because having Christopher Steele's name earlier may just have spared another young man's life.

THE CRIME SCENE flickered in and out of Jake's focus like a candle flame. His concerns for Sheila and Frank were pulling at him.

And I am working with Lacey Ray! How the hell has it come to this?

'Jake, are you with us?' Gardner said.

'Yes, sorry, ma'am. Just shocked by what I'm seeing.'

Steve Crawford had been ravaged. Unlike Samuel, he still had all his limbs, but huge chunks had been bitten out of him. The killer had chewed deep down into his right eye, leaving a cavernous, bloody hole. Nearly his whole cheek was missing, and the braces on Steve's teeth shimmered through the opening.

Lance Reynolds usually danced around the victim to take his photos, but he was restricted here because Steve had been killed in a narrow corridor leading from the bar into the back. So, he simply hovered in as close as possible without disturbing the pool of blood and fried everyone's retinas with his flashbulb. 'He looks like he's been attacked by something inhuman.'

Patricia Yorke had been contacted to attend the scene, but she was dealing with a family crisis, so another pathologist had been sent up from Southampton. Pathologists were usually hardy when it came to bodies, but such was the state of this body, he'd rushed for air. He did manage to establish the cause of death before fleeing the scene, even if it was obvious. Jake looked down at the bloody hammer beside the body.

Gardner took a deep breath which whistled through her facemask. 'So, as I was saying, Jake, he probably wanted to feed for the reasons Mike went through back at HQ. For freshness, potential of rejuvenation ... Jesus, I can't believe I'm saying all of this.'

'Go on,' Jake said, still trying to focus his distracted mind.

'But maybe the killer hadn't the time to go to work with the saw and needed a quick fix.'

'Ah for God's sake, look at that neck,' Lance said, zooming in. 'He chewed right through it. Look, you can see what's left of the Adam's apple.'

Jake and Gardner took this as a cue to step away from the body, bumping into a queue of SOCOs behind them, desperate to get into that narrow space and hunt for trace evidence. Jake suspected that once they'd squeezed their way in there, they'd be desperate to squeeze out again.

They went outside to continue their conversation. The Southampton pathologist passed them on the way. He nodded a greeting but didn't say anything. He looked too green at the gills for that.

Outside, Gardner said. 'I hope Mike is right. I hope that it is Christopher Steele and grabbing him tonight will put an end to this fucked-up business.'

'It looks like it is him.'

'Yes ... but if there's one thing I've learned over the last couple of years on major crimes, it's never that simple.' Gardner's phone rang. 'Excuse me, Jake.'

Jake leaned against the wall of the public house and waited for Gardner. He could hear her in a heated exchange with Topham. She was telling him to get himself home, and that she'd see him later. Judging by the frustration in her tone during the next parts of the exchange, he wasn't complying with the request.

Jake sighed. Everyone was preoccupied when people were dying, violently, around them. It really wasn't the best show for a usually capable team. Would Yorke also be drawn away by the family crisis that was affecting Patricia?

His phone vibrated. He pulled it out of his pocket and read the message on the screen.

These words had a worse effect on him than the body lying on the floor in the pub.

15

FTER LOOKING AROUND at the carnage in the treatment room, Lacey said, 'I think that this may just be the most beautiful room I have ever been in.'

Simon Young certainly didn't see the funny side. 'I've just killed my best friend.'

'Come on Simon, you've done worse.'

'When all this is done, I'm going to kill you, do you know that?'

'Simon, your threats have never worried me.'

'They should.'

'Leave your gun on the body and let's go. I'll take you to your son. You can have him back, and then you and me ... well ... we will never see each other again.'

Young relinquished his silenced pistol and they headed to the front door. There were several men outside the house. Young instructed them to fall back.

'And if they follow us, Simon, I'll simply stop directing. And if I stop directing ... well ... tick tock ...'

'You heard the lady,' Young said. 'If any of you follow, and my son dies, I'll kill your children too.'

'Spoken like an employer who really cares about the mental wellbeing of his staff,' Lacey said.

Once in the car, Lacey told him to drive straight on.

After she'd taken him on a wild goose chase through Salisbury city centre, to ensure that nobody followed, she started fiddling with the radio. The car filled with eighties classics. 'Tobias likes music,' she said.

'Fuck you.'

'Next left.'

It was at this point, Lacey texted Jake and waited for him to respond with his location. If he was all the way up at HQ, that would affect timings and she'd have to keep the wild goose chase going a while longer. He texted back quickly. He was ridiculously near.

'Who are you texting?' Young said.

'Who is in charge here?'

'You will die slowly.'

'Every experience is worth savouring. Next right ... and stop there.'

After exiting the vehicle, Young went around to the boot, opened it and reached in. He pulled out an axe.

'Wow,' Lacey said.

'Fuck you if you think I'm going anywhere unarmed.'

'Yeah, I get that, but an axe?'

'You made me leave my gun.'

'So you didn't pack a spare gun, you packed an axe?'

'I wasn't always what I am today, bitch. There was a time, long ago, when I was more down-to-earth.'

Lacey thought about the axe. Yes, she preferred him disarmed and she could possibly push for it, as she had done back at Caroline's house ... but she had to admit, she was quite impressed. Besides, it might come in handy as her plan evolved. 'Why not?'

'Wasn't a choice as I said.'

'Well, you may want to keep it under your jacket or something because we still have a five-minute walk and I don't want to get arrested before we get there.'

'*Five minutes?*'

'Yep. As if there isn't a tracker on that car ...'

She noticed his eyes narrow.

'You haven't got a great poker face, Simon. Also, take your phone out and chuck it in the boot. You'll get your son, I promised, but none of your friends are coming – this isn't going to be the OK Corral.'

AFTER GARDNER PROVIDED a further update on the damage wrought on Christopher Steele's second victim, Yorke completed his journey to the Steele Farm with the fast food from earlier clawing its way back up his throat.

Already CCTV footage had thrown up images of Christopher worming his way into the public house, and less than an hour later, away from it. Unfortunately, he'd then become lost in the winding streets around the pub and could have hopped into a vehicle off-camera. Door-to-door was already flaring up with intensity to establish the trajectory of this elderly killer.

Considering how the case had evolved to date, Yorke was unsurprised to find the Steele property another disused farm in need of severe renovations.

Yorke had already acquired the Steele family history. Well-meaning crop farmers who, like the Bennetts, had something of a respectable reputation. Again, their son had been rather reclusive but unlike Robert, he'd attended school despite the PVS. Medical records had already confirmed that Christopher had PVS but had not attended a hospital or doctor appointment in over ten years. Not since his parents had died.

So, Yorke thought, *we have another Ray, and we have another recluse. What box of delights are we about to open at this home?*

Yorke was not the first on the scene. Local officers had already attended the property to try and arrest Christopher if he was there. He wasn't. One female officer was leaning over a male officer, consoling him. After he parked up, and approached them by foot, Yorke realised she was not actually comforting him, she was holding him as he vomited.

Another officer joined this pair and logged Yorke. She then informed him what they'd found.

'Human?' Yorke said.

'No, animal,' the officer said, turning grey, and spinning to one side to gulp air. 'Sorry.'

'No need to apologise, officer. Can you show me?'

She nodded.

SOCO and the rest of major incidents were yet to arrive. Yorke was happy to see that all the officers had worn their protective clothing. He followed their excellent example and pulled on his paper suit.

As the officer led Yorke through the house, he thought about Christopher and Robert.

Twins separated at birth. One a deranged cannibal like the grandfather he'd never met. And the other? Well, what was Robert Bennett? He wasn't a killer, just someone who feared for his wife's life and supported this monster in these unthinkable acts.

Robert Bennett's childhood had not exactly been a barrel of laughs, so what was different for you, Christopher? What triggered you to become what you became? How did your path diverge from that of your brother's?

There was an odour which intensified the further he was led into the house. He swatted away a few flies that crossed his path. Eventually, Yorke and the officer stopped by a door under the stairs.

'The basement,' the officer said. 'I don't think I can go down there again.'

Yorke nodded and opened the door.

The stench was overwhelming. He put his hand over his nose and desperately tried to seek out the fragrance of the last bar of soap he'd washed with. He failed and gagged. Things had died down there. And then rotted.

The flies rose in a wave from the basement. He brushed more out of his face with the hand that wasn't pinned to his mouth.

The officer reached over Yorke's shoulder and switched the basement light on. 'Sorry.'

She turned and left Yorke to descend the steps.

And what happened after your parents died, Christopher? Going through their belongings did you find some truths? A diary, perhaps? A letter from Father William asking if all was well? Something that told you about your illegal adoption? How did you feel when you discovered the truth of where and who you came from? Did you find yourself inspired by your evil heritage? That you were directly descended from the most notorious monster this part of the world had ever seen ...

Yorke neared the bottom of the stairs. He tried to hold the vomit in. He was literally breathing through the palm of his hand and feeling rather lightheaded for it.

And your brother? How did you find out about him? Was he in these diaries or was it a chance sighting?

On the final step, Yorke looked around the room. He gripped the bannister to steady himself.

There was a large oak table, not unlike the one at the McCall Farm, except this one heaved under the weight of meat and bones. There were smashed rib cages and punctured skulls; and mounds of rotten offal that appeared to pulsate as hundreds of flies fed on it.

Around the sides of the room were chains coming out of the stone walls. Some empty, some still gripping on to a rotten animal. There was a lamb which had had its two hind legs sawn off; a piglet which had been disembowelled, and a foal, missing an entire head.

So, Christopher, is this where you spent your last ten years? What the hell were you doing?

There were only two possible answers to this question. Either, he was trying to satiate his desires without committing the unthinkable like his grandfather had done; or, he was practising.

Yorke turned away. He could feel something inside himself splinter.

The chains.

Holding something against its will, as it was fed on.

So many chains.

No one had paid Reginald a blind bit of notice on his journey to Sarah and Paul Ray's house. That was one of the only advantages of being old, people found it too awkward to stop and pay you any attention, and they were happy to let you blend into the background. Even with his face!

He smiled. With this face, there'd have been a time that he could have scored a fantastic job with a travelling freakshow and people would have paid money to behold him. But that era of exploitation had long since passed.

Reginald had been careful to avoid getting blood on his clothes by removing them before feeding. After, he had towelled himself down with dishcloths from behind the bar; there'd been a tap so he'd been able to scrub the blood from his hands and rinse his lesion-covered face until most of the blood was gone. Some of the dishcloths stank of beer, but that didn't matter; it helped mask the scent of Steve's innards.

After dressing, he'd looked in a mirror and was pleased that his clean clothes hid most of the bloodstains on his body. He'd also treated himself to five minutes so he could examine his face. It was working. Slowly but surely. His skin seemed to be healing.

He cursed all those wasted years feasting on live, youthful animals, trying to absorb as much of their freshness into him as possible. The process had been too slow. Why had he delayed for so long? Samuel, and now Steve, had shown him what was truly possible. His grandfather had been right.

He felt truly wonderful. He really was Reginald, now. No question. Let them all deny it. He knew the truth.

It took him over an hour to reach Paul's house in Wilton. During that time, the day had died, and darkness had spread its inky talons over the sky. Now, standing around the back of the house, he considered the impact of taking Paul as his next victim.

He was a Ray, and one not affected by the affliction that had plagued his own existence. Could consuming him bring an even greater boost to the rejuvenation process?

Well, there was only one way to find out.

He tried the back door and was relieved to find it

unlocked. His second option had been to draw them out of the house by knocking over the bins and creating a racket. A far riskier play.

He stepped into the dark kitchen. There was light breaking under the kitchen door and he could hear muffled voices. The air was tarnished with the smell of curry, and Reginald curled up his top lip. Disgusting. Yes, he was bloated from Steve, but curry had always repulsed him anyway.

He could hear the muffled voices gaining some clarity.

Were they coming now?

He reached for the nearest weapon he could find. He took hold of a corkscrew with the cork still attached. *Bit early for a drink now, isn't it?*

He looked around the kitchen for somewhere to hide. He could duck behind the island in the centre and spring out. Alternatively, he could slide himself behind the kitchen door when it opened and wait for them to spot him before pouncing. Or ...

He looked down and opened the cupboard beneath the sink. There was certainly space for a diminutive old man such as himself alongside the water pipes. He clambered inside, pushing aside some bleach and spare bin bags.

He closed the cupboard door, unscrewed the cork from his weapon of opportunity, and waited for the Ray family to make an appearance.

He would kill Sarah first. She was unnecessary, and then he would ask Paul to join him again. Unlike last time, he would be lying. Reginald did not give second chances. While Paul was mulling over his limited options, Reginald would wing the little fucker ...

And then ... and then ...

Fuckity-fuck – I'm so excited!

JAKE'S PHONE was buzzing on the passenger seat, but he couldn't be bothered looking at the screen. He knew it was Gardner because her mouth had been hanging open as he'd nodded a farewell at her through the car window.

As he approached his home, he killed his lights. He wasn't about to announce his arrival by flying into his driveaway, so he opted to park near the bus stop over the road from his house. He took a quick look at his semi-detached newbuild. The outside light was on, the front door was closed, and the living room window glowed. Everything looked normal. Jake knew it was anything but.

Lacey had sent him a text message: *Young is here. He has me. He's taking me to yours to get Tobias. Where are you?*

Why would Simon Young allow her to text? Were they working together? And if they weren't, what had possessed her to lead him directly to Tobias?

What the hell was she playing at?

He took another deep breath, left the car and retrieved a tyre-iron from the boot. The road was well-lit by streetlamps, so he didn't bother seeking out shadows, he just moved as quickly as he could.

He darted over the small garden at the front of his house, weaving around some gnomes that Frank had relocated from the edges to the centre, and slipped through the gate at the side. When he hit the back garden, the outside light flared into life. He'd expected this. Every option carried a risk but going through the back gave him more of a chance than going through the front door.

At the patio door, he took some hope from the fact that the lights in the back room were off. The kitchen light was also off. The intruders may still be none the wiser to his presence.

He pulled out his keys and thumbed through to the patio door key. Due to his shaking hands, it took him a moment to get it into the lock. After turning it, he slid the door aside as quietly as he could and slipped past a red curtain into the darkness.

16

'DIDN'T YOU HEAR that?' Sarah muted the television, stood up and wandered over to the window.

'What?' Paul said from the sofa. He felt out of it on pain killers and wasn't about to jump up and join her.

'That tapping?'

'No.' Paul watched his mother surveying the garden for a minute. 'Can we just put the television back on—'

'*There! Look!*'

Despite his grogginess, Paul rose from the sofa and joined her at the window.

Sarah was pointing out of the window. 'Our garden wall ... look at it ... it was tapping on our window ... *I'm bloody sure of it.*'

Paul's eyes widened. His mind spiralled back to a moment in his dreams, and the moment he was knocked unconscious outside the Ray farmhouse.

Was that a raven standing on the garden wall?

For DI Michael Yorke the world was constantly in flux.

Every time he dared to believe that he had a handle on everything and that he could move forward, another curveball was thrown, and he'd be standing there with an empty hand, as the ball spiralled off into the night behind him.

Something he had seen in that animal slaughterhouse had really bothered him. It had caused a seismic shift in everything he thought he'd understood up until this moment. Everything.

It wasn't so much the blood and violence. That was part and parcel of the world Yorke inhabited, and had been for a long time.

It was something buried much deeper than that. And it was something he didn't want to face head on, not just yet. Simply because he didn't believe it. Didn't want to believe it.

He phoned Collette Willows at HQ.

'You sound shaken up, sir.'

'I am, Collette, more than you could ever imagine.'

'Can I help?'

'Yes, but I want you to tell me what I want to hear, rather than what I know you're going to tell me.'

'Sir? You're not making any sense.'

'No, I'm not,' Yorke said. 'Can you pull up the Samuel Mitchell crime scene report? Could you also get Paul Ray's witness statement?'

'Of course. Why? What are we looking for?'

Yorke looked out of the window at the farmhouse where Christopher Steele had orchestrated a catalogue of atrocities.

'Chains, Collette. That's where I think the truth lies. With the chains.'

'YOU STAY THE FUCK BACK!'

Jake didn't spend long in the back room. His wife's shouting brought him quickly out of the darkness.

Despite his quick movement, he was careful not to blow his cover just yet. The door to the front room was ajar. Still holding the tyre iron, Jake peered in through the crack between the door and its frame.

Sheila was pressed up against the fireplace; one of her hands was on Tobias's shoulder, and the other was on his son's. Frank was pale and curled himself tightly against his mother; whereas, Tobias hung loosely, and his eyes were lowered and appeared unfocused.

The two people that Sheila was screaming at were nearer to the door where he stood. Even though Jake saw them from behind, he recognised Lacey's shaved head and tattoos immediately. The smaller man standing to her left wasn't familiar, but he assumed this was Simon Young, if Lacey's text from earlier was to be believed. Young had an axe over one shoulder. Jake felt everything inside him tighten.

'They say hell hath no fury like a woman scorned,' Young said. 'But that is nothing compared to a father having his son stolen.'

'I didn't take your son,' Sheila said. 'He was delivered to us by Millie. That woman next to you.'

Jake recognised the tone in Sheila's voice because he was often on the receiving end of it. It was sharp and showed no weakness. Despite this terrifying situation, Jake felt pride and love for this woman. She was a fighter.

'*Millie?* Is that what she told you?' Young said. 'She's a good liar. She *told me* my son was buried alive in a black box. Unless you have just dug him up, I guess you're not the only one not being led on a merry dance around here.'

'Who is she then?' Sheila lifted her hand from Tobias, who didn't seem to notice and moved it slowly behind her back towards the fireplace.

The fire poker, Jake thought. *No, no, Sheila ... slow down. If he sees ...*

'Lacey Ray,' Young said.

Sheila's eyes widened. 'Jesus, *really?* ... not again ... Lacey ... do you ever fuck off?'

'Watch your language in front of the children,' Lacey said.

Jake watched Sheila's strong veneer splinter.

Young laughed. 'Tell me about it! She really is on a different planet, isn't she? If she wasn't due to die before the hour was up, I might have reemployed her.'

Lacey tutted. 'Now, now, Simon, we've discussed this already. That's a non-starter.'

Young looked to his right at Lacey. He had beady eyes that darted about while the rest of his face remained stony and still. 'Listen bitch. You are still alive simply because I do not want my boy to witness the things that I am going to do to you.'

'He's seen worse ... I can assure you of that.'

'*Do not tempt me!* The good-humour and relief I feel over finding Tobias alive has a short shelf life.'

Any suspicions that Jake had regarding Lacey working with Young evaporated. Why had she brought the gangster here and put herself and Tobias in danger? And then invited Jake along too? Surely, she hadn't expected him to march in and arrest Young on his own? And she would have known he couldn't bring his colleagues as that would have been a one-way ticket to jail. So, what was her play? Why had she orchestrated—

And then it hit him like a bullet. She *wanted* Jake to overthrow Young with her.

A long time ago, Jake had accused Lacey of being emotionally stunted. Every time she came back, she reminded him of this criticism – threatened him with death. But death wasn't the ultimate revenge, was it? The ultimate display of power and revenge would be to control him and turn him into her fucking puppet.

Lacey was playing them all.

Sheila lifted the fire poker and pointed it at the two intruders. 'Get out of my house.'

Young said, 'Give me my son, and I'll do just that.'

'I'm not going to let a little boy walk out of here with an axe-wielding maniac now, am I?'

'Suit yourself.' Young brought the axe down off his shoulder. 'Let the fun and games begin.' He tapped the axe-head against his hand.

Then something surprising happened. As Jake turned into the room, holding his tyre iron, Tobias suddenly awoke from his stupor, charged forward and threw his arms around his father.

Lacey looked at Jake and smiled. 'Hiya lover.'

Sarah banged on the window. The black bird stood its ground. 'I don't think I've ever seen a raven around here before, have you?'

Paul shook his head.

'You're pale again, son. Are you okay?'

'The painkillers are wearing off.' He held his bandaged stump up to his mother. 'And it's starting to throb like a—'

'*Don't even!*' Sarah said. She already had her palm in the air.

'Not just the once? I mean if losing your hand isn't reason enough for a profanity or two then I don't know what is!'

Sarah hugged her son and then held him by the shoulders. He looked up at her, and then brushed away a tear which was running down her face. 'Not again, Mum. Keep looking at the raven. I'm going to the kitchen to get some more painkillers.'

In the kitchen, he switched the light on.

His mother was right about the raven – he didn't remember seeing any around here before. He'd seen one the night he was knocked unconscious, staring at him as he knelt before the hooded figure. He'd also seen many in that dream, picking at Reginald's face ...

He went over to the sink and poured himself a glass of water. He held it up in the air. The water was cloudy, so he placed it on the draining board to settle. He noticed that the outside light was on. He looked through the kitchen window at their tiny back garden and saw that one of the bags in the bin was torn open. Cats.

Following that dream, and since returning from hospital, he had Googled ravens. He'd discovered that ravens could operate in teams and had been known to hunt down game too large for a single bird.

'You best be careful out there, cats.' Paul picked up the glass of now-clear water. 'It seems the ravens are about.'

He turned away from the sink and took a couple of steps to the island. He smiled over the memory of the "easy-to-assemble" island they had bought from Ikea only a few months ago.

Easy to assemble, he thought, *over an entire day!*

His smile turned to a grimace when he recalled his stump. He wouldn't need to worry about DIY anymore. Nobody would be asking for his help. With his left hand, he opened the drawer and reached in for his painkillers—

He heard a noise behind him.

He turned quickly and saw that the cat was back, burrowing into the bin liner. He stepped forward and knocked heavily on the window. The cat scarpered. 'And after I told you about the ravens too!'

Feeling the door of the cupboard under the sink pressing against his leg, he looked down and saw that it was ajar. He pushed it closed with his knee.

And it came ajar again.

This time, he tried with his remaining hand. No luck. He considered rearranging the contents of the cupboard, so it closed easier, but he decided he was too tired, and his stump throbbed like a *motherfucker.* He grinned over the profanity his mum wouldn't let him use.

He turned back to the island, stepped over and popped two tablets from the packet of painkillers in the open drawer. These would make him sleepy too. He fancied falling asleep in front of the television. He closed the drawer—

The patchy face of Reginald Ray looked up at him. The monster was lying on his side on the kitchen floor. 'Hello Paul.' He smiled, revealing his loose-fitting white teeth. 'You left without saying goodbye.'

With his heart thumping in his chest, Paul glanced back at the open cupboard door. He must have just crawled out of there—

There was an excruciating pain in his leg. He screamed. Reginald was propped up on his right elbow as he worked the corkscrew into Paul's calf.

Paul tried to pull his leg away and lost his footing as the corkscrew tugged him back. As he fell, the metal ripped free from his calf with a sucking sound. He landed on his front and the wind was bashed out of him.

Then, he felt the old man crawling up his back.

'You know,' Reginald said. 'I thought we had a connection. You made me believe in you. And you let me down.'

Paul tried to roll over but couldn't. Despite Reginald's small size, he felt heavy. The painkillers in his system, and the shock of the deep flesh wound in his calf, were working against him.

'I treated you like royalty,' the old man said.

'You tried to make me eat someone ... that poor boy ...'

'Tried?' Reginald said and cackled. 'Tried? I've never seen anyone enjoy their dinner so much!'

'Liar. I refused. I never touched—'

'*Refused?* You gorged and gorged. Fuckity-fuck! You were one of the goddamn family.'

Paul felt the tip of the corkscrew pressed against the side of his neck.

'A real Ray if I ever did see one,' Reginald said. 'It's just a shame it has to end—'

There was a clunking sound. Paul felt the weight lift from his back. He looked left and saw Reginald was lying alongside him now with blood running down his face.

'Who are you?' Paul said.

'I'm Reginald Ray.'

Paul looked into his eyes. 'No, who are you really?'

'That doesn't matter.' He coughed as blood gushed

down over his scaly face. 'What matters is that I am Reginald Ray. *We are* Reginald Ray—'

There was a flash of metal and another clunk. Reginald's forehead caved in but his eyes remained fixed on Paul's. His next words were weak, and seemed breathed, rather than spoken. 'You are Reginald—'

Another flash. One of Reginald's eyes vanished inside his face and the other one protruded out. '*Ray.*'

Paul rolled over and looked up at his mother. She was holding an iron in her hand. She lifted it above her head, and brought it crashing down again. This time, Paul didn't watch the damage it caused.

Instead, he saw the glass of water he'd poured himself, slip from the top of the island and tumble down towards him.

He didn't have time to move so blackness came instead.

DESPITE KNOWING that this was exactly what Lacey wanted, Jake targeted Simon Young. He didn't have a choice. Wielding an axe, the bastard presented a clear and present danger. With the tyre iron primed, Jake brushed Lacey aside and charged.

'Go get him tiger,' Lacey said.

Young's eyes widened, he pushed Tobias away and raised the axe to block the tyre iron. There was a loud clunk as metal met metal.

'JAKE!'

Screaming was the wrong thing for Sheila to do because when Jake looked over at her and his son, he let his guard down.

The thrust of Young's axe against his tyre iron was

sudden, and he slumped back. Then, the gangster stepped forward and swung. There was a whooshing sound as the axe sliced the air but fortunately not him. He'd managed to hop back another step and suck in his stomach.

Lacey pounced and shoved Young. He stumbled sideways, drawing dangerously close to Sheila and Frank. He was yet to bring the axe up for another swing and the weight of it wasn't helping with the stumble. When he was within touching distance of Sheila, she swung the fire poker and clipped him round the face.

'BITCH!'

Clutching his cheek, Young staggered back towards Lacey and the axe slipped from his grip. Jake ducked and darted inward, relinquishing the tyre iron so he could swoop the axe up with his empty hand.

Lacey clapped. 'Teamwork!'

Young stopped and shook his head. He stood in the middle of them all. 'And now what?' He smiled. His teeth were red with blood. 'Are you all going to kill me? Do you really think that if I die here today that is the end of it for you all? Every single one of you will be rounded up, the young boy included, and cut into pieces for your—'

He grimaced and reached around to his back. He started to stagger and moan.

Young turned around to look down at his son. Jake saw the knife sticking out of the small of his back.

'Mummy's little soldier!' Lacey clapped again.

'What the—' Young gasped for air. 'Tobias ... I'm your father ...' He reached out and grabbed his boy by his neck and pushed him towards the front room window.

'Jake!' Lacey looked directly at him. 'He will kill Tobias.'

Tobias flailed in Young's grip. His face was reddening, and his tongue had slipped out between his lips.

Young said, 'Who are you? ... What's she done to you? ... You're not my Tobias.'

Jake turned the axe and swung the back of the head downwards, intending to knock Young unconscious. Young shuffled closer into Tobias at the last moment and Jake missed the centre of his head. Instead, the back of the axe head scraped down past his ear and crashed into his left shoulder with a sickening crunch.

Young released Tobias. The boy crumpled to the floor and gulped for air, while his father released a long, guttural moan. Eventually, when Young turned, Jake saw that his arm was hanging dead from his smashed shoulder and that most of his ear had been torn off.

Young reached behind himself again and managed to pull the knife from his back this time. He stumbled towards Jake. Despite the wounding, his eyes continued to flare with life, darting everywhere, still trying to bore into everyone who met them.

'It's over,' Jake said. 'Just put the knife down.'

Young reached up to feel his ear and it came away in his hand. He turned to Lacey, threw it in her face, and lurched at her with the knife.

Jake swung the axe again, but this time failed to turn it in time. It buried itself deep into Young's back. Behind him, Sheila gasped. He threw a look in her direction. Thank God she was covering their son's eyes.

The clatter of the knife hitting the parquet floor brought his attention back to Young.

Lacey stepped forward, smiling. She pushed Young gently in the chest. He stumbled backwards and swayed. 'I thought you were going to kill me.'

He opened his mouth to speak, but only a trickle of dark red blood emerged.

'Shh.' She placed a finger to her lips. 'I will take good, good care of Tobias. It is time for you to sleep.'

He slumped to his knees and looked up at Jake. The energy in those eyes had gone. And then, behind those dead eyes, the man vanished too. The body fell forward.

Lacey looked at him and raised an eyebrow. 'I'm proud of you, Jake—'

'DON'T YOU FUCKING DARE!'

Jake heard his son burst into tears behind him.

Lacey smiled. 'I always knew you had it in you.'

17

BEFORE HE'D EVEN finished his conversation with Willows, Yorke had started his journey to Wilton. The world was in flux, the curveballs were continuous, he'd heard enough to know that Wilton was where he had to go to steady this ship but the knowledge, *the agony*, of the truth was still too much to bear.

The chains ...

He asked Willows again. 'Clarify it for me one more time.'

'Of course, sir ... sorry, sir.'

'Why do you keep saying sorry, Collette?'

'Because I know what this means to you.' She was tearful.

'It's just our job—'

'Nonsense, sir.'

Yorke sighed. 'Yes, you're right. It's nonsense.'

He pushed his speedometer to seventy on a country lane. He had sparked up a two-toned siren and fired up a flashing blue light on the front grille.

Most people made way but those that didn't, probably

because their music was too loud, were provided with a sudden shock as he streaked around them.

'There were no chains at the Samuel Mitchell crime scene.'

Yorke kept his car as straight as an arrow, a sharp turn could send him spinning to his death. And he wouldn't let that happen. He had to live long enough to put all of this right.

'And Paul definitely said he'd been chained to that chair?' Yorke said.

'Definitely.'

Yorke braced himself as he screeched around an Audi. He threw the stunned driver an angry look.

Yorke chewed his lip. 'Where the bloody hell is that chain?'

'I'm sorry, sir. Also, having looked at his hospital records again, there was no bruising around his ankles which would have been in keeping with his story that he had fought the chains and bashed the chair against the wall.'

'But *there was* a broken chair at the crime scene?'

'There was, but the medical report suggests there were no bruises on his back despite what Paul told you ...'

'Jesus. So, what we are saying is that he never broke out of that chair? That he was never chained up?'

'Sorry, sir.'

Yorke punched his steering wheel. He approached a turn and should have slowed more than he did. He felt himself pressing against the side of the car as he took it sharp. 'How the bloody hell have we missed this?'

'There's been a lot to process in such a short space of time—'

'*And what the hell does it all mean?*'

'I don't know, sir.'

'I'll be at Paul and Sarah's in fifteen minutes. Dispatch some officers.'

'Will do, sir.'

'Yes, sir. And sir?'

'Please don't say I'm sorry again. Please don't.'

'Okay, sir – I won't.'

'Thanks.'

———

PAUL RAY WAS in the air.

He knew it was a dream because it wasn't possible that he could be this high up, but he welcomed the change in scenery after witnessing what his mother had done.

Beside him, a raven hovered. The muddy brown eyes stared into his. Ahead, he saw the Ray farmhouse. Below him, looking up at him, were the soldiers.

The horror began to dawn on him. He was hanging from a tree.

He reached up to claw at the rope around his neck. It was thick and taut, so his fingers made no difference. He tried to speak but realised he couldn't. Then, he realised he couldn't breathe either.

Below, the soldiers were cheering for his death. He wanted to scream at them. 'You have the wrong person! It's not Reginald. It's me. Paul. I'm innocent!'

He recognised Gladys too. Reginald's long-suffering wife watching him, the wrong man, die.

Alongside him swooped another raven. *No*, he thought as he fought the rope, *no, no, no! You will not take my eyes ... my tongue ...*

My life.

He went into a frenzy, battled as hard as he could but

253

it was useless. The blackness was closing in. Below, alongside the soldiers and Gladys, was a young man looking up.

It was him.

But how can that be? Because if I am there, how can I be here too?

Unless ...

We are Reginald Ray.

Ravens circled him now. They were ready to consume him. Take him into themselves.

I am Reginald Ray.

The ravens closed in.

———

AFTER THE MURDER, Sarah had dragged Paul all the way from the kitchen into the lounge and onto the rug in the centre of the room. Then, she'd placed a cold towel over the cut on his head and wrapped the bloody hole in his leg up in several tea towels. Finally, she'd phoned the emergency services. They wouldn't be long away.

Now, she sat beside him on the rug, cradling his head. She sighed in relief when he finally opened his eyes. 'My baby boy.' She kissed him on the cheek. A tear ran down her face and soaked into the towel on his forehead. 'It's all over now ... don't worry ... the whole thing is finished.'

He moved his eyes from side to side.

'Something fell on your head. You're probably concussed.'

He took a deep breath through his nose.

'Please lie still—'

He sat up. Sarah jerked back to avoid a clash of heads. Without saying anything, he sat there for a time, staring ahead. Tentatively, she stroked his back. 'Please Paul, you're all I have. Wait for the ambulance—'

'I feel fine.' Paul stood up. He groaned as he tested out his injured leg several times, before limping past her towards the window.

'Watch the leg, honey, he did make a bit of a mess of it.'

'Stop fussing woman. I don't think I've ever felt better.'

Sarah flinched. 'But ... Paul—'

'Did you not hear me?'

She put her hand to her mouth. The sooner the ambulance arrived, the better.

Silence hung there for a time while she allowed him some breathing space to look out of the window. But, eventually, impatience got the better of her. 'What are you looking for?'

He didn't reply.

She stood up and approached him from behind. 'Are you looking for the raven?'

He still didn't reply so she put a hand on his shoulder. 'Paul, please come and sit down. You're tired.'

He turned around and stood close to her. Blood streamed down the left side of his face from the cut on his forehead. *'It's gone.* Thank fuck.'

With tears in her eyes, Sarah reached up and took Paul's face in both of her hands. 'You're not yourself. And you're bleeding heavily. Please, listen to your mother.'

'There's something about you woman.' He placed his remaining hand over one of Sarah's hands on his face and leaned in to kiss her.

At first, she welcomed his affection but when she felt his tongue press against her lips and then slip into her mouth, she lurched away. *'Paul, what are you doing?'*

His top lip curled up into a snarl, but his eyes didn't

look angry. They looked hungry. He licked his top lip. 'I always said Rays taste best.' His snarl morphed into a ravenous smile.

'You've banged your head really hard, Paul.' Her words trembled.

'Yes, so?'

'You should sit down.'

He snorted. 'What fun can we have sitting down?'

She took a step away. 'I don't understand—'

'What's not to understand, woman?' He licked his top lip again and took a step towards her.

She lifted the palms of her hands. 'Paul, this isn't you!'

Paul's hand darted out and gripped one of Sarah's wrists. 'Fuckity-fuck! You only just worked that out?'

'Let go of me, Paul, before I—'

He jerked her in tightly against him. He then released her wrist and sent his remaining hand down to her backside and pulled her in sharper still. She could feel her son's crotch against hers. He was aroused. A wave of nausea washed over her and terror froze her limbs.

He thrust his face in against hers. 'Loosen up, woman, dance with me.'

'*Paul!*'

'I've never felt so *alive.*'

She tried to pull away but couldn't. He now held the back of her head in the crook of his arm. She could feel him licking her neck.

'*Stop, Paul.* I am your mother ... I am your *bloody* mother!'

Still supporting her head with his arm and pushing his erection against her, he yanked his head back so he could look at her straight-on. 'Fuckity-fuck, you've got some fight in you Sarah.'

By nuzzling her, he'd smeared his own blood all over his face, reddening him like a devil. Despite looking less like her son by the second, she told herself to fight the doubt. *This was her son. It was. And he needed her help.*

Paul sucked in a deep breath through his nose. 'Did Joe ever see this side of you?' He smiled and touched his blood-stained front teeth with his tongue. 'If not, you really should have shown it to him. If he knew what a feisty bitch he had on his hands, he might not have fucked half of Wiltshire.'

'Paul, you need—'

There was a blinding flash as her son's forehead smashed into her nose. She tried to pull away, but he just yanked her in harder. Her nose and temples throbbed. She could feel the blood gushing out.

With her mouth filling with blood, she said, 'You're injured ... Paul... you don't know what you're doing ...'

There was another flash. This time she felt his forehead bite into her top lip. Her head was swaying, so she kept her eyes closed. She felt herself starting to fall but he held her tightly enough to prevent that happening. She could feel him gyrating his crotch against her.

'I am Reginald Ray. You will use my real name when I fuck—'

'*Paul!*' She opened her eyes. The headbutts had splintered her vison and divided her son into two. 'You're not ... Reginald.' She paused to allow the blood and tears from her mouth to dribble down over her chin. 'You are ... Paul ... my son.'

He darted in again. She could feel him nuzzling her and licking her, surely tasting her bodily fluids as they poured from her nose, lip and mouth. She then felt him nibbling her.

'Paul ... this isn't ...'

He jerked back and looked at her. 'Paul is here, but he won't be for much longer, not when he realises what I've done to you.'

She spat at him. 'Leave my son alone.'

He opened his mouth and flew in again. She felt a burning sensation around her collar bone. 'GET ... OFF ... ME!' Vomit oozed from her mouth as he gnawed at her. Her vision blurred further. If it wasn't for Paul holding her up, she'd already be on her knees. Or her back.

She started to welcome the blackness she was descending into, when he suddenly released her backside and let her stumble backwards. She was just about to fall, when he reached up with his remaining hand to grip her hair fiercely.

He drew back his handless arm.

'I love you, Paul.'

He swung his elbow. Everything flashed.

She gulped air. 'I *said* I love you, Paul.'

Flash.

'I love—'

Flash.

She opened her eyes. The world had turned inside out. There was little comprehension of what she was seeing now, and little comprehension of what was truly happening.

'Dance with me,' she heard her son say.

She felt his warm arm around her neck.

'Yes ... of course ...'

She couldn't see him now, but she could see the white wall.

Flash.

Her head and face burned.

She saw the wall again, smeared in blood.

Flash.

Flash.

Nothing.

Jake shielded Young's body as best he could from his wife and son. 'Wait outside for me.'

'Why?' Sheila was still covering Frank's eyes. 'What happens next?'

'He doesn't know.' Lacey stepped alongside Jake. 'But I'd do as he says, if I were you. And please, take my son with you.'

Jake turned to scowl at Lacey, and then looked back at his quivering family. He couldn't tell if it was Sheila that was shaking, or his son, or both. 'Please leave.'

'Why? What are you going to do with *her?*'

Lacey snorted. 'He's hardly going to start fucking me next to a man with an axe sticking out of his back, is he?'

Jake turned, and drove Lacey back against the wall. 'Shut up. Shut up, or I'll ...'

'You'll what? Maybe you're right, Sheila, maybe I ought to be worried.'

'Well if you're not worried about him,' Sheila hissed. 'You best be worried about me.'

Lacey clapped like she'd done earlier when they'd worked together to bring down Young. '*Go team Pettman!* I really underestimated you guys.'

Jake looked at Sheila again. 'Leave.'

'*Okay,*' Sheila said, 'but be quick. I'm phoning the police.'

'Good,' Jake said. 'Stand outside and wait for them.'

Sheila held out a hand for Tobias, who stood over his father's body.

'Tobias,' Lacey said, looking at the child she'd stolen. 'Go.'

Tobias turned from the corpse and took Sheila's hand.

As she led Tobias and Frank from the room, Sheila said, 'Don't do anything stupid, Jake. You're already in enough trouble.'

Jake closed the door behind his wife.

'She's got a point hasn't she Jake? You do find yourself in quite a pickle.'

He approached Lacey, avoiding the puddle of blood spreading out from the corpse. When he was within a metre of her, he paused and kept his eyes down. He didn't want her to see the fury in them. 'So, what's the plan, Lacey?'

'Plan, Jake? Why would you think that there's a—'

Jake slammed his fist into her stomach. It sucked the air out of her, and she fell to her knees. He stared straight down at her. *What's the plan, Lacey?*'

Once she'd got her breath back, she looked up at him. 'Wow – I knew you were changing, Jake, but this is really something—'

He kicked her hard in the abdomen, and she fell sideways. 'WHAT'S THE PLAN, LACEY?'

Gasping for air, she struggled, but managed, to get some words out. 'What do ... you think ... it is?'

Jake put the palms of his hands on the wall and leaned over her. 'Let me guess, Lacey, you want us to run away together into the sunset?'

She turned onto her back so she could look up at him. Grinning and with her breath back, she said, 'Now, there's an idea I hadn't considered. You then have a ready-made son. You'd only really be trading like for like.'

'*Like for like?* You and that boy you abused for Sheila and Frank? Are you out of your mind?'

'Do you really have to answer that?' She sat up and shuffled over to the wall.

Jake sighed. 'You've ruined my life; do you know that?'

'Hang on, champ. I didn't lead you to Caroline. You did that all on your own.'

He looked at the door, paranoid that Sheila was listening in, before looking down at the body on the floor and realising that was the least of his worries.

He turned his back to the wall, and slipped down it, so he was sitting alongside Lacey.

'Your first?' Lacey said, prodding the top of Young's head with her shoe.

'My last,' Jake said. 'Did you plan all of this?'

She raised her eyebrows.

'Actually, don't answer that. I suppose the one consolation is that you're going to jail too. And it'll be a different one to me, so I'll probably never have to see you again. Every cloud has a silver lining, I guess.'

'Unless—'

'*No.* No more, please. I've had enough.'

She put her head on his shoulder. 'Okay, let's just wait for the end.'

Jake looked down at her head. '*Bollocks.* Any moment now you're going to try to talk me into something? Can't see you breaking the habit of a lifetime.'

'Can you remember some of the things I talked you into back—'

'Not now, Lacey.'

'Later then. When I write to you.'

Jake sighed. 'At least that boy, Tobias, will go back to his mother.'

'Yes, and the crime syndicate that surrounds her. Out of the frying pan and into the fire.'

'Still. At least his real mother might help him feel emotion.'

Lacey laughed. 'You really have me all wrong, you know that?'

'Do I?'

'It's not too late to make this work for all of us.'

Jake snorted. '*There it is!* Go on then Lacey, enlighten me. What fantastical move do you propose?'

'Simple really. You wipe that axe handle clean and I'll put my hands all over it. Job done.'

'Is that it! What a load of bullshit. After all this, you'll just roll over and go to jail, and let me walk?'

'Who said anything about jail?' Lacey lifted her head off his shoulder. 'I'll walk out of here with Tobias and you can go back to being DS Jake Pettman and his broken family as if all of this never happened.'

Jake sighed. 'There are no limits to your ambition, are there? And how do you propose I make that work? Why were you, Young and Tobias here in the first place? How did you just walk away?'

Lacey kissed him on the side of the head. 'Jake, you are one of the most intelligent men I have ever met. I'm sure you can work something out. After all, it's a bloodbath back at Caroline's and my DNA will be there too—'

'Caroline?'

'I didn't touch a hair on her head.'

Jake shook his head. 'I can't just let you walk out of here. Not after everything you've done.'

Lacey kissed him again. 'Can't you, lover?'

18

YORKE NEEDED TO hold onto something just to feel some semblance of control. *Something ... anything.* No matter how fleeting. No matter how false.

He chose the top of the television, which was still switched on, although muted. Two politicians were facing off with their plans to put the world to rights.

They aren't in this room, Yorke thought. *They aren't seeing what I'm seeing. If they were, they'd know that they were facing an impossible task – the world could never be put to rights again.*

Sarah Ray was dead. To know that, he didn't need to check her pulse, but had done anyway. Someone had rammed her head into the wall.

It could have been Paul who'd done this.

Yorke gripped the television so hard that his knuckles glowed. He took deep breaths. Control. He needed it. The world was in flux. *Steady ... steady ... steady—*

A car roared into life outside. He flew to the window and saw a white Kia under the streetlight on the other side of the road. Paul was at the wheel. He must have headed out of the back door and around the side of the house when Yorke had come in.

He sprinted out of the front door and then to his car parked at the top of the driveway. Paul was already at the end of their terrace turning onto North Street before Yorke had fired up his engine. His siren shattered the silence of Wilton and his flashing lights burned through the darkness.

Yorke raced up the gears and turned hard left onto North Street. He could see Paul's rear lights in the distance. Many vehicles had pulled over to the side already due to Paul's erratic driving, and this allowed Yorke to slip past them.

Yorke jammed his foot down. Townhouses and small stores flashed by.

When he reached the turn off, Yorke saw that Paul had already caused three cars to rear-end each other on the A36. Other vehicles behind the pile-up, and on the opposite side of the road, had all ground to a halt to avoid getting involved in the carnage. This allowed Yorke to turn immediately. His wheels screeched and the smell of burnt rubber filled his car.

The rear-view lights of Paul's Kia grew larger. Yorke pushed the car almost to eighty and was inches away from Paul's bumper. Yorke felt adrenaline burn every nerve in his body when he saw the roundabout looming close. He suspected Paul would simply tear over it or they would both be goners.

He was wrong. Paul's brake lights glowed.

Yorke stabbed his own brake as he watched Paul enter a skid but manage to take the Kia left off the roundabout.

Yorke didn't feel so lucky. His wheels were locked, and he was now entering his own skid. He felt dread, like acid, melting his insides. After almost ninety-degrees, the car righted itself and he was now on The Ave.

He didn't have time to breathe a sigh of relief, instead he punched the accelerator again. He pressed a button on his dash. Fortunately, Gardner was the last person he phoned, so there was no need to scroll.

'*Emma! I'm chasing down Paul Ray.*'

'*What?*'

'*No time to explain, just get to the Ray house in Wilton. Sarah is dead—*'

'*God, no!*'

'*Emma, just bloody listen!*' He was in the centre of the road. Traffic continued to make way for Yorke. Rows of whitewashed houses blurred on his left. Paul was metres away. '*I've just come off the A36 at King's Road onto The Ave, and I'm approaching the bridge over the railway. You need to get the road blocked ahead.*' He gave the registration number of Paul's vehicle, which was unnecessary as they would be able to access Sarah's vehicle details, but it might buy them a few extra seconds.

As they passed an industrial estate, Paul started to slow down.

'What the?'

Paul stopped at the entrance to railway bridge. He climbed out of the Kia and headed up the bridge.

'He's stopped, Emma. Get someone here now.'

He hung up, pulled over behind Paul's vehicle and jumped out of the car.

PAUL WASN'T QUITE sure what was happening as he staggered up the bridge.

He remembered Reginald on the floor, looking up at him. He also recalled being stabbed in the leg, hence the limp. But he wasn't sure what had happened since that point. He had a throbbing pain in his head, and he could taste the blood running down his face and into his mouth.

Why had he driven out to the railway? And what had happened to his mother and Reginald?

He put his hands against the barrier of the bridge and vomited over onto the train track several metres below.

My mother!

He felt his spine turn to ice.

With that old man ...

'Paul! It's me, Mike!'

Paul turned towards the bridge entrance. Sure enough Yorke was standing there.

Paul swayed and steadied himself against the chest-high brick barrier to stop himself tumbling. With his eyes closed to fight the sudden disorientation, he remembered a moment long ago, when Yorke had rescued him from that vile pig farm, and given him his life back ...

Emergency vehicles spread like a rash and everything changed. Darkness and desolation were replaced with the beat of light and life. By the ambulance, his mother had her arm hooked around that poor girl, Martha.

'I thought we were going to die in there,' Paul said. 'Thanks.'

'Don't mention it,' Yorke said. 'You were the brave one in all of this. The care you took of your mother was incredible. She must be so proud ...'

'Where is my mother, Mike?'

Yorke approached. 'Paul, you need to come with me. It's not safe up here.'

The question had not been answered. *My mother ... Reginald ... please, God, no ...*

'Mum?' Tears filled the corners of his eyes.

Yorke's response was delayed. It wouldn't be the truth. 'She's worried about you. As am I.'

Paul's tears started to fall. 'She's dead, isn't she?'

A car drove past them. It beeped its horn but didn't stop.

Yorke put a hand on Paul's shoulder. 'All I know right now, Paul, is that you aren't well. I've come to get you ... and help you.'

Paul could see the sadness in the detective's eyes.

'Tell me the truth, Mike. I was in the kitchen and that man came back.'

'Who?'

'Reginald.'

'At the house?'

'Yes, I saw him in the kitchen. He'd been hiding. He stabbed me in the leg, and now I can't remember anything.'

Yorke put a hand on Paul's shoulder. 'Come with me. We will find out what is happening soon enough.'

Yorke started to lead the frail boy down the railway bridge. Another car came past. This one stopped, and the driver leaned out the window. 'Everything okay?'

'Yes. Police,' Yorke said.

The driver took him at his word and moved on.

'What's wrong with me, Mike?'

Yorke was desperate not to engage Paul in this conversation. Not here. Not right now. He wanted him behind closed doors, with several of his colleagues, and the necessary professionals to deal with this psychological issue. The fact that this poor, young man had no recollection of what he'd done made Yorke feel physically sick.

'You've been through a lot, Paul. And not just this week but back then, all those years ago. Let's get you somewhere warm.'

Paul ducked under Yorke's arm and retreated several steps. 'And then what, detective? Administer some old-fashioned police justice? Oh, I've been on the receiving end of that before. More than once. It wasn't particularly pleasant, but it was *invigorating*, I can tell you that.'

Yorke didn't move. Paul was only several metres in front of him. He wanted to keep it that way. He didn't want to have to chase.

'Punch the man with the fucked-up face ... it was a national pastime back then! Well the man with the fucked-up face has started to punch back, and let me tell you, sir, I feel so much better for it.'

'Paul, there is nothing wrong with your face.'

'Now, now, detective. Don't play dumb. You know damn well who you are talking to.'

'I'm talking to Paul.'

He laughed. 'Do I really sound like that little, pathetic weasel? I'm Reginald.'

'Reginald Ray is dead. He died a long, long time ago, Paul. There is a man called Christopher Steele who is descended from Reginald. It was him who took you from the Ray farm. It was him that made you watch as he murdered Samuel Mitchell.'

'I know who Christopher Steele is! The feisty bitch just caved his head in in her kitchen and this little shitbag can't even remember seeing it!'

Yorke hadn't made it into the kitchen back at the house,

so he guessed this was possible. That would verify what Paul had said moments ago about being stabbed in the leg.

'Listen Paul. It was Christopher Steele who taught you what kind of man Reginald was. He got into your head in what must have been a horrendous situation. It's that evil influence that has caused this in some way.'

'*Fuckity-fuck,* for the last time, you are not talking to Paul Ray. Like a little maggot, he's hiding away, like he always does. He can't remember anything, but I can you see. I remember *everything.* Everything I do *and* everything he does. Now's the time to help him along with that ...' He smirked.

'Paul, if you can hear me, please listen. I am going to have to take you now to the station. I would prefer it if you didn't resist.'

His smirk fell away. 'Mike?'

'Yes! Paul, is that you?'

'Mike?' His face blanched. He took two steps back. His eyes widened. 'I remember ... oh, God ... I REMEMBER!'

Yorke flinched.

'I can *see* everything.'

Yorke could hear the rumble of a train in the distance. 'Listen, Paul—'

'*My hand, Mike!*' He was holding the palm of his one remaining hand in Yorke's direction. 'There's blood on my hand. Mum's blood. *I can see everything!*'

Yorke took a step towards Paul. 'You're ill, Paul. Your trauma has caused Dissociative Identity Disorder. You've fractured into two personalities—'

'OH GOD, MUM.' He put his remaining hand to his forehead. 'WHAT HAVE I DONE?'

Yorke took another step and stretched out a hand to him. 'When you were with Christopher Steele, in that

269

room, he created this other personality. I don't think he did it intentionally, but I think you acquired his traits. I can only imagine the trauma of what you must have gone through to cause this.'

'I remember. I ate Samuel. He fed me pieces of that poor boy and I ate him.' His hand flew to his mouth. 'I'm a monster. My god, I'm a monster ...'

Yorke shook his head. 'You're not a monster. You're sick. The other personality is becoming dominant, controlling you.' He managed to get to Paul and put his hand on his shoulder. 'You need help, you need to come with me.'

Yorke felt the air quiver as the train thundered nearer.

Tears were streaming down Paul's face now. Yorke, too, wanted to cry but he had to remain in control.

'I hurt Mum. I hit her and hurt her. My own mother. She loved me. She kept telling me she loved me. I kept hitting her and then ... the wall ... oh God, WHAT HAVE I DONE?'

'It wasn't you, Paul. It was something else. A part of you that needs taking out.'

'Where is she?'

'The hospital.'

'You're lying.'

The entire bridge lit up. Yorke looked right. The train had roared out of the darkness.

Paul took a deep breath and stared up at Yorke. 'This time you were too late, Mike.'

Yorke felt a carnivorous emptiness in his stomach growing and consuming. 'No, I'm here *now*, Paul.'

'*No*, you are too late. I'm the same as all the rest. Just another Ray.'

'*It's not true. I can help—*'

'No one can help, Mike.'

Yorke felt a searing pain in his knee; Paul had kicked him and broken away from the hand on his shoulder. 'There's only one way now. It's just like you said.'

'Like I said?'

'It has to be taken out.'

He said something else, but Yorke couldn't hear it over the sound of the approaching train. Yorke pounced, and was quick, but Paul was quicker. He evaded Yorke and so his hand closed on empty air.

'PAUL, I CAN HELP YOU!' Yorke prayed he could be heard over the sound of the train.

Paul stared at Yorke as he backed away.

'PLEASE!' Yorke shouted.

Paul let himself fall back over the brick barrier to meet the train head on.

19

AFTER GARDNER HAD seen both bodies, she stepped outside, crossed the road and climbed into the car. She hadn't yet decided whether she was going to burst into tears, or vomit.

She wasn't long off a decision though.

On the journey to this crime scene, where both Sarah Ray and Christopher Steele had perished as a result of catastrophic head wounds, she had received notification of two other crime scenes.

There had been two bodies recovered at the house of a beauty therapist in Salisbury, and a body had been recovered at the Pettman's.

Jake, Sheila, Frank and another young boy called Tobias were at the hospital. Jake had given a statement already. From what Gardner could gather, Lacey Ray had returned to Salisbury with two criminals from Southampton. The first man had been dispatched by Lacey at the beauty therapist's home, along with the beauty therapist; and the second man had been executed, with an axe, in Jake's house. The boy, Tobias, had been the victim's son, and the child kidnapped by Lacey a few years ago.

Jake was unable to provide a reason as to why Lacey would take this infamous man along to his house to kill him, but as he had succinctly put it, 'Does a woman like Lacey need a reason?'

He was right with that one, Gardner thought. *Lacey quite often acted outside the boundaries of reason.*

Jake hadn't been able to get involved with what transpired in the house as the criminal in question had knocked him unconscious with a fire poker. Gardner could only imagine the terror Sheila and poor Frank must have felt as they watched Lacey end a man's life in so brutal a fashion. Apparently, Jake was beating himself up for not being awake to stop it and his concussion was only adding to his poor state of mind. Lacey had fled the scene but had been collared only minutes later. She clearly hadn't anticipated the speed of the police response following the emergency call from the Pettman's. Jake was one of their own after all, and so was entitled to the Full English. Lacey had had nowhere to run and would now, God willing, be spending the rest of her life in jail.

While Gardner had been standing over Sarah's body back in the house, thinking that things could not possibly get any worse, Yorke had phoned her, and delivered the news.

The fact that Paul had gone was devastating enough, but the manner by which he'd departed had hit her hard. She'd struggled to keep the phone in her hand as Yorke had relayed his discoveries.

Dissociative Identity Disorder ... a fragmented, malignant personality born from traumatic experiences ... an identity in the form of Reginald Ray after being exposed to

Christopher Steele in his slaughterhouse ... his other personality made him believe that he was chained up ... the other personality fed on Samuel Mitchell ... the other personality did this to his mother...

The other personality showed him everything before he died.

Paul had to live through everything he did.

She felt vomit in her throat and tears in her eyes.

Her phone rang. The screen informed her that it was Topham.

'Tell me you're at home.' Gardner couldn't believe she delivered the instruction with such force. She felt fragile and her body shook.

Topham didn't respond.

'Mark?'

'I'm sorry, Emma.' There was no force in Topham's voice.

'What for?'

'For not listening.'

'Mark, what's wrong? Where are you?'

'Goodbye, Emma.'

'*Don't you do this, don't you say this to me, Mark Topham! Where the hell are you?*'

'You're the best of us.' Despite his voice being brittle, his statement came with conviction.

'Mark? *Mark?* MARK?'

Nothing.

She tried ringing him back but was sent straight to Topham's spritely voicemail request. It sounded like a completely different person.

After the beep, she said, 'Ring me back!' She hung up. 'Shit! Shit!'

Deciding to go to Topham's house, she started the

engine. Her phone rang as she started to accelerate. She hit the brakes and answered. 'Damn it, Mark, don't you hang up on me!'

'Err ... sorry, ma'am.'

'Collette?'

'Yes, ma'am.'

'Sorry, Collette, me and Mark just had a disagreement ... anyway ... is everything okay?'

'Not really, ma'am. We have another body.'

'You're *fucking* kidding. What is happening around here? Where?'

'The Blue Forest Hotel in Salisbury. It's a relatively new place. Commotion was heard from one of the rooms and they phoned it in. A young man. His name is Dan Tillotson. He's a male prostitute from Southampton ...'

Gardner's vision started to swirl. 'Say again?'

'A male prostitute—'

'*How did he die?*'

'Beaten, ma'am. To a pulp.'

No ... no ... no. 'Any indication of who has done it?'

'We have witnesses seeing a tall man going in with the victim and leaving alone. CCTV footage will clarify—'

She'd moved the phone from her ear and pressed it against her thigh so she couldn't hear Willows anymore. Gardner thought her ribs would splinter under the force of her beating heart.

I'm sorry Emma ... for not listening ... you are the best of us.

She cracked the car door, allowing in some air.

She threw up first and then started to cry.

20

YORKE SLID PAST Patricia after she opened the door. He saw her bewildered expression and apologised, but he was already halfway up the stairs before he could catch her reply.

Out of breath, he knocked on Ewan's door.

'*Go away.*'

He knocked more forcefully.

'*I said go—*'

The last word never came. Yorke was already in the room, looking down on his adopted son, who was lying on the bed with a magazine beside him.

'Not now, Mike. Not now.'

Yorke sat down on the edge of the bed beside Ewan.

'Are you listening to me, Mike?' He felt Ewan pushing him from behind, urging him away. 'Leave me the *fuck* alone.'

Yorke turned on the bed and slipped his hand around the back of Ewan's head. He tried to pull his boy's head towards him, but he resisted.

'Get off me!' He slammed a fist against Yorke's chest.

Yorke didn't.

'*Get off me!*' He hit him again.

Yorke increased his efforts and forced Ewan's head towards his chest.

The young man relented and crumpled against his adopted father. 'Mike ...' He started to cry. His entire body shook.

Yorke had never seen Ewan in such despair. Not even when he'd woken in hospital to discover that his father, Iain, had died.

Ewan's whole body seemed to fold in on itself. Yorke held him as tightly as he could, terrified that if he didn't, the young man would disintegrate in his arms. 'Mike ... I feel alone ... so ... *fucking* alone.'

'I know you do,' Yorke said in between mouthfuls of his own tears. 'But you're not alone, and I want to make sure that you never feel this way again.'

EPILOGUE

TODAY, FOR A change, the Orchard Care Home felt more welcoming than usual. The colourful orchard remained pretentious and the meandering white corridor was still sterile but, as he sat beside Hayley Willborough, Yorke felt a sense of contentment which he'd not felt for months.

Hayley was at peace. Her passing had brought her the closure she'd longed for since her youth when Andrew Ray had stolen her innocence, and a finality that had continued to evade her as she lay locked inside her own body.

Yorke clutched her withered hand.

When Yorke had learned of her death, he'd requested a moment alone with her. They were happy to allow him that time.

He'd had the journey here to reflect on why he'd made this request, but it hadn't taken him particularly long to reach a conclusion.

This woman, who had endured so much, and had fought so hard for the child she had borne but could never name as her own, deserved a final farewell. And with

Robert Bennett incarcerated, and everyone she'd ever known or loved gone, Yorke felt that the responsibility fell to him.

Hayley had offered him the truth, even when that truth seemed so desperately out of reach. She'd summoned up the energy within her dying body to communicate with Yorke in so grotesque a situation.

She deserved this moment of respect.

So, Yorke stroked the back of her hand, told her of Ewan and Patricia and the embers of happiness that still glowed in his own life and occasionally, leaned over to kiss her cold forehead.

Then, after Yorke had bidden her a final farewell and left the hospital, his thoughts turned to his late mother and sister too, as they so often did, and he shed a tear for them all on his journey home.

———

When Robert Bennett learned the news of his mother's passing, he was granted compassionate time alone in his cell.

Since the death of his wife, his own health had been declining rapidly. His skin ailment had worsened, he was gripped by nausea for the most part of every day, and the weight had relentlessly fallen off him. As he reclined back on his bed, with tears in his eyes, he struggled to even stay conscious.

But he did. Because if anyone deserved the last dregs of his life and fight, his mother did.

He spent some time reminiscing over the countless times she'd sat beside him at the window, offering him the companionship that no one his age had ever offered him.

She'd teach him, yes, but they'd also talk for hours, about his greatest love, animals, and about the joys of life that awaited him when he was old enough to leave the prison his adoptive parents had created.

Robert felt a twinge in his chest. He knew that it was his heart. It'd happened yesterday but he hadn't bothered to report it. The sooner the better as far as he was concerned.

His mind turned to Christopher Steele, his twin brother. The bastard who had taken his wife. This man had been his flesh and blood. He should have come to him with open arms, not with an appetite for destruction.

What had caused the evil to flourish within Christopher? Was it destined to come to him too?

The Ray family, he thought. I'm not even the last one, am I? There's another. A woman. In prison too—

There it was again. The twinge. Fiercer, this time. He could feel it spread along with a rising tide of nausea. He felt the numbness in his arm ...

Robert Bennett turned over and pushed his face into the pillow so no one could hear him having a heart attack.

Knowing that he was escaping the evil that had ravaged the minds of so many of his kin, he died content.

JAKE STOOD and watched the large black birds tearing lines through the low-hanging moonlit clouds. He didn't think he'd ever seen anything quite like it.

He looked back towards the tree that Reginald had swung from and his own car beneath it. He'd parked where Paul had parked several nights earlier. Jake lowered his head. Paul's tracks were still fresh and yet the boy was no more.

He glanced also at another part of Paul's handiwork: the blackened, skeletal remains of the farmhouse. Then he did what he'd come here to do.

He fell to his knees and yelled. There were no words. For days his emotions had remained caged within him so now they came as a roar.

Lacey had blackened him. Turned him into a murderer. And she thought she'd just walk away? Again? He'd accepted her offer. Allowed her to put her DNA on the axe that had ended Simon Young, but then he'd turned the tables on her. He'd grabbed Tobias and refused to allow him to leave with her. She'd become desperate, threatened his life, as she so often did but she'd been forced to run when the sirens came.

But you didn't run fast enough, did you?

For days, he'd waited for his colleagues to turn up on his doorstep and lead him away in handcuffs. It never happened. Why? He had no idea. Why would she not tell them everything? The bitterness she must now feel towards Jake must have been eating her up inside. Maybe, she just wanted to save him for herself, but that wouldn't be happening any time soon. Not with her incarcerated.

Jake stopped roaring and gasped for air.

You deserve everything. You are the last of them and you deserve to be locked away in nothingness.

He imagined her sitting in her sterile room. Alone. No one to visit her. Living off emptiness and fiery memories.

He smiled. She would burn under the weight of those memories and the longing for what she could never have again.

Burn like this farmhouse had burned.

And when she finally became ash, he wouldn't be there to say goodbye.

He would rejoice with the rest of the world over her demise, knowing that she was the last of the Rays.

They wouldn't allow her a pen to write a letter. A potential weapon, they said. You could also commit suicide with one, they claimed.

They told her that a phone call was the best they could offer. She told them it wasn't good enough and continued to kick up a fuss until they relented.

Tomorrow, they told her, she could dictate a letter to a guard which would then be posted to the recipient.

So, Lacey sat alone in a room which had been stripped of everything but a mattress and planned out what she would put in her letter, the first of many, to Tobias. A letter, she knew, they would never actually send. Yet, still she would rejoice in its creation.

Later, she descended deep into her Blue Room.

They were all there tonight. Her parents, Lewis Ray, Billy Shine, and some of her more recent kills from the Southampton snuff set. All of them sat hunched over in chairs, looking solemn. They bathed in blue light but did not find the comfort that Lacey found from this colour.

She moved among them, and when she moved past Simon Young, she smiled.

When she wasn't writing letters to her son, this is where she would stay.

She could be happy here.

Well ... at least for a little while.

Tobias watched the woman they called his mother fuss over him.

First, he was shown to his new bedroom. The walls, and bedsheets, were decorated with robots.

'Transformers,' she told him. 'We can change them if you want?'

Tobias approached a toybox in a corner. He picked up a plastic figure which was a cross between a robot man and a plane. After staring at it for a few moments, he put it back.

'They belonged to your father,' she said, 'when he was your age. He loved them.'

He looked up at his mother. He certainly didn't recognise her, and he wasn't sure if he liked her. Her face looked too gentle. He reached up to touch it. It felt too soft.

She closed her eyes and sighed. 'I love you, son.'

He turned and looked out of the window. The garden, and the surrounding bushes, were large. He noticed some cats enjoying the space.

He liked animals. Liked to play with them. He thought about what games he could play.

'I think we will be happy again, Tobias,' his mother said from behind him. 'Even after everything that has happened, we can be happy.'

She felt her kiss the back of his head.

'Welcome home, Tobias Simon Young.'

Tobias turned slowly to look up at his mother. She smiled. He didn't smile back. She opened her arms to him. He didn't go to her.

'It's Tobias Ray,' he said.

YOUR FREE DCI YORKE QUICK READ

To receive your FREE and EXCLUSIVE DCI Michael Yorke quick read, *A Lesson in Crime*, scan the QR code.

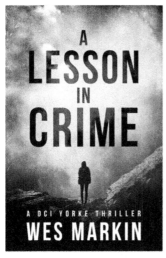

Scan the QR to READ NOW!

CONTINUE YORKE'S STORY IN DANCE WITH THE REAPER

How do you stop a perfect killer?

After the terrible events of the past year, DCI Yorke's team are on the verge of finding peace. But after a terrifying act of violence shatters their equilibrium, they are forced to dance with a skilled assassin who knows no equal.

After it becomes clear that this hitman is connected to the most shadowy of criminal organisations, Yorke is forced to dive into his own past, and face a future in which he is either alone, or dead.

Can Yorke and those he holds dearest survive the Reaper? Or will this be one dance too many?

Rise of the Rays is a true edge-of-the-seat, nail-biting page turner.

Scan the QR to READ NOW!

START THE JAKE PETTMAN SERIES
TODAY WITH THE KILLING PIT

A broken ex-detective. A corrupt chief of police. A merciless drug lord.

And a missing child.

Running from a world which wants him dead, ex-detective Sergeant Jake Pettman journeys to the isolated town of Blue Falls, Maine, home of his infamous murderous ancestors.

But Jake struggles to hide from who he is, and when a child disappears, he finds himself drawn into an investigation that shares no parallels to anything he has ever seen before.

Held back by a chief of police plagued and tormented by his own secrets, Jake fights for the truth. All the way to the door of Jotham MacLeoid. An insidious megalomaniac who feeds his victims to a Killing Pit.

And the terrifying secrets that lie within.

Scan the QR to
READ NOW!

JOIN DCI EMMA GARDNER AS SHE
RELOCATES TO KNARESBOROUGH,
HARROGATE IN THE NORTH
YORKSHIRE MURDERS ...

Still grieving from the tragic death of her colleague, DCI Emma Gardner continues to blame herself and is struggling to focus. So, when she is seconded to the wilds of Yorkshire, Emma hopes she'll be able to get her mind back on the job, doing what she does best - putting killers behind bars.

But when she is immediately thrown into another violent murder, Emma has no time to rest. Desperate to get answers and find the killer, Emma needs all the help she can. But her new partner, DI Paul Riddick, has demons and issues of his own.

And when this new murder reveals links to an old case Riddick was involved with, Emma fears that history might be about to repeat itself...

Don't miss the brand-new gripping crime series by bestselling British crime author Wes Markin!

What people are saying about Wes Markin...

'Cracking start to an exciting new series. Twist and turns, thrills and kills. I loved it.'

Bestselling author **Ross Greenwood**

'Markin stuns with his latest offering... Mind-bendingly dark and deep, you know it's not for the faint hearted from page one. Intricate plotting, devious twists and excellent characterisation take this tale to a whole new level. Any serious crime fan will love it!'

Bestselling author **Owen Mullen**

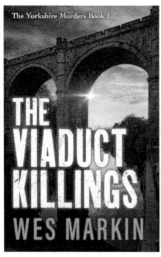

Scan the QR to
READ NOW!

ACKNOWLEDGMENTS

As always, massive thanks must go to my family - Jo, Peter, Janet, Ian and Eileen for their encouragement and patience. Not forgetting my little people, Hugo and Beatrice, who keep me laughing even when the work becomes overwhelming.

Thanks, as always, to Jake, who is always there for support and encouragement, even though he is inundated with his own stuff to do! Huge appreciation again to Cherie Foxley, who continues to astound me with her ideas for the Yorke covers. Thank you to Aubrey Parsons who is in the process of bringing Yorke to life on Audible.

Thank you to Jo Fletcher, Jenny Cook and Kath Middleton for their savage – but necessary – edits. Thank you to all my Beta Readers who took the time to read early drafts and offer valuable feedback – Keith, Carly, Cathy, Donna, Yvonne, Holly and Alex. Thank you to the bloggers who continually support me – Shell, Susan, Dee, Caroline and Jason. Thank you, and farewell to Nik Plumley, a loyal reader and a great person. You will be sorely missed by many.

Lastly, thank you to every reader, and every wonderful blogger, who continues to read my fiction. I hope *Rise of the Rays* entertained, and I hope you all join me and Yorke for a *Dance with the Reaper* in July ...

STAY IN TOUCH

To keep up to date with new publications, tours, and promotions, or if you would like the opportunity to view pre-release novels, please contact me:

Website: www.wesmarkinauthor.com

facebook.com/WesMarkinAuthor

instagram.com/wesmarkinauthor

twitter.com/markinwes

amazon.com/Wes-Markin/e/B07MJP4FXP

REVIEW

Without a huge marketing budget, it is difficult for indie authors to compete with the big publishing houses, no matter how worthy our books are. But what we do have is an army of loyal fans and readers, and it is with your help we can continue writing and publishing books for you to read. So, if you enjoyed reading **Rise of the Rays** please take a few moments to leave a review or rating on Amazon or Goodreads.

REVIEW

If you enjoyed reading **_Rise of the Rays_**, please take a few moments to leave a review on Amazon, Goodreads or BookBub.

Printed in Great Britain
by Amazon